smoking Hot

KAREN KELLEY

sourcebooks
casablanca

Published by Sourcebooks Casablanca, an imprint of Sourcebooks, Inc.
P.O. Box 4410, Naperville, Illinois 60567-4410
(630) 961-3900
Fax: (630) 961-2168
www.sourcebooks.com

Library of Congress Cataloging-in-Publication data is on file with the publisher.

Printed and bound in the United States of America.
VP 10 9 8 7 6 5 4 3 2 1

There are just some people who are too much fun to be around—but I'm a glutton for punishment *grin*. This book is dedicated to those people: Melissa (who is always smiling!), Sally, Samantha C., Samantha S., Allison, Heather, April (I miss you on dayshift!), Yo-Yo Yolanda, Dimisha, Nicole (a fellow romance book glommer), Theresa, Hector, Lorena, Sandra, Lakisha, Barbara, Jordon, Chelsy, Rebbecca, Jennifer...

To the pill pushers (legal!): Esther (did you know you blush when you talk about reading my books?), LaKendra (you're too funny!), Pam (I love ya!).

Maria (Thank you!)

Fellow Compadres: Art, Brittanie, Angela, Julia (who needs to change shifts!), Irvina, Marsha, and Megan.

To Toya—who heals all wounds (literally) and makes the world a better place!

To Debbie—who makes life easier. The ruler of the South.

Chapter 1

RAINE MCCANDLESS NEVER REALLY thought about dying—until she moved back to Randolph, Texas. It wasn't just a sleepy little town, it was comatose. Funny, she always figured a bullet would get her; she'd never considered boredom.

Old Red's front tire suddenly dipped into a pothole and threw Raine against the door of the pickup.

"Damn," she muttered as a stab of pain shot down her arm. She gripped the steering wheel a little tighter and dodged the next one. That was what she got for not paying attention.

You shouldn't even be here, the voice inside her head complained. *Your life is in Fort Worth, Texas, patrolling the streets on the north side where the landscape is skid-row bars and gang graffiti.*

Remember what it was like to roll on a call when your life was in danger, the adrenaline flowing through your veins? The rush, the excitement?

She drew in a deep, calming breath, trying to still the warring emotions between regret and her duty to family. The problem was that she did remember and guilt was tearing her up inside.

Her father told her being in law enforcement was in her blood. He'd been the sheriff of Randolph back then and he taught her everything he knew. After becoming a police officer, Raine moved away because she wanted to experience more than what the small sheriff's office in Randolph could give her.

Now she was back. She'd come full circle. Not that she had a choice. Grandpa needed her and he was family. So what if she had to make a few sacrifices? As far as she was concerned, he always came first. She topped the small rise, then stepped on the clutch and brake, surveying the land and buildings before her. This was home. The tightness inside her began to ease.

She'd been on McCandless land for the last quarter mile. Every rut, every pothole, every scraggly bush belonged to her grandfather and would someday belong to her. That is, if they didn't lose it to the creditors. If that happened, it would destroy Grandpa. All he ever talked about was the ranch. There were a lot of memories here. It didn't matter the old two-story house needed a new roof, or the barn leaned a little too far to the right, or both needed painting.

"So much needs to be done." She slumped back against the brown leather seat that was almost silver from the duct tape patches and took it all in. The plumbing was shot and the electrical system was a joke. Then there were the fences. Her brain ached worrying about all the holes from downed barbed wire, and posts that were rotting.

Fixing fences gave a man time to think, Grandpa always told her. She smiled wryly. With so much fence that needed mending on the one hundred and twenty-two acres, Grandpa had plenty of thinking time.

Maybe that was his problem. Thinking always got him into trouble. He'd rescued a starving horse, and the owner filed charges for horse stealing. The owner got a hefty fine for animal abuse and the horse was taken away. Grandpa had still committed a crime and was put on probation. Someone suggested she sell the place and put him in a nursing home.

She gripped the stick shift and shoved it into first gear as a surge of anger rushed through her. No one would be putting

Grandpa in a nursing home. He was *not* senile. Forgetful at times, maybe, but everyone forgot things. No one, not one damn redneck son of a bitch was going to tell her what she needed to do. She let off the clutch and brake, and started forward again.

It didn't matter she was stuck in this little podunk town where people still remembered that Sheriff McCandless's wife ran off with a traveling salesman and the sheriff proceeded to drink himself into an early grave, unmindful he still had a daughter to raise. Her heart squeezed painfully. Yeah, well, life sucked sometimes. There were only two certainties: taxes and long memories for scandal, especially in a small town.

Nothing ever changed, except now she was so exhausted she could barely put one foot in front of the other. Working nights patrolling the streets, then coming home and taking care of the ranch and Grandpa was draining her energy. The way her life was going, she'd probably die here.

Without him, Raine was going to die tonight.

She was going to be pissed when she discovered a stranger in her home, too. Dillon's plan was to warn her, then get out—fast. He'd be lucky if she didn't shoot him, and bullets stung like a son of a bitch.

"You're an idiot," he muttered. "A fool to even care."

The closer she got, the louder the pickup rumbled. Raine needed a new muffler. The rusty-red hunk of scrap metal swerved to miss the deep ruts like a drunk trying to walk a straight line. Baling wire kept the right side of the bumper tied on and a dirty rag served as a gas cap.

Raine finally managed to pull the pickup to a jarring stop near the gate in front of the weatherworn ranch house. Dillon braced himself. He hadn't been involved in anyone's life in a long time, but Sock McCandless was a persistent old coot. Dillon frowned. More like a pain in the ass. Yeah, that was closer to the mark.

Raine shut off the engine. The pickup rattled to a coughing, sputtering death as if someone had their hands tight around the engine choking out any life that might still be left.

Dillon drew in a deep breath, then exhaled.

And waited.

Raine sat in the truck, staring straight ahead.

Why wasn't she getting out? He wanted this over and done.

Her shoulders suddenly sagged and she leaned forward, resting her forehead against the steering wheel. Weariness rolled off her in waves, coming closer and closer to him. He took an involuntary step back. Dillon wasn't about to get caught up in a lot of emotional baggage. He'd been through that once before and it was more than enough to last several lifetimes.

Raine pushed away from the steering wheel, then squared her shoulders as though attempting to gather enough energy to climb out and trudge the short distance to the front door.

She didn't look strong. Not a bit. Sock said she was capable, but needed help. He didn't mention vulnerable. Dillon had a sinking feeling his plan wasn't going to work. His timing was off; nothing new there. He should come back later, when she was rested. When she was...

He jerked the black Stetson off his head and raked his fingers through his hair. His life had been okay up until the point the old man started badgering him. Damned persistent prayers! The man would not stop.

Answering mortals' prayers was a lamebrained idea. Dillon wondered which one of his three friends came up with that one. He was thoughtful for a moment, vaguely remembering one of them bringing up the subject and how he'd argued the point they were nephilim, half angel, half man, so they should be answering prayers.

"A dumbass idea," Dillon muttered. They weren't real angels, if anyone wanted to get specific. Their fathers were angels who mated with mortal women. The women had children and a new race was born, the nephilim. Some said they were demigods. Yeah right, if they only knew. There wasn't an angelic bone in his body. He had all the vices of man. If there were rules to break, he broke them, then invented new ones as he went along.

But someone in the group thought their life would be less boring if they answered prayers. His eyebrows drew together. Chance had always been sort of their leader. He might have suggested they help mortals. He doubted it was Hunter. Hunter would rather spend all day watching reruns of *Survivor* or with his animals. It was eerie the way he could communicate with them. Ryder probably started the whole business. He'd always wanted to be like *real* people, as he called them. What the hell did that make them? Yeah, it was probably Ryder.

Dillon liked fighting demons a hell of a lot better than answering prayers, but the demons were laying low because Chance killed one of their leaders a few months ago. Since there were no demons to fight, Dillon's day-to-day routine had gotten a little boring.

A *little* boring? If he was honest, his life was a whole lot boring. But it was safe, uncomplicated. There had to be a trade off.

The pickup door creaked open. He moved closer to the window and pulled back a corner of the dingy lace curtain, dislodging a wisp of dust. The tiny speck danced about in front of his face before he waved it away.

His gut churned as Raine stepped out of the truck, tugging on the bill of her dark brown hat. She couldn't have been much more than five feet four and a half inches. He'd thought she would be taller, heavier, sturdier. From everything Sock told him, she carried a heavy load. From this distance, she looked fragile. Fragile wasn't good. Fragile almost killed him once, but that had been a long time ago. But not long enough that he'd forgotten.

This wasn't his only option, he reminded himself. He could leave. There was still time. Raine would never know he'd been there. He could send her a note.

A note?

He snorted. What the hell would he say? *Heads up, you're going to die tonight.* Dillon quickly dismissed that idea.

As much as he wanted to forget the whole thing, he couldn't. He'd made a promise. A stupid one in a moment of weakness. But it was still a promise. He'd do what he had to do, then disappear. Quick and easy. He settled his hat back on his head with renewed determination. She was just a female. Nothing more.

Not quite what he expected after everything Sock told him. Dillon imagined a big-boned female who tossed bales of hay onto a trailer as if they were ten pound bags of potatoes.

One booted foot rested on the running board as she leaned back in to grab the key from the ignition. His gaze moved over her gently rounded backside. She stretched farther, and the material tightened. Her ass wiggled.

"Aw, hell," he muttered. The hairs on the back of his neck tingled. His bad feeling grew stronger. This wasn't going to be quick or easy.

When Dillon had first made the decision to help, he figured the job might take five minutes at most. Then he could blink himself back to the ranch and enjoy a little peace and quiet with his friends again. The sprawling ranch was his sanctuary. The four nephilim bought the land together a few decades ago. It was their idea of normalcy, he supposed.

Until Sock's prayers found him.

Dillon refocused his attention when Raine closed the pickup door and made her way across the uneven ground toward the house. The sun was just breaking through night's fading shadows and the early morning patches of fog that clung to the air.

He couldn't see much of her face under the hat. The loose beige shirt and black pants of her uniform managed to hide all traces of feminine curves. She also had a 9mm Glock holstered snugly on her hip. The gun would be enough to scare off most men. Dillon wished he could've been most men because he really didn't want to be there.

He could close his eyes and think about Mount Everest. He'd be so high up, Sock's infernal prayers couldn't reach him! Only sweet, blissful silence.

He frowned. She did have a nice ass, though.

Nice ass or not, Raine would cause him more problems than he needed. She was female, and all women meant trouble.

Like right now. She was a cop, and she didn't survey the area to make sure anything hadn't changed from when she'd left for work. Raine thought she was safe. She wasn't.

She stepped from his line of vision. Keys rattled right before the door creaked open. He grimaced. A little oil would fix the noise. Why alert an intruder? People thought they were protected once they closed the front door. That wasn't always the case.

When she flipped a switch, light flooded the hall. Dillon stepped back into the shadows. The light didn't quite reach his corner. He'd give her a few minutes, then gradually let her know he was in the house. He shook his head. That didn't sound like a good plan either. No matter what he said, she was going to be pissed.

What possessed him to promise Sock McCandless anything? He was a crazy old man. Dillon dismissed that notion as quickly as it popped into his head. No, Raine's grandfather was a sly old codger. He knew exactly what to ask and when to ask it. The old man had caught Dillon in a moment of weakness.

He heard her keys drop on top of the entry table, followed by a deep sigh before something else landed on the scarred surface. The heels of Raine's black cowboy boots made a dull thud on the hardwood floor. He thought she would walk past the doorway, but she suddenly stopped. Had he inadvertently made a noise? He didn't think so, but just the same her body stiffened as her senses went on high alert.

Raine scanned the space, as though sensing something wasn't right. Her gaze swept past where he stood, then jerked back. Her hand moved to the gun on her hip. In one smooth motion, she flipped the snap and pulled the weapon from the holster, pointing the gun in his general direction. "Step out of the shadows. One wrong move and I'll shoot."

She'd taken off her hat. He studied her, regretting his promise more and more as he watched the silver lights dance in her pale green eyes. Her full sensual lips would be a temptation for any man, mortal or immortal. Heat began to spread over him. No, no, no. She was supposed to be a big husky woman with a straw of hay hanging out one side of her mouth. The kind of woman who would think nothing about chewing tobacco and spitting out the juice while laughing over an off-color joke. Raine wasn't at all like that.

Sock had told him she took care of the few animals left on the ranch. She fixed fence. He bragged his granddaughter could outride and outshoot any person he knew, and if someone really made her mad, she could throw a punch just right and knock a grown man to his knees.

Dillon's gaze swept over her again. This little thing? Nah, Sock had fed him a line of bull. Raine didn't look as though she could fight her way out of a wet paper bag, even if she did carry a big gun.

But she did have some things going in her favor. Like a sexy ass… and pouty lips. The kind of lips made for kissing. It had been too long since he slowly undressed a woman, revealing each hidden secret. What did Raine hide under that uniform?

Flames sparked inside him, spiraling quickly downward. He shook his head. Chance was right: he needed to get laid. That had to be it. She wasn't his type. He liked tall curvy women with porcelain skin. Raine was tiny and tanned. Not as big as a minute.

Her scent drifted over to him. He inhaled. A taunting fragrance of oils and spices—jasmine, clover, and sweet honey—curled around him, tempting him to step nearer and lose himself in her essence. Some nephilim could be more susceptible to the pheromones mortals released. It rarely happened, but it wasn't unheard of.

"Step into the light," Raine ordered. When he didn't move, she added, "I won't tell you again."

He shook his head in an attempt to clear it. Yeah, it could be her scent throwing him off guard. Or the way she stood with her knees slightly bent, both hands firmly holding the gun. He shouldn't be turned on that Raine had him at gunpoint, but he was. He hadn't expected her voice to be raspy, sultry, and tempting as hell either. Its resonance rippled over him like a warm massage.

Chance would have a field day with this one. Dillon was on the brink of salivating over a female who should have zero sex appeal for him. The fact that she had a gun pointed at him would only make Chance laugh harder. His friend had an odd sense of humor. Dillon's gut feeling was right. He should've kept his distance.

Chapter 2

A RUSH OF ADRENALINE surged through Raine. The exhaustion she'd felt when she turned off Old Red's engine was gone the instant she came inside and sensed someone else in the house. Every fiber of her being was on high alert.

"Show yourself!"

He stepped out of the darkness.

Her eyes widened and her mouth dropped open, then snapped closed. She'd expected an unbathed drifter with a scraggly beard, not a cowboy who looked like he was made to fulfill any woman's fantasies. He wore his clothes as if the black T-shirt and dark jeans had been made to fit his broad shoulders and muscled thighs. She hadn't seen anything so delicious since being talked into going to that male strip show in Fort Worth.

She quickly regained her composure. He might be easy on the eyes, but he was still trespassing. "Who are you?" she asked. When he continued to stare, she wondered if he had a few missing brain cells. "Do you understand what I'm asking," she said, speaking slowly.

His eyebrows drew together, then relaxed as a lazy smile formed, as though he realized exactly what she was thinking and the joke was on her.

She bristled. He stood in the middle of *her* living room as if *he* belonged there and then had the audacity to smile, completely disregarding the fact she held him at gunpoint. She aimed the gun lower.

His smile vanished.

That was better. He wouldn't think the situation was so damned funny if she blew his balls off. "I never miss what I aim at," she added for good measure.

"The bank is going to be robbed," he blurted.

Robbed? Yeah, right. Why would anyone want to rob the bank? The risk would be higher than what they could steal.

He suddenly closed his eyes.

What the hell? He acted as if he was about to leave. Was he planning to plow right past her? She tightened her grip on the gun. "How would you know the bank is going to be robbed?"

He opened his eyes, looking put out that she'd guessed his intentions and foiled his plan to escape. "Trust me," he said.

"You break into my home, then tell me to trust you. I don't think so, cowboy. Turn around and put your hands on the wall." It was a shame the guy was a few bricks shy of a load because he was damned attractive. Not that his appearance would influence her. She'd met her fair share of good-looking criminals who tried to talk her out of handcuffing them. Their charm never worked.

"The Randolph bank is going to be robbed tonight," he repeated his warning.

Okay, she'd play his game and see exactly what he was up to. "And how do you know this?" He crossed his arms. She tightened her grip. "Don't make me nervous." She motioned for him to lower his arms.

The slow smile appeared again, but this time it reached all the way to his eyes, crinkling them at the corners. The stranger was starting to piss her off. Their gazes locked and she found it difficult to look away. His eyes were an intense blue, mesmerizing. He broke the connection. His gaze slowly drifted downward as if he mentally removed everything she wore.

Her body began to ache with a need that burned low in her belly. When he finally raised his head, he wore an expression that said he knew exactly what effect he had on her and that she'd stopped thinking about shooting him. Maybe, but that didn't mean she wouldn't start up again. She raised her chin, daring him to try something and see what she was capable of doing.

"You're not willing to trust me?" he asked with a slow Texas drawl. He slipped one thumb into his pocket, his fingers tapping lightly against the denim.

Against her will, she watched, mesmerized by the motion of his fingers tapping, then brushing lightly against his pocket. With supreme effort, she forced herself to concentrate on getting him in handcuffs. She stifled a groan. That thought created a wealth of unwanted images.

Somewhere between Fort Worth and coming home she'd lost her edge. A month ago she would've had this guy in custody by now and be reading him his rights.

"How do you know the bank will be robbed?" she asked, deciding the more she knew, the better off she'd be.

He reached up with his free hand and removed his hat.

She jerked, almost pulling the trigger. "Be careful your next move isn't your last." He had no idea how skittish he was making her.

He paused, then slowly brought up his other hand and raked it through thick, dark blond hair before settling the hat on his head once more. He wore a pained expression.

Oh right, *he* was feeling put out. She was damn sorry she'd interrupted his plans to steal her blind. Next time she'd make sure she called out before entering the house in case there was another intruder.

"I'm telling you this because I promised someone I'd look out for you."

"For me? Really?" That was laughable. This kept getting better and better. The guy was lying through his teeth. "You'll be glad to know I can take care of myself."

He shook his head. "Not tonight you won't."

"What's so different about tonight?"

"You'll be shot and killed."

A flash of fear swept through her. She felt the color drain from her face, even knowing the guy was lying to throw her off guard.

He muttered something about that not coming out right, then cursed. "I didn't want to get involved." He drew in a deep breath. "Just be careful tonight, okay?" Then he apologized in an offhanded way. "I didn't mean to scare you."

Her hand trembled, then steadied as she took one hand off the gun and reached up to her shoulder. "You did get involved, though, and I don't scare easily." She pushed the button on the mike clamped to a loop on her shirt. The cord curled down to the radio hooked on her belt. "This is Raine," she told the dispatcher, dispensing with formalities. "I need backup at the ranch. I have an intruder." Her voice was firm, authoritative. She released the button.

The radio crackled. "10-4, Raine," a man's voice came across the air waves.

The radio crackled again and another man began to talk. "Put me en route. I'm already in my car."

"10-4, Ethan."

Ethan Miles was the last person she wanted to back her up. The lead deputy was a jerk. He always found fault, always pushed her buttons until she wanted to scream. But she didn't. Instead, she did her best to fit in. She was the outsider. It didn't matter that she'd grown up in Randolph. She had a feeling that was the main reason most of the deputies resented her. She *had* grown up in Randolph and they hadn't. But right now, she'd take whatever deputy they sent.

"You didn't have to do that," the intruder said. "I won't hurt you." He took a step toward her.

Raine's eyes narrowed. "But I *will* hurt you if you move any closer."

"Will you?" He took another step. "Look me in the eyes, Raine. Can you pull the trigger?"

She automatically looked up, then found once again that she couldn't look away. She blinked several times, but the longer she stared into his eyes, the more relaxed she felt.

"Your eyes are beautiful." His words were soft, as though he didn't want to break the spell he cast. "They're a very unusual shade of green with tiny silver sparkles."

"Stay back or I'll shoot." Her voice sounded as sluggish as she felt.

"I can't blame you if your finger gets a little itchy. Just not when you're holding a loaded gun pointed at me."

Shoot him! a voice inside her screamed, but she had no strength to pull the trigger. The man stopped in front of her and took the gun from her lax hand. He was right. She was going to die, but he wouldn't wait until tonight. He'd shoot her where she stood.

When she stumbled, he grabbed her arm to keep her from falling and followed until she backed herself against the wall. "You always have to be the one in control." He spoke the words so softly she had to strain to hear. "I'd love to show you how it feels to lose control."

"Who are you?" she managed to say. He was too close, invading her space. He was a scorching summer day, his breath warming her skin while waves of erotic heat shimmered down her body.

He set her weapon on a nearby table, but he never let her eyes break contact with his.

"I'm just someone who wants to help."

Some of her equilibrium returned and she raised her chin. "I don't need anyone's help. I've always taken care of myself."

"And your mother, too."

A cold chill trickled down her spine. "What do you know about my mother?"

"And your father. You took care of him. Now you're taking care of your grandfather. When will someone take care of you?" He touched her cheek.

A jolt of electricity shot through her. She flinched.

What was wrong with her? She could take this guy. One quick jab to his midsection and then one solid punch to his jaw and it would all be over. Only problem was her arms felt like she held fifty pound weights. "I don't need anyone to take care of me," she said with as much defiance as she could muster.

"Don't you?"

He reached to the back of her head and pulled one of the pins from the tight bun. "You're not a simpering Southern lady with a creamy complexion. Not that I've seen any. Just heard about sweet Southern belles. Maybe they don't exist." He shook his head as he studied her. "There's nothing pale about you. And you have a very determined chin." He removed another pin. A few dark auburn strands escaped to lie against her cheek. "Beautiful."

She managed to raise her arm. Her hand brushed his. "Stop."

"Why? Afraid I'll discover who you really are?" His gaze drifted lazily over her as his hand encircled her wrist. "Or are you afraid of what I can make you feel?"

Heat rose up her face because she knew there was some truth to his words. The guy was dangerous. Her movements were lethargic, but she defiantly raised her chin. "Release me or I'll make sure you're locked away forever and I'll be the one who throws away the key," she ground out.

"If you were in the cell with me, forever wouldn't be nearly long enough to enjoy making love to you." But he did as she asked and released her wrist.

She swallowed hard as images of the two of them naked in bed filled her thoughts. She forced them aside. "I'm an officer of the law and you're trespassing."

"You're right, but trespassing with you would be so damn sweet."

In the distance she heard a car. *Backup.* She should've felt more relief. What the hell was wrong with her?

He picked up her Glock off the table. Fear raced through her, but he only placed the gun in her hand, then stepped away. "A shame we couldn't have more time. I'd show you delights you've never even thought about.'

She held her gun tightly. She was right. The guy was crazy.

"Be careful when you patrol the streets tonight," Dillon warned. "There will be two men near the vault when you investigate a light. They'll be wearing black ski masks. One of them will be tugging on the collar of his dark sweatshirt as though the material is scratching his neck."

Raine squared her shoulders. How had he gotten the drop on her? And why did he return her gun? Was he crazy enough that he would play games?

"You'll have the drop on the bank robbers," he continued.

"Where do you fit into all this?" she finally asked, her voice scratchy.

"There will be a man behind one of the desks who sees you enter the bank," he continued, not bothering to answer. "When he bumps the chair behind the desk, you'll turn toward him. His gun will go off." He drew in a deep breath. "The bullet will hit you center chest. You'll be dead before you hit the ground."

"There are doctors who can help you," she said, then wondered if they might help her, too, because she had no idea how he was able to get her gun away from her. "I have to take you in." She motioned with her gun. "Turn around and place your hands on the wall, feet spread. Don't make any sudden moves or…or…I'll shoot." Her words lacked conviction and her hands were shaking. Her gut instinct kept telling her that if he were going to hurt her, he would have already had plenty of opportunity. What game did he play?

He closed his eyes.

The light in the hallway flickered, then popped before going out. She was suddenly surrounded by darkness. "Don't move!" she threatened as cool air swooshed around her.

Chapter 3

THE FRONT DOOR SLAMMED open. Bright morning light spilled from the hallway, momentarily blinding Raine.

"Officer Miles," Ethan called from the front porch.

Raine ducked into the hallway, leaning against the wall, heart beating faster than when Billy Ray asked her to the senior prom. What the hell happened?

Get ahold of yourself! You still have an intruder!

For just a minute, he hadn't seemed like an intruder.

He'd caught her off guard, nothing more. She was tired and he wasn't your run-of-the-mill intruder. The cowboy was sexy and he definitely filled out a pair of low-riding, snug-fitting jeans, but breaking and entering was still a crime and that made him a criminal. She knew there was more to it. He'd played her. That pissed her off. No one got the better of her. No one.

She shot a look into the living room. There were too many dark corners and too much furniture. He could be hiding behind anything. The living room was a hodgepodge of pieces that were only good for gathering dust. She should've hauled most of the stuff to the attic, but her grandfather had looked so pitiful when she mentioned downsizing that she didn't have the heart to make any changes. She was getting soft.

"Raine?" Ethan asked. "You okay?"

She'd forgotten her backup was still on the porch.

"I'm okay, but I don't see the intruder," she said. "The bulb blew in the hallway and the room went dark. He probably used the opportunity to hide. The hallway is clear." Her grip tightened on the gun. There was no way the guy could've made it past her. "He has to be in the living room."

Ethan moved down the hall to stand beside her. Raine had to admit the man was all business when it came to answering a call. He was a good cop, but knowing what he was doing didn't make him less of an ass.

"You need to fix the front door so it doesn't squeak," he chastised.

"I'm right on it," she told him and was privileged to receive his infamous cold-eyed stare. One look from his steely gray eyes would have criminals ready to sign a confession. "Can we take care of the intruder before I start the projects on my to-do list?"

His eyebrows drew together, and for a second she regretted her sarcasm. But only for a second. She was used to rocking the boat. When she had come home to Randolph and was immediately hired by Sheriff Barnes, the other deputies were pissed. Todd Bell from the next county over had planned to take the job. It didn't matter that he found a better paying one in Dallas with a chance for more training. She was pretty sure they still blamed her because Sheriff Barnes and her father were once friends and the other officers probably thought that gave her special privileges. Maybe it did, but she'd needed the job, so she took it.

Holding his gun with one hand, Ethan pulled his black Maglite from the loop on his belt and turned it on. He was all business.

"Was he armed?" he asked.

"No." She frowned. "I don't think so." His expression made her cringe. It was worse than the steely eyed look. Ethan always made her feel like she lacked a key ingredient to be a good cop. She raised her chin and met his gaze head on. "There wasn't a visible weapon. It doesn't mean he didn't have one on him."

He didn't comment, telling her exactly what he thought without words. Not that she cared. She only wanted the intruder behind bars so she could crawl in bed for a few hours of sleep.

The beam of Ethan's flashlight made its way around the room. Nothing. "If you're in here, you might as well show yourself. It'll go a lot easier on you."

Silence surrounded them like a graveyard at midnight. He reached inside and flipped on the light switch. Brightness filled the space, chasing away the shadows. He cautiously stepped farther inside. Raine braced herself, expecting the stranger to jump out at them any second, but as Ethan looked behind every piece of furniture, her anxiety grew.

"The man was right where you're standing. Tall, maybe six two or six three. Dark blond hair. Black cowboy hat." Raine hated the fact that she sounded apologetic. "He was right there," she said, but with less conviction.

"You just got off duty," Ethan said. "You're tired. Maybe you just thought you saw someone."

"I know what I saw. He spoke to me." She gritted her teeth to keep from saying more.

"Are you positive you didn't imagine him?"

The biggest slap in the face was when Ethan holstered his gun. He might as well have told her that he didn't believe there ever was an intruder. "No, I didn't imagine him."

"Did the man say anything?" Ethan asked.

She started to tell Ethan about the man's dire warning, but stopped herself at the last moment. What could she say? The bank would be robbed? She would be shot and killed? Ethan would *really* think she'd lost her marbles. "Not much. Nothing specific."

Maybe he'd slipped out of the house when Ethan drew her attention away after all. The stranger could've gone past her.

She'd gotten maybe four or five hours sleep the day before. Last night her shift dragged by. Now that it seemed her intruder was gone, she no longer felt the adrenaline rush. Raine was so tired she could barely stand.

He sighed with exasperation. "If he didn't say anything, then can you describe him a little better? Did he have a beard? Was he unkempt?"

Hysteria bubbled inside her. The stranger could have posed for a tropical paradise ad. A blond hunk with an amazing tan walking on the beach, white shirt flapping open in the breeze, no shoes, slacks rolled up to his ankles. He didn't look like he belonged in a freakin' line-up!

Before she could say another word, footsteps sounded on the stairs behind them. They both whirled around. She pointed her gun up the stairs at the same time Ethan drew his gun back out of his holster.

Her grandfather stopped halfway down the stairs, his eyebrows drawn together. "What's all the blasted commotion? A body can't get a decent night's sleep around here anymore."

"Grandpa, what are you doing home?" Raine holstered her gun as relief and a twinge of anger filled her. Her grandfather was getting forgetful and frail. He was supposed to stay at Tilly's on the nights she worked, which kept him out of trouble. Did she have control of any situation?

"I had Tilly bring me back last night. This is my house. I don't need a dang babysitter." He continued down the rest of the stairs. "I don't like sleeping in a strange bed, either. Makes my joints ache. Besides, you've been doing all the chores and working at the sheriff's office. I was up at four this morning and got them all done. Now you can get some decent sleep."

"You're okay, Mr. McCandless?" Ethan asked.

"Why wouldn't I be?" Grandpa groused. "I look okay, don't I? I ain't too old to milk Bessie or gather a few eggs."

Something close to a snort escaped before Ethan covered it with a cough. "You look fine, Mr. McCandless." He put away his gun.

Ethan treated Grandpa a lot like he did her. Or was she imagining the tone of his voice? She was tired and on edge. She directed her attention back to her grandfather. She would talk to him later about staying at Tilly's. "Did you hear anyone in the house, Grandpa?"

"I did." He came down the rest of the stairs. When his feet were solid on the floor, he reached down and massaged one knee with a grimace. "Damned arthritis," he mumbled.

"You're okay, though?" Ethan asked.

"No. I'm getting old. Arthritis ain't a bit fun. Pills don't help, neither."

Her heart skipped a beat. Grandpa didn't understand the seriousness of the situation. "There was an intruder. He was dressed like a cowboy. Ethan wants to know if he hurt you." Raine's gaze ran over him, looking for any sign of injury, but other than being bothered by his arthritis, Grandpa looked fine.

"No, why would he hurt me? I'm the one who asked him to come."

Her eyebrows shot up. "You asked him?"

"Yeah, I asked him. I prayed for a miracle and he showed up. I had to do a fine piece of talking to convince him to help. Can't rightly say why he decided to, but something must've changed his mind. All I wanted him to do was watch over you."

Finally, they might actually get somewhere. Grandpa would talk to anyone. The intruder was probably looking for work but found a trusting old man he could take advantage of by convincing

Grandpa he would watch out for her—if they paid him, of course. Her grandfather was a little gullible at times.

Ethan's eyes narrowed. "Can you describe him?"

Grandpa scratched his chin. "Describe him, you say." He hesitated, as though he was thinking about the man. "He was tall. Dark blond hair. Blue eyes. Black cowboy hat."

"It sounds like the same man," she confirmed.

Grandpa looked at her. "Of course it is. Who else would be in the house?"

"Was he armed?" Ethan asked.

"Now why would an angel need a weapon?" Grandpa looked at Ethan as if he was bonkers. "We had us a beer out there under the oak a few days ago and I told him 'bout the troubles Raine's been having." He sent a glaring look toward Ethan. "Not that this is any of your business."

Her stomach flipped over. Her grandfather's cognitive abilities were rapidly declining and it broke her heart. If Ethan said one word to him, she…she'd knock him into tomorrow. She had a hell of a right hook!

Deep breath. Exhale. She had to stay calm, get a grip on the situation. "Grandpa, think about how that sounds. An angel drinking beer?" Her voice was soft, as though she spoke to a child.

"I ain't crazy, if that's what you're thinking, and he ain't really an angel."

She let out a whoosh of air. Good, her grandfather hadn't completely bought into the stranger's story.

"He's a nephilim."

"Excuse me?" Ethan's eyebrows drew together.

"A nephilim," Grandpa repeated, enunciating the syllables as though Ethan was a little slow. "He's only part angel. The other part is man. You see, the way he told me was that his father, who was an angel, came down and bedded this beautiful mortal woman. Well, she had a baby who was mixed race, you could say. Dillon can answer prayers. That's why he came. I prayed for a miracle."

"And you had a few beers together." Ethan looked as though he had it all figured out and there were probably more than a few beers involved.

"The mortal side of him still likes all the pleasures of the flesh—like drinking."

And sex? The thought crossed Raine's mind before she could stop it. She shifted her weight from one foot to the other, telling herself not to let her thoughts drift in that direction. She must really be tired.

Ethan pushed the button on his mike. "False alarm, Art. I'll take a look around but I doubt I'll find anything."

Raine raised her chin in defiance. There had been an intruder. She didn't care that Ethan chose not to believe her.

"I don't guess you need me," Ethan said when he was off the radio. "How many people can say they have their own guardian angel?" He snickered as he walked to the door, but stopped before going out, then turned to look back at her. He studied her for a moment as though he was trying to decide if she was crazy, too. "Just in case, I'll check the outbuildings and drive down the surrounding roads. *If* there was an intruder, the highway isn't that far. He'll probably hitch a ride with someone."

"Ass," she muttered when he was out of hearing range.

She didn't imagine the intruder. He'd been in the living room. She might have imagined him taking her gun...

A cold chill swept over her. She looked past the screen door to the trees outside, but not a leaf stirred. There was something about the stranger's eyes. Such an intense shade of blue. They drew her in and held her captive. One time when she was swimming in the ocean and the tide was going out, she'd gotten caught in the undertow. She struggled to get to shore and finally made it. The intruder had that same kind of pull, almost hypnotic.

She frowned. But then he'd broken the connection. No, she didn't think she imagined any of it.

Raine forced herself back to reality. She was practical, and she certainly didn't think any man could sway her like he had if she wasn't so blasted exhausted. If she didn't get some sleep she'd start believing Grandpa's story about the intruder being an angel. No, Grandpa called him a nephilim. Half angel, half man.

There was only one logical explanation. The stranger was a drifter who drank Grandpa's beer, then almost got caught. He made up the crazy story about her getting shot and killed, hoping it would distract her.

Damn, damn, damn! She wanted this guy caught and locked away. No one took advantage of her. No one!

She glared at the light fixture. It was just luck that the bulb blew out and he could make a run for it. Ethan was probably right about the guy heading for the highway. What she wouldn't give for a moment alone with the intruder so she could show him exactly who was in charge of the situation.

"Never did like that boy," Grandpa mumbled, breaking into her thoughts.

She shook her head, having forgotten her grandfather was in the room. She definitely needed more sleep.

He nodded toward the front door when she didn't comment. "When your father was alive, he would've put Ethan in his place fast enough. People respected him. He was a fine sheriff." He swayed, then grabbed the newel post.

Raine rushed forward. "You okay, Grandpa?"

"Of course I'm okay. Why wouldn't I be?"

Raine slipped her arm around his waist. He was frailer than he had been a month ago. A moment of panic seized her. What would she do when he was gone? Grandpa was the only family she had left.

"Your dad was the best sheriff this town ever had." He slipped his arm across her shoulder and squeezed.

"Yes, he was." For a moment, the past rushed back. She looked down the narrow hallway and could almost see her father's jacket hanging on a peg, his holstered gun on another. Hank McCandless had been larger than life, and when the sun sparkled off the silver badge pinned to his shirt, Raine thought he must be part of Heaven above. A bright star that fell from the sky to shine on her life.

"Then your mother ran off with that greasy salesman," Grandpa said, drawing her back to the present. "I told Hank the guy was bad news. Lucy never needed none of that junk the salesman sweet-talked her into buying. Hank couldn't afford to spend that kind of money on her, but he did anyway. He never was the same after she took off."

A deep ache began to build inside her. *No, don't let the past come back!*

Except she couldn't stop it. Raine's world tumbled down around her the day Lucille McCandless hugged her and said she had to find her own life, that Lucille felt suffocated on the ranch. Raine had been eleven.

At the time, Raine didn't understand what she meant. Lucille made a phone call and left. Her father rushed in the house twenty minutes later, taking the stairs two at a time, then came back down, stumbling. The paper drifted from his limp hand as he sat hard on the stairs, as though his legs wouldn't hold him.

Raine picked up the note and read her mother's words, then folded the sheet into a small square and tucked it inside her back pocket. Her mother wasn't coming home. She drew a deep breath and climbed the stairs to sit beside her father. His hand was frigid, and the cold seemed to reach all the way to her heart.

His tears were the hardest for Raine to accept. That day her father stepped down from the pedestal she'd put him on. He was only human after all. She swore no one else would hurt him and took up the reins. But she couldn't keep her promise.

A few years later, when he was lying in his casket, she remembered thinking his hand felt as cold as the day her mother walked out. It stood to reason, since that was the day he changed from a loving father to a walking corpse.

"I know the people in town say crazy runs in our family, but your dad weren't any crazier than me," her grandfather said.

Startled, she looked at him, having forgotten the thread of their conversation.

"What?" she asked.

"Crazy don't run in the family," he stated more forcefully.

She hugged him. "Of course it doesn't."

"Dillon will fix everything."

"Dillon?"

"Yep. Our angel. Now, let's get something to eat. I'm starved."

Oh yeah, the angel who hypnotized her with his blue eyes. The one who told her she would die tonight.

Maybe crazy did run in the family because she wasn't thinking about dying. Her thoughts were centered on how Dillon had made her feel for one brief moment.

She rubbed the cold chills that popped up on her arms and hoped like hell she never laid eyes on her intruder again. She didn't like losing control, ever.

Chapter 4

"So, you've entered the land of the living," Chance said as he leaned back in the saddle.

Dillon studied the man he'd called friend for a few centuries. If Chance was being sarcastic, Dillon didn't see it. "Yeah, it would seem I have." He nudged the sides of his horse. The mare reluctantly raised her head from the clump of grass she'd been chewing and set off at a nice easy pace. Chance nudged his horse's sides and they rode in silence for a few minutes.

"It's about time, too," Chance commented.

Dillon looked around at the hills dotted with pecan and oak trees, thick green grass dancing on the breeze that rolled across the land. Longhorns grazed where their ancestors once roamed. Above them, a hawk soared across the deep blue sky, floating on a current of air. The landscape was incredible. He felt as though he was seeing it anew.

Dillon's thoughts immediately turned to Raine. She'd made him feel alive for the first time in a long time. *As alive as Lily had made me feel?* He sucked in a deep breath as soon as the thought crossed his mind. He tried not to think about her because inevitably pain and guilt followed.

Besides, Lily and Raine were as different as night and day. There was nothing strong about Lily. She was a fragile orchid in a garden filled with weeds. Mortal men worshipped her, ready to do her bidding. And then she captured the heart of a nephilim. Dillon knew he wasn't supposed to interact with mortals, but he couldn't resist her beauty. Because of him, a demon also noticed her.

He gripped the reins a little tighter. Demons were soul stealers. They promised mortals a better life with untold riches until they gladly signed a contract with the devil. The demons failed to disclose all the facts, though. They would get nothing until they met their own quota of souls. After that, they would be cast into the fires of Hell until all semblance of humanity was charred from their bodies. Only after that would they become full-fledged demons, but by then they would be as hollow as the demon who recruited them.

He didn't care that the demons were keeping their distance and it was unlikely they would bother Raine. He was finished and refused to become emotionally involved with another mortal. They carried way too much baggage.

The other three nephilim, Chance, Ryder, and Hunter, said he needed to let go of the past. That wasn't always easy. But if they thought answering an old man's prayer to watch over his granddaughter was returning him to a life he'd just as soon forget, then he was better off. It would give him a rest.

"Be careful." Chance shifted in his saddle and met Dillon's gaze.

In other words, don't let his emotions rule. There was no chance of that happening again. The others never let him forget. Sometimes they reminded him of overprotective fathers.

Chance and Ryder had known each other longest. Dillon joined up with Hunter when a pesky demon almost fried his ass and Hunter jumped into the fray and saved him. Hunter didn't say a whole lot. He didn't mingle much, either. Dillon and Hunter had run into Chance and Ryder late one evening when they were scrounging for food.

They were just kids back then who left home once they realized they had special powers. Chance and Ryder were afraid their town would come under attack by demons. The demons were afraid of the new race created to keep mankind safe. They liked nothing better than to kill the young offspring of angels. And why not? It seemed the angels were not overly concerned with their young's welfare.

Dillon left because he couldn't stomach the spiteful aunt who cared for him after his mother died. She was always jealous of her beautiful younger sister. When she discovered her sister's son was fathered by an angel, her jealousy turned to anger because she wasn't chosen. She took every opportunity to tell Dillon his father left him to fight against demons without the skills he needed to survive. Before he left, he told his aunt that his father gave him exactly what he needed, an aunt who was worse than any demon he would ever meet. He never saw her again.

Hunter became his family. Then when Dillon and Hunter met up with Chance and Ryder, they figured four nephilim trying to survive were better than two, so they joined forces. They had each others' backs.

Except Ryder was gone. He left behind a gaping hole of ache. "Do you miss him?" he suddenly asked, knowing Chance would know who Dillon meant.

Chance didn't say anything.

Dillon wondered if Chance heard his question until he noticed Chance gripped the reins until his knuckles turned white. His grip loosened and the color returned.

"Yeah." Chance cleared his throat. "I miss him a hell of a lot."

They rode in silence for a few minutes, each lost in his own thoughts, until the cry of a hawk broke their reverie.

"Don't let this woman get to you," Chance said, turning the conversation back to Dillon.

"That won't happen."

"You're sure?"

"She reminds me of the runt in a litter." She did in the beginning, anyway. Dillon thought he'd be safe when he saw her getting out of the pickup. Raine did a good job of downplaying her looks. The hat cast her face in shadow, hiding her delicate features. The loose-fitting shirt didn't add anything remotely inviting.

"That bad?" Chance asked.

No, not bad at all. He frowned. "She smells good. Like jasmine and honey. Intoxicating." And she had a nice ass, but Dillon figured he'd keep that to himself.

"Sometimes all it takes is a woman's scent to drive a nephilim insane with desire. It's rare, but it can happen."

"Not with this woman. She's not my type."

"How so?"

"She's kind of mannish. I like them a little more feminine. She likes taking charge."

"Be careful."

"I always am. Besides, I've warned Raine about tonight. The rest is up to her." She might not have believed him, but he bet she would be more cautious. *There's nothing I can do. It's in her hands. I'm out of her business...and safe.*

If that were the case, then why the hell did he feel as though nothing good would come out of this? He kicked the sides of his horse and yelled, "I'll race you."

"You can't win!" Chance grinned as his horse lunged past.

Dillon didn't care. He just needed to feel the wind on his face. Most of the time, he tried to stay away from mortals. Raine's grandfather had been persistent, though. For some strange reason, Sock's prayer kept attaching itself to Dillon's every thought. No matter how hard Dillon tried to block his plea, the old man's voice penetrated until Dillon had to answer or go stark raving mad.

Then Dillon met him. He should've walked away, but he'd hung around because he liked listening to the stories the old man told. Tales about when he bought his ranch and how he worked the land. Dillon understood exactly how Sock felt. The land could take a broken man and make him feel whole again.

That quickly changed as soon as Sock started rambling on about his granddaughter. Dillon had felt a heavy thud hit him center chest, a premonition, then nothing. He knew Raine would die soon if he didn't intervene. He grimaced. Raine didn't need a guardian angel; she needed a full-time sitter to keep her out of trouble.

Dust swirled when Chance pulled back on the reins in front of the barn. As soon as the air settled, he turned in his saddle with a wide grin plastered on his face.

Dillon slowed his horse, patting the animal's neck when they came to a complete stop. She was a good mount, but couldn't beat the other horses. It didn't bother him. He never let much of anything annoy him.

"Like I said, you can't win."

Dillon grinned. "Then let's get a beer."

"Yeah, I bet you swallowed plenty of my dust."

"I'm glad I have my boots on because the bullshit is getting deeper." He swung to the ground, then drew in a deep breath of country air. This was where he was supposed to be, at their ranch, not answering prayers. Mortals were a strange breed. Why Ryder had been so intrigued by their lives was beyond him. They carried way too much baggage. He was glad to be finished with Sock and his granddaughter.

After they took care of the horses, they walked to the house and straight to the den. Chance was the first to the refrigerator, too. Coming in second didn't bother Dillon, especially when Chance handed him a cold beer. Dillon twisted off the cap and took a drink. Yep, the most he wanted to worry about was if it might rain. Even that didn't overly concern him.

Chance broke the silence. "So, you're not returning?"

Dillon carried his beer to the lounge area and sat in one of the overstuffed chairs, stretching his legs out in front of him. "Returning where?"

"To the girl."

"Raine?" He shook his head. "Why would I do that?"

"You had glimpses of a bank robbery. You said she would get shot."

He took another drink, trying not to think about Chance's words. "I warned her."

"You think she listened?"

"She's not stupid."

Dillon watched him from the corner of his eye. Chance took a drink, then sat on the sofa across from him. "She can take care of herself," he finally said when Chance didn't continue the conversation.

"I'm glad." Chance shifted to a more comfortable spot, then sighed.

Anyone would think Chance had dropped the subject, but Dillon wasn't buying it. He waited for round two until he could no longer stand the silence. "Hey, I answered a damn prayer. What more do you want?"

"We're not keeping score," Chance calmly pointed out. "Answer prayers if you want. It's not a requirement. We only started answering them because we were bored."

"I know what you and Hunter have been thinking."

One eyebrow shot up. "Really? You can read minds now?"

"Both of you figure I'm afraid to get involved. That I don't want to screw up again."

"You didn't screw up the last time. It wasn't your fault."

Dillon slammed his beer down on the end table and came to his feet. "Don't you think I know that? She gave up her soul because it was easier than trusting me. She bought the demon's lies easy enough, though." He should've protected her better.

"Because she wanted what the demon offered: wealth, power, to always be beautiful," Chance quietly said.

As though Chance swung a sledgehammer toward him, Dillon flinched and turned away. "She wasn't like that. The demon made her that way."

"You never could see the truth when it came to her. She manipulated you. She still is. It's time you forgot about her."

Dillon's head jerked around. Their eyes locked. "Forget Lily?" His laugh was bitter. "I can't." He was the reason she'd been swayed by a demon. He'd failed, and it cost Lily her soul. Dillon would never understand why the others couldn't see just how fragile and beautiful Lily had been.

"Stop feeling guilty."

"Don't you think I would if I could?" he answered honestly. "Every day it eats away at me." That was why he didn't talk about her. If he kept her in a little box at the back of his mind, maybe he could bear the blame he felt.

The room began to close in on him. He had to get away. "I'm going to the cabin." He closed his eyes.

"Don't," Chance said. "Dammit, you've never been able to see what she was…"

His words trailed off as Dillon transported. The wind rushed past, lights swirled. A few minutes later, he stood on solid ground and was finally able to breathe again.

He opened his eyes and looked around. The land was rough and rugged, the terrain uneven. Oaks reached out with gnarled limbs, scraggly cedars stood like aged sentinels, and mesquites were like unruly children ready to poke the unmindful with their thorny branches.

He stood in front of the cabin. The structure was small, only one room and a small bedroom that branched off. There was a fireplace for cold winter nights and a kitchen with the basic appliances. This was all Dillon wanted. Peace settled over him. Here was his sanctuary. Nothing could touch him.

There was a small barn next to the cabin. He went inside and grabbed a tool belt hanging from a peg on the wall. He eased more tension fixing fences for one hour than he could doing anything else.

He worked until sundown then dove into the cold river to wash off the sweat and dirt. When he crawled into bed, there wasn't an ounce of stress left inside him.

Except for a persistent humming that had been with him most of the day. Now that he was still, the humming sound began to evolve into words.

Dillon groaned, grabbing the pillow and turning on his side. "Go away, Sock!"

The old man's voice grew louder and louder.

"Damnation! I did what you asked! Leave me be!" But he couldn't block the infernal man's prayers. His words droned like angry bees.

Chapter 5

"THANKS, MR. UNGER." RAINE gave one more tug on the tarp that covered the sacks of feed they'd loaded onto her truck.

"Yeah, no problem. Your papa was a good man. He made sure the deputies watched my feed store every night. Not one break-in since I opened. Sheriff Barnes is a good man, too. Anytime you want, I'll stay here. Not everyone would come home to take care of family. You're a good kid."

She smiled and didn't try to explain she wasn't the same little girl who would stop by every once in a while to say hi. She was a grown woman. Mr. Unger was nice and he stayed past closing hours so she could get feed before her shift and not have to make a special trip into town.

She turned the key and, after a couple of false starts, the pickup started. She waved to Mr. Unger who smiled and waved back. Next stop, the drugstore. It was only a few minutes away, but then everything in town was only a few minutes away. She parked the truck and went inside.

"How can I help you?" the clerk asked.

"I need to pick up pills for Sock McCandless."

The girl nodded, moved to a row of white paper sacks, and glanced through them. "Here they are." She looked at the ticket. "It'll be twenty-two fifty."

They'd gone up again. Figured. Raine reached in her pocket and pulled out her cash. She hated to part with her last twenty but she didn't have a choice. She handed the girl the money and left the store.

She climbed in the pickup again and slipped the key in, but this time the damn motor didn't even try to turn over.

"Having problems, ma'am?" asked a male voice with a lazy Texas twang.

"It won't start, so yes, I'd say I have a problem." She turned to glare at the man, but as soon as she shifted in her seat and got a good look at the guy, she knew who it was and her stomach began to churn uncomfortably.

Raine lost her virginity to Dwayne Freeman in Grandpa's barn one hot summer day. She was fifteen and he was seventeen. The rumor going around was that Dwayne had experience. The rumor was true.

That summer she fell in love for the very first time. He taught her a lot in those three months, but then school started. Dwayne made the football team and started dating a cheerleader. He never gave Raine a second look. She'd cried for weeks.

A few years later, he and his two younger brothers inherited the salvage yard when his mother died. His brothers were still in high school and would be for another three or four years. They were a little slow on the uptake.

Dwayne thought his looks and expertise in bed would carry him through life. They didn't. Carousing all night with his buddies was aging him fast. His hair was thinning and he carried a definite paunch. He looked fifteen years older than Raine instead of only two.

"I heard you were back in town." He leaned against the door.

"Looks like you heard right, then, doesn't it."

He grinned. "You've gotten kind of uppity since you moved off to the city."

She cocked an eyebrow.

He laughed as he swaggered to the front of the truck and raised the hood. He disappeared for a few minutes, then stuck his head out from under the hood. "Now try it."

She turned the key and the engine fired up. "Thank goodness," she mumbled. She couldn't take another expense.

Dwayne looked around for something to wipe his hands on, then leaned against the door again. "You should bring it by the yard and I'll go over it real good. I'll take care of you, Raine. You know I can. Besides, I'm working on old vehicles now. Going to get me another business on the side. I should be rolling in greenbacks in a few months. We could have us a lot of fun. Catch up on old times."

Barf. His lines might have worked when she was an innocent kid, but the grown woman was a little smarter and a whole lot wiser. "I've got to get to work," she said.

He wiggled his fingers. "Got anything I can wipe my hands on?"

She didn't point out that they weren't that clean before he stuck them under the hood; instead she reached into the floor of the pickup and scooped up a white rag, shoving it at him. "Uh, thanks, Dwayne," she called out as she quickly shifted the pickup into reverse and backed out of the space. And she *was* grateful. But not grateful enough she wanted to be friends or anything.

It was sad to think Dwayne starting Old Red was the best thing to happen to her that day. It wasn't going well at all. She couldn't convince her grandfather to stay at Tilly's. Grandpa had a mind of his own and he wasn't about to let her talk him into leaving his bed. Not that Raine blamed him. She would probably be just as stubborn if she lived to be seventy-five years old.

She parked the pickup, got out, and went inside the sheriff's office. She headed straight for the coffee pot. She was drinking her second cup when Darla, the night dispatcher, came inside.

A door slammed.

Raine flinched.

"You're jumpy tonight," Darla said as she grabbed a soda from the refrigerator.

What would Darla say if Raine told her an angel said she would die tonight? An angel—*really*? You would think he could've come up with something a little more plausible.

Raine studied the thirty-year-old divorcee. Knowing Darla, she would probably ask if her intruder was single and worry about the rest later. Darla went through men as fast as she did packages of chewing gum.

Raine held up her cup and kept her thoughts to herself. "Too much caffeine." The last thing she needed was another person thinking she was crazy.

Darla puckered her mouth. "Coffee goes with working the graveyard shift. If it's not a man screwing up my nights, then it's the frigging hours I work." She chuckled at her own joke.

There was something Raine liked about Darla, although they had absolutely nothing in common. Darla had been married three times and had two children. She loved men and she didn't mind telling people. She lived by one rule: she didn't date coworkers. Everyone else was fair game.

"I heard someone broke into your house. You okay?" Darla watched her as if she thought Raine might suddenly break into tiny little pieces.

She shrugged. "He was probably a drifter. I took one of the horses and searched the area, but he was long gone. I doubt he'll come back since he knows I'm armed." She drained her coffee and carried her cup to the sink.

"And Grandpa?"

Raine rinsed her cup. The first time Darla met Raine's grandfather she'd given him a great big hug, then blushed. It was rare that anything embarrassed Darla. Grandpa had good instincts, though. He guessed Darla needed roots after bouncing around from town to town when she was growing up. He hugged her back and told her and the boys to call him Grandpa, which absolutely thrilled Darla.

"He's fine," Raine said, drying her cup before returning it to the cabinet. "He wouldn't go to Tilly's though."

Darla nodded, then began to chew her gum so fast Raine was afraid she might break a tooth.

"What?" Raine asked.

"What's what?" Darla repeated.

"Your jaw will be sore if you don't slow down." Raine could almost see the light bulb go off in Darla's brain.

"Oh, my gum. When I get nervous I chew faster."

"I know."

Darla chewed faster, then realized she was doing it again. She spit her gum into the gray trash barrel.

Raine had never known Darla to be this skittish. Something was on her mind. "What's bothering you?"

"Is Grandpa getting old-timers?" Darla finally blurted. She twined her fingers together, biting her bottom lip.

Old-timers? "You mean Alzheimer's?"

She nodded, bleached blond ponytail bouncing around her head. "Yeah, the disease that makes people forget everyone."

"Of course not," Raine reassured her, hoping she spoke the truth, but the same thought had crossed her mind more than once. He didn't leave water boiling on the stove, and most of the time he told her where she left *her* keys. No, he wasn't losing his mind. He was a little gullible but that didn't mean he was crazy.

"Ethan said your burglar told Grandpa he was an angel and Grandpa believed him. Not that I believe everything Ethan tells me, but I think the other deputies do. Ethan said Grandpa should be in a nursing home so people can look after him. He said Grandpa's a danger to himself and if you wouldn't do anything about it, he might not have a choice. What did he mean?"

Nursing home? Locked away? Ethan might do it, too. If he called in Adult Protective Services they might think the same thing. In any case, it would be more problems for her to deal with and she had more than enough now. The room swam in front of Raine. She put her hand on the counter to steady herself.

"You okay? I didn't mean to upset you. Are you going to be sick?"

Raine turned the water on and began washing her hands. "I'm fine. Ethan is an idiot. Grandpa trusts people more than he should, but it doesn't mean he's losing his ability to function." She yanked a paper towel from the roll and dried her hands. When she faced Darla, Raine's emotions were under control. "There's nothing wrong with Grandpa except he's getting old. Ethan doesn't want me working here and this is another way he's trying to force me to quit."

Darla's features relaxed. "You're right, but I was worried there for a moment. Ethan better leave Grandpa alone or I'll send him on calls to the end of the county." She grinned. "Maybe he'll get lost and never come back."

Raine doubted that would happen. Her luck wasn't that good. "I'm going to make a couple of runs through town."

"And I need to get back to the dispatch desk." She rolled her eyes. "Justin hates being there by himself. Did you know he's barely out of high school? Lives will be in his hands when I get through training him. He told me that manning the call center terrifies him." She chuckled. "Does he think someone's going to rob the bank?" Darla was still laughing as she left the break room.

Raine didn't see the humor.

She left the station and climbed into her patrol car to begin her rounds. Raine and Leo were the two deputies on the night shift. He was probably on the other side of town at the truck stop. There was a new waitress and it was a well-known fact he liked to flirt.

As she turned the corner, her cell phone began to ring. She slipped it out of her pocket. "Hello?"

"I was worried about you," her grandfather said.

His voice brought a smile to her face. *He* was worried about *her*. "I'm fine. Why aren't you asleep? It's after midnight."

"Restless, I guess. Seems like the older I get the less sleep I need. I went out to the barn. I sort of found a stray tonight."

Grandpa was bad about *finding* strays. He once nursed a raccoon that got its paw mangled somehow. Her father hated the animal and told Grandpa he'd better get rid of it or else. The raccoon stayed and her father never pushed the issue.

Raine guessed the raccoon was just so old and tired of fending for itself that the animal decided he would hang around for a while since he got free food and a warm straw bed in the barn. A couple of years later the old raccoon passed away in his sleep. Her father was the one who dug the grave behind the barn and put fresh straw inside the hole. Grandpa and Raine made a cross out of two twigs and tied them together with string.

"What kind of stray?" She barely made enough money to feed them and the livestock. Another animal was out of the question, and this time she would be firm.

"I'm going to call her Lady."

"Grandpa, we can't—"

"She's a beauty, little girl."

Grandpa was playing dirty using the nickname he'd given her. His ploy wouldn't work. They couldn't afford to nurse another animal.

"She's a golden retriever and has the sweetest nature, but right now she's a little scared of people. I...uh...think she might have been abused. Mind you, I don't know that for sure 'cause I don't know who the owner could be, but she's a little skittish."

Abused? Like the horse he rescued? Oh no, that was the reason he was on probation.

No, Grandpa wasn't foolish enough to steal another animal. He'd promised. That didn't mean they could afford to feed another animal. She mentally calculated the cost of a bag of dog food. A golden retriever would eat a lot. No, they couldn't keep her.

"Her front leg is cut kind of deep. I put a poultice on it."

She heard the hopeful note in his voice. He'd lost so much over the years. His wife, his son. "We can only keep her until she's healed," Raine finally told him.

"Of course," he quickly agreed. "I better go check on her."

"Grandpa, I don't want you wandering around outside at night."

"I know, I know. That's why I brought Lady inside."

She opened her mouth to tell him the dog absolutely could not stay in the house, but couldn't bring herself to say the words. "Are you sure she doesn't have rabies or something? No tags, identification of any kind?"

"I'm positive. She doesn't have a thing wrong with her other than a cut leg."

Maybe the dog would watch over him. She knew a little

about the breed and they were good animals. When did life get so complicated? "Okay, Grandpa, I'll see you in the morning."

"Be careful."

"I will." She touched *end* and tossed her cell phone in the passenger seat as she turned the corner. They would manage somehow. She supposed if the dog didn't stay long, the cost wouldn't break them.

Her radio crackled and drew her attention back to her job. She waited for Darla to talk.

"Hey, Raine," Darla's voice came over the radio. "I almost forgot. Ethan wants you to go by Dwayne Freeman's and ask if he knows where his brothers were last night. That new math teacher's house was papered and whoever did it got a little carried away. They busted a taillight on her car and shoe-polished that antique light at the front of her house. The teacher said she put the boys in detention for a month, and the rumor going around is that they were going to get even with her."

Raine stifled her groan. She had enough of Dwayne's company earlier tonight. "Yeah, sure," she muttered. "I'm on top of that one." But she didn't say what she was thinking. She pushed the button on the mike. "I'll head that way now."

"If you need backup, let me know."

Backup? Dwayne was a jerk, but she could handle him.

She slowed as she drove past the bank. A flicker of light caught her attention. It was so brief she thought her imagination was playing tricks. Who wouldn't see boogeymen when the seed was planted? And the stranger had planted a whole row.

The rational side of her brain said keep going. Follow up on Dwayne's brothers. Why would anyone want to rob a bank in a small town?

She pulled around the corner and stopped. This was stupid.

Totally insane. She grabbed the mike and spoke. "Unit eight will be—" She paused, knowing Darla never remembered the ten codes.

"What's that, Raine?" Darla asked.

Raine counted to three, then keyed the mike again. "I thought I saw a flash of light inside the bank. It's probably nothing, but I'm going to check it out." So much for protocol.

"Want me to get Leo to back you up? He's over at the truck stop."

"I'll let you know if I find anything."

"Okay, sweetie."

Darla didn't sound worried. Neither should Raine. The last major crime in Randolph was when Dwayne's brothers robbed the laundromat and got a bag full of quarters. They might have gotten away with it, but two of them were going around town buying gas and junk food. They paid the merchants in quarters. It didn't take a rocket scientist to figure it out. Ethan had brought them in. He said they confessed as soon as he read them their rights. Every day after school they picked up trash along the side of the road. They might think twice about their actions after six months on clean up detail.

Raine brought the windows up and locked the car. She had an obligation to see if her mind was playing tricks or if the flash of light was real. So what if the other deputies taunted her tomorrow about her imagination working overtime. She shook her head. What was a little more fuel added to an already burning fire?

She slowed her steps as she went around the corner, scanning the area, but all was quiet, peaceful. The bank was a beautiful old building built in 1886 using brown brick hauled all the way from Mexico. It sat between the pharmacy and a dry goods store. Between the pharmacy and the bank was an alley, a shortcut to the sheriff's office when Raine was still in school.

She'd sit in her father's office doing homework until he left for the day, then he would take her home in the patrol car. Her mother hated the relationship Raine and her father developed. Lucille forbade any talk about work. How could they not talk about it? Law enforcement was in their blood. Maybe that was why she left them. If they talked about the weather, would she have stayed? Doubtful.

As Raine drew closer, the hairs on the back of her neck stood up. She stopped and glanced around one more time. Nothing. She tried to shake the bad feeling crawling over her, but couldn't. The intruder's words echoed in her head.

There will be two men in the bank near the vault when you investigate a light.

Unless the intruder was involved, how would he know? And why warn her? Maybe he'd developed a guilty conscience. Something told her there was more going on with him, but every time she tried to figure out what it could be, her head pounded until she gave up.

She flipped the snap on her holster, peering around the side of the pharmacy and down the alley. Empty. Her hands trembled. She leaned against the building and took a couple of deep breaths. She'd once been described by a fellow officer as fearless. She wasn't, but she loved the adrenaline rush.

She walked down the alley until she was at the side door of the bank. It would take an explosion to unhinge the reinforced steel. Someone would have heard the noise. She tested the knob. Locked.

Of course it was locked. This was Randolph. They didn't have crime. At least, none that would make headlines in a major newspaper. She started to turn away, but hesitated at the last moment when the hairs on the back of her neck tingled. Her dad used to tell her she had a natural instinct when something wasn't quite right. He also told her to always trust her feelings.

Instead of going back to her car, she tested the door once more. Again, nothing budged. The tingling persisted. "What am I missing?" she murmured as she ran her hand over the rough-textured brick that framed the door.

One of the bricks shifted. Her heart skipped a beat. She slowly moved her hand over the bricks, dislodging two of them. The door might be heavy duty reinforced steel, but the brick surrounding it had been there a long time.

Loose bricks didn't mean there was a bank robbery in progress, she told herself. That didn't stop the fluttering in her stomach. There was one way to find out. She carefully removed four bricks and set them on the ground.

She looked through the opening, but it was too dark to see anything. She cringed at the thought of sticking her arm inside a dark hole. It reminded her too much of gathering eggs and sticking her hand beneath a hen. The stupid birds always pecked her.

Just like gathering eggs, she gritted her teeth and did it anyway. The lock wasn't hard to release. It was a little too easy, in fact. As if someone made sure the lock was oiled. She opened the door and stepped inside the narrow hallway. At the other end was an open door that led into the main part of the bank. The lights were always left on low in the lobby. Only a scant amount of light spilled out. She glanced down the shadowed hall. It seemed to stretch for miles.

Something else bothered her. The door that led to the lobby was always kept closed. An employee could have left the door open. Friday night, the end of their week, a hot date—it happened.

A streak of light flashed past the opening.

Raine sucked in a breath, not daring to exhale. Muffled voices drifted from inside the bank and down the hallway.

She eased back outside, heart beating faster. Once she was out the door and halfway down the alley, her breath came out in a whoosh. Trembles raced over her as she pressed the button on her mike. "Darla, you there?"

There was a moment of silence. She was starting to worry when her radio crackled.

"She went to the bathroom," Justin's voice squeaked over the airwaves.

Darla would really appreciate him telling everyone in the county who owned a scanner that she was peeing. Raine almost pitied him.

She reached into her pocket for her phone and realized it was still on the passenger seat. What the hell was happening to her?

"Darla's been gone for a while and should be back pretty quick—"

Raine heard the door to the dispatch office slam against the wall.

"What the hell are you doing?" Darla's voice came over the airwaves. "I told you I would answer any calls on my portable radio."

"You didn't, though."

"Because I flushed the toilet and I didn't want to broadcast my location," she snarled.

Raine gritted her teeth and waited for Darla to realize Justin still had the mike open and their conversation was being broadcast for everyone's amusement. Until Justin released the button, Raine couldn't communicate with dispatch. At this rate, she would have time to jog back and get her phone.

"Sorry," Justin said.

"Don't let it happen again."

"Yes, ma'am."

"Ma'am? Did you call me ma'am? You're not *that* much younger than me. I'm not sure you even—"

There was a moment of silence.

"Why are you still holding the button down?" Darla's voice trembled with suppressed anger.

"Sorry."

It hadn't taken Darla long to figure out she was quickly gaining notoriety as late night entertainment. She might not be too smart when it came to picking husbands, but she knew dispatching inside and out. Darla once said she'd been a screw-up all her life. Being a dispatcher made her feel as though she could finally do something right.

Except for the ten codes. Someday they would work on that.

"Take…your…finger…off…the…button." Darla spoke slowly, clearly. There was a distinct clicking noise, then Darla's voice came over the radio, still shaking. "I'm sorry, Raine. Did you need something?"

It was about time. "There's a burglary in progress at the bank."

"You're serious?"

"Very."

"I'll send backup."

"I'm going to investigate. I'm turning off my radio." Raine didn't wait for Darla to respond before she turned the knob. She'd wasted too much time already. Darla would go into a long spiel about Raine waiting for backup and she didn't have time to listen. She removed her gun before moving back to the door and eased inside the building.

When her back was pressed against the wall, she realized how vulnerable she would be if she continued forward. There would be no place for her to run if the burglars realized someone was in the hallway.

She could turn around and wait for backup. Ethan was probably on his way, definitely Leo. They would keep her safe and have her guard the front while they checked out the inside of the building. She would be completely out of danger. They might be jerks ninety-nine percent of the time, but they would make sure she was out of harm's way.

As if she was going to let that happen! Why the hell should she let them have all the fun?

Her respiration increased as she swiftly made her way down the hallway. She didn't stop until she was at the open door. She could feel the blood rushing through her veins, releasing adrenaline. Energy flowed through her body. The cop who said she was fearless definitely had it all wrong. It wasn't fearlessness. It was the excitement, the danger of the job that sent her pulse racing. Living on the edge was a high like no other.

A flash of light in the other room ricocheted and bounced off the wall before continuing on. She forced her breathing to slow, then took a quick look into the other room, but didn't see anyone.

The bank was one large room, except for three offices on the east side. Four teller windows were on the north, and the walk-in vault was on the west side. The floor was still the original hardwood. Carpet would have muffled her steps a lot better. Old floors had a way of squeaking at the wrong time.

There was a silk wisteria in a gray planter not far from her. The branches were covered in green leaves and purple silk blooms that draped down like clusters of grapes. The tree would give her a better vantage point to determine exactly what she was up against and it would get her out of the hallway.

After making sure the coast was clear, she quietly moved into the open, keeping low, moving quickly. Once she was in position, she drew in a calming breath. The adrenaline rush, the release of endorphins was heady, but she knew from past experience that feeling invincible didn't *make* her invincible.

The view from behind the tree was better. She could see Flashlight Man standing near the vault with his back to her. He was built like a bulldozer, but other than a dark blob, she couldn't tell anything else about him.

"In and out," he whined. "That's what you said. You know I don't like closed-in spaces. I'm claustrophobic." He turned in her direction, swinging the flashlight around the room.

Raine quickly ducked. The beam of light swept past her without pause. She tentatively raised her head. Bulldozer had his back to her again. She didn't recognize the voice, but that didn't mean a thing because the black ski mask he wore muffled his words.

Another man stepped from the vault. He was dressed similar to Bulldozer—dark clothes and a ski mask pulled over his face—but he wasn't as large. He shined his light directly on Bulldozer.

Bulldozer stumbled back a step. "I've got asthma and this mask is making it hard to breathe, and this sweatshirt itches." He tugged at the collar.

They'll be wearing black ski masks. One of them will be tugging on the collar of his dark sweatshirt as though it's scratching his neck.

A cold chill of foreboding enveloped her. She quickly shook off the feeling. It was only a coincidence.

"Will you shut the fuck up? As soon as we get these bags loaded we can get the hell out of here. Quick and easy, just like I told you." He grabbed the flashlight out of Bulldozer's hand and shoved against his shoulder. "Now get in there and fill those other bags."

Apparently, he was the leader.

Bulldozer quickly ducked inside the vault. "It's dark in here" came his muffled voice.

The leader mumbled something Raine didn't catch, but she would bet it wasn't pretty. She was starting to feel like she'd been cast in a bad B-movie and she already knew the ending. What? Was she actually starting to believe the intruder? Maybe he was right about the bank being robbed, but not about her dying tonight. No one was that good at predicting the future, and she had a different ending in mind.

She weighed her options. There were two burglars and one of her, but she had the advantage since they didn't know they were being watched. Foiling a bank heist might get the other deputies off her back. She hated office politics.

As much as she wanted to take these idiots in without asking for help, it wouldn't be the smart move. Raine knew she had to go back the way she came and wait for the perps to leave. They wouldn't stand a chance when they made their escape down the alley because she and the other deputies would be waiting.

She was nearly to the door when the quiet of the night was shattered by a souped-up car zooming down the street a few blocks over. The car's muffler growled like a lion ready to feed. She knew the car from the sound—a red 1980 Mustang that belonged to seventeen-year old Cory Bradley. He had way too much time on his hands and extremely indulgent parents.

Raine froze at the same time the thief's flashlight made another sweep. The beam swept past her before she could get out of its path. The light swung back in her direction.

She had no choice. "Hands in the air," she yelled as she faced the robber, her gun pointed directly at him. He reached for the ceiling. "You, inside the vault, get out here where I can see you."

"I told you this wasn't a good idea," Bulldozer said as he stepped out.

"Shut up!" the leader growled.

"Hands in the air," she said again. "If you don't think I won't put a bullet in you, just try me. I haven't shot anyone since I patrolled Fort Worth's north side and I might be a little trigger happy." She'd never actually shot anyone, but this was a need-to-know situation.

Bulldozer reached toward the ceiling.

The hairs on the back of her neck tingled again. She frowned.

There will be a man behind one of the desks who sees you enter the bank. When he bumps the chair behind the desk, you'll turn toward him. His gun will discharge. The bullet will hit you center chest. You'll be dead before you hit the ground.

Bulldozer's eyes strayed to her right, toward the desks.

Her lungs felt as though they were deflating. She couldn't draw in a breath deep enough to get oxygen to her brain. Everything around her slowed.

There was a dull thud as a chair bumped a desk.

You'll be dead before you hit the ground, you'll be dead before you hit the ground, you'll be dead before you hit the ground sing-songed inside her head, but she was frozen in place.

If she could relive her life, she would have sex a lot more often. Odd how she would think about sex right before she died.

Chapter 6

STRONG HANDS SHOVED HER forward as the deafening report of a gun echoed through the bank. The side of her head slammed into the hard floor. Bright lights flashed in front of her eyes. The room blurred and voices faded.

"Fuck! I didn't mean to shoot her," someone said.

"Idiot! Someone probably heard your gun go off!" someone else yelled. "Grab the bags and let's get the hell out of here."

The voices all sounded the same as they ran together. Did that mean she had a brain injury or something?

"Do it! Now!"

Her head pounded harder. *Please be quiet*, she silently prayed as the thudding inside her head grew louder and the sound of running feet grew faint. The bank robbers were getting away. She blinked, trying to force her vision to clear. Where was her gun? She reached out to feel along the floor but a sharp pain shot down her arm.

Oh God, had she been shot?

She gingerly felt the side of her head. No blood. She wiggled her fingers. Nothing wet ran down her arm, either. If she'd been shot there would be blood. Her head pounded as she sat up. She'd really whacked it good. She waited for a wave of dizziness to pass, then looked around for her gun. Her intruder was right about everything except being shot and killed. She was still alive.

She needed her gun. Moving to her knees, she looked behind

her. The air left her lungs with a whoosh when she spotted a body and the puddle of blood. She remembered someone pushed her out of the way. "Oh crap," she whispered. He took the bullet for her.

She scooted to her knees and knelt over him. There was a lot of blood. Too much. "That was a stupid thing to do!"

The intruder from her home opened his eyes. "I didn't think so at the time. It'll only sting for a minute."

He was going into shock. Blood oozed from the center of his chest. He was going to die because of her. Where was her backup? *Please, please,* she silently prayed, *don't let him die because of me.* She turned on her radio then pushed the mike. Nothing. She must've jarred something loose when she hit the floor.

"Help is on the way," she said. "Why the hell were you robbing a bank?"

A smile tugged at his lips. "Haven't you figured it out? I didn't rob the bank. I'm an angel. Sort of. I'm a nephilim."

He was already hallucinating. "I know that's what you told Grandpa."

"He's a very persistent old man."

"Shh, don't talk. Help will be here soon." But would it be soon enough to save him? "I need to call an ambulance."

He grimaced. "Won't do any good." He took her hand in his and squeezed. "We'll see each other again. I promise." His eyes closed.

"Don't you dare die on me!" She jumped to her feet, then swayed as though she'd downed a six-pack. She weaved to the nearest desk and grabbed for the phone, missed, then connected on the second pass. Her stomach lurched. She swallowed hard, forcing herself not to be sick, and punched in 9-1-1.

"Hello?" Justin answered, then cleared his throat. "I mean, 9-1-1, what is your emergency?"

"Bank robbers. Man shot. Need ambulance," she mumbled as the room began to spin. Her head felt too heavy to hold up. If she could just rest it on the desk she would feel better in a few minutes.

"Did you say that you've been shot?"

Had she been shot? No, she didn't think so. "The angel. Someone shot my angel." She aimed for the phone's cradle but missed. Not that she cared. Her head rattled worse than Old Red.

She grabbed a pink sweater that had been left on the back of the office chair and weaved back across the room. "If you die I'm going to be really pissed," she mumbled as she moved to her knees. "Promise me you won't die."

He opened his eyes. "I promise I won't die."

She folded the sweater and placed it over his wound to stanch the flow of blood. He was going to die and she knew there wasn't a damn thing she could do about it. She'd seen people with gunshot wounds center chest like this one. Hell, she was surprised he was still talking.

"Your name is Dillon, right?" She thought that was what Grandpa called him. For a moment the man was silent, and she wondered if she was having a conversation with a dead man, then he dragged his eyes open.

"Yeah."

"Why the hell would you take a bullet for me?"

He smiled, but it quickly changed to a grimace. "Why, don't you think you're worth saving?"

She shook her head. "Not if it means your death." Where was the ambulance? If Justin screwed up calling one she would strangle him with her bare hands.

"Kiss me," he said, words strained.

"What?" She jerked back enough that her head felt as if

someone was shooting a game of pool inside and they just dropped three balls into the pockets.

"Grant a dying man his last wish. Kiss me."

She frowned down at him.

"I saved your life and this is all I ask in return."

Ah hell, it was the least she could do. "You don't have a disease or anything?"

"I'm clean. I promise."

It wasn't as if she would ever see him again. She was immediately filled with guilt. Thinking hurt way too much. She leaned down and brushed her lips over his, surprised by the warmth of his. She thought they would be cold.

His hand went behind her head and brought her closer. He deepened the kiss. Warmth spread over her when his tongue began to caress. *He damn sure doesn't kiss like a dying man*, she thought as shivers of pleasure ran down to her belly, then settled lower, between her legs. Everything around her vanished from her mind. It was just her and him all alone and…

The sound of a siren broke into the fantasy building inside her mind. She scooted away from him, but swayed when the room swam around and around. Her palm rested on the floor until the room stopped spinning.

"Good-bye, Raine."

"No, not good-bye. The ambulance is here and you're going to be fine." He had to be fine. She refused to let him die saving her life. "I'll show them the way. You just lie still."

She came to her feet, wobbled again, then started down the long hallway that led outside. She had to hurry and let the paramedics know someone was dying. A sick feeling grew inside her belly, curling into a tight ball. She was nearly to the door of the bank when it was kicked open. She stumbled forward and would have fallen through the opening if someone hadn't grabbed her arm and jerked her out of the bank, shoving her against the outside brick wall. Her head cracked against the brick exterior. Her body throbbed from the force of his attack.

"Oh hell, the bank robbers came back to finish me off."

Her stomach rumbled as she blinked past the fog surrounding her and met the ferocious glint in Ethan's eyes. Not the bank robbers, then. She glared at him. Who the hell did Ethan think he was— Rambo? He was always kicking down freakin' doors. "What are you doing?" she said, pushing against him, but for some reason she had no strength. And her head was pounding so hard her vision blurred.

"I didn't know who was coming out," he said. "You okay?"

"I need an ambulance. Hurry."

His gaze swept over her. "Where are you hurt?"

"Head."

"Raine, stay with me." Ethan jiggled her shoulder.

Her head pounded. She opened her eyes. "Stop shaking me."

"Who was shot?" Ethan asked.

"A man. Inside the bank. I think he's dying." She fought back the bile that rose inside her. *Please don't let him be dead*, she silently prayed. He was probably one of the bank robbers, and he had broken into her home, but he saved her life and she didn't want to live with his death on her conscience.

"One of the robbers?"

"No. My guardian angel." He was now, anyway.

"There's no one in the bank," Leo said as he rushed out as if he'd been running for a long time. "The vault is open and money's scattered on the floor. We better call the sheriff."

"I did before I arrived," Ethan said. "Just in case."

Just in case? What, did he think she made up a robbery in progress?

Raine glanced at Leo. She hadn't heard the other deputy go inside the bank. She must've knocked her noggin pretty good. Leo royally screwed up this time if he hadn't spotted the guy on the floor with a bullet hole in him. "You didn't trip over him?"

"Huh?"

"Never mind," she said.

Leo glanced toward Ethan. "I swear, I searched everywhere and there's no one in there."

Ethan ran his fingers over her head, stopping when he grazed the bump above her ear.

"Ow!"

"Head injury," Ethan pronounced.

"I bumped my head when the guy shoved me out of the way. He took the bullet. If not for him, I'd be dead."

Flashing lights and the whine of a siren filled the alley. The ambulance screeched to a stop, turning off the siren. A good thing, because much more noise and she was going to pass out. Her eyes were already crossing.

Two men got out, grabbing the cot and jump kit out of the back. Raine recognized the crew but she couldn't remember their names, and her head was still pounding so she didn't try.

"Where's the gunshot victim?" the taller one asked, practically pinging off the wall.

"She's hallucinating," Ethan told them.

"No, I'm not. He's in there." She pointed toward the door and lost her balance. If Ethan hadn't grabbed her, she would've fallen. The paramedics quickly lowered the cot. Ethan guided her until she was sitting on the thin mattress.

"We have to check it out," the ambulance driver told Ethan.

Bless him! Dillon could be dead by now. She swayed again. Ethan put her feet up, forcing her to lie back.

Leo shrugged. "Go ahead, but there isn't anyone in there."

Her eyes narrowed. Leo looked her way, but as soon as he caught her angry expression, he turned away. Something bothered her about him. "What took you so long to get here?"

"Flat tire," he mumbled.

"I'll stay with her, you check out the bank." The paramedic's partner eagerly took off.

The name tag on his shirt had Raymond J. Smith on it. "I'm RJ, deputy," he told her. She liked his voice. "As soon as I get your blood pressure do you think you can tell me what happened?" He strapped a cuff around her arm.

"I'm okay." Frustration filled her. They should all be looking for the injured man.

He smiled, but didn't say anything as he pumped air into the cuff and stared at the dial. A few seconds passed before he released the air. "Your blood pressure is only a little high. That's a good sign."

"I've been trying to tell everyone I'm okay. I would have been shot if he hadn't pushed me out of the way. He took the bullet meant for me."

"And you hit your head?"

Finally, someone was actually paying attention. "Yes."

"Pretty hard?"

"Hard enough."

"Were you knocked out?"

She was dazed, but she remembered hearing the bank robbers running away. Then nothing. "Everything blurred and my head hurt, but no, I was aware of what was going on."

"But you're not positive?"

"Not absolutely." She rubbed her forehead, then grimaced when the pounding started again.

"Nothing," the medic said with more than a little disappointment as he came out.

Leo was right behind him. "It's as I said, there's no one in there that has been shot. The only person inside is Mr. Aimsley."

"Damn!" Ethan exploded. "He's going to contaminate the scene. Why did you let him go inside?"

Now he questioned Leo's intelligence?

"He must've come through the front. He's the owner and has his own key, you know." He didn't try to hide his sarcasm.

"Stay with her." Ethan stormed inside.

She closed her eyes. Where could the guy have gone? She brushed her fingers across her lips. They tingled in response.

"Did he give his name?"

She opened her eyes. "Who?"

"The man who was shot."

"My guardian angel?"

Leo snorted. He was a real ass.

"Dillon," she said. "His name is Dillon."

"Matt Dillon?" Leo smirked.

She opened her mouth, then snapped it closed. "Dillon is his first name. I don't remember his last name. Grandpa might know."

"Your grandfather was in the bank?" Leo asked.

"No, the man was at my home this morning." She suddenly realized how she sounded. "He's not really my guardian angel, but he did save my life," she told RJ. She sighed and closed her eyes. No one was going to believe a word she said. It sounded too ludicrous.

"We'll take you to ER and have Doc check you out." RJ and his partner wheeled the cot to the back of the ambulance and loaded it. She was glad when RJ was the one who climbed in with her. On the ride to the hospital she couldn't stop wondering what happened to the man who saved her life.

The next few hours were a blur. She'd never answered so many questions in her life. Even Sheriff Barnes grilled her about the bank robbery.

Then Grandpa came to the emergency room after she told him not to, but at least he called Tilly to bring him. The woman was a blessing. Not only did she take in guests at her bed and breakfast, but she let Grandpa stay if she had a spare room and at no charge when Raine worked. She said it was nice to have a man around. Apparently, they were no longer angry with each other.

Grandpa and Tilly went for coffee. Why, she had no idea. The caffeine would keep him up for hours. She glanced at the clock. The doctor agreed to let her go home after she badgered him, but only if she stayed another thirty minutes for observation. She'd already been there two hours, wasn't that enough?

"It was the angel who saved her," Grandpa stated boldly from the other side of the curtain. "Her guardian angel pushed her out of the way and saved her from a bullet."

"Where is the angel now, Mr. McCandless?" a man asked.

Raine's eyebrows drew together. "Grandpa, who are you talking to?"

"That guy from the *Randolph Tribune*. He's doing a piece on the holdup." He cleared his throat. "Dillon, that's the angel's name, he wasn't in the bank. He disappeared. Whoosh! Maybe he went back to his ranch."

"The angel owns a ranch?" The reporter barely contained his humor.

"Grandpa, I think that's enough with the stories."

"It's fine, baby girl."

"The ranch?" the reporter urged.

Raine moved the pillow from under her head and covered her

face. Was it possible to suffocate herself? Or would she pass out first? It might be worth a try.

"Oh, yeah, he owns a ranch with some other nephilim."

"Nephilim? I thought you said he was an angel."

"Young fella, don't you read your bible? It's as plain as the nose on your face. You can read all about them in the Good Book."

"Grandpa," she wailed.

"Now, Sock, what are you doing that's causing so much distress to your granddaughter?" Tilly asked. "My goodness, I go to the powder room for a few minutes, and look what trouble you get into."

"Weren't no trouble. I was just tellin' this reporter fella about the angel that saved Raine."

"Did you see the angel?" the reporter eagerly asked.

"If I did," Tilly said, "I certainly wouldn't be telling you. Now shoo before I spill my coffee."

The curtain slid open. Raine kept the pillow over her face. "Take me home," she said, pretty sure they could understand her. She wanted to go home and crawl under the striped down comforter on her bed and sleep for at least ten hours. Her body ached from when she'd landed on that blasted hardwood floor.

But an hour and a half passed before she got her wish. She barely remembered the drive home or falling into bed. She finally dragged her eyes open at ten the next morning and pulled on her clothes. When Grandpa proudly showed her the front page of the newspaper, she wished she could go back to bed and sleep forever.

"Lookee here, baby girl, you're famous."

The headlines were big and bold.

BANK ROBBED! DEPUTY SWEARS ANGEL SAVED HER LIFE!

Raine groaned. It reminded her of the cheap tabloids at the checkout in the supermarket. Grandpa unfolded the paper.

When had the reporter snapped a picture? She peered a little closer. She was on the ER cot and her eyes were closed. The damn reporter had added a caricature of a grinning angel standing beside her bed.

Raine wished the blasted angel would go to Hell!

Chapter 7

DILLON HADN'T BEEN PLAGUED by Sock's incessant prayers, so he supposed the old man didn't have anything to complain about. "I'm glad someone is happy," he muttered, bringing his hammer down hard enough to bury the staple in the cedar post. "Yeah, they always take and take and take, then forget about you after they get what they want." He reached inside the leather tool belt tied around his waist and brought out another staple, but dropped it.

What was wrong with him? He should be thrilled he didn't have to listen to the old man's monotonous stories about life before corporations began to take over the world and run the government. He'd been there, too. He paused, hammer drawn back. Sock's stories were a lot more fun to hear, though. He was a born storyteller.

Dillon frowned. The old man was still a pain in the ass, though, and he *was* glad he didn't have to listen to him.

Or feel Raine's body pressed against his or imagine how it would feel to sink inside her body...

"Damnation!" Why did he even think about her? She wasn't his type. From what Sock said, she could get bossy and she was a workaholic. So what if her skin was soft beneath his fingers?

He was thinking about her again. It seemed that was all he did lately, no matter how hard he tried not to. He shoved his hand inside the tan leather pouch again and brought out another staple, spilling several on the ground. He didn't bother to pick them up. Before the day was finished, he *would* stop thinking about her! He reared his hand back and brought the hammer down as hard as he could.

The hammer slammed into his thumb.

Throbbing pain shot up his arm, then spiraled down to his toes before shooting back up to the top of his head. He bellowed out a string of curses, threw the hammer down, and grabbed the post as lights flashed in front of him. His thumb burned to hell and back.

Nephilim could feel pain, and right now he was feeling a hell of a lot. He closed his eyes and clamped his lips together, waiting for the healing to come. *Deep breath*, he told himself. *Deep breath and focus.*

The ache slowly began to ease. This was only his thumb and he knew it wouldn't take long to heal. Not as long as it took him to heal after getting shot during the bank robbery. Man, bullets stung.

His strained muscles relaxed. He eased his glove off, but he didn't need to be careful. His thumb was fine. To be certain, he moved it back and forth. No pain. Nothing. As good as new. Nothing ever changed.

He leaned his arm against the post, drawing in a deep breath. No, nothing ever changed. Answering prayers was a thankless job. Had he done the right thing helping them? As soon as that thought came to him, he quickly dismissed it. Taking the bullet that night had been his only choice. He couldn't let Raine die. A tender smile curved his lips. Her reaction had surprised him. Concern and worry shone in her eyes. He couldn't remember the last time anyone cared about his welfare. Sure, Chance, Ryder, and Hunter cared, but they shared a bond of loyalty and brother-hood that was unbreakable. Their feelings were expected. Raine was an outsider. He barely knew her, and most of that was from what Sock told him. Why should she care what happened to him? A stranger?

There he went, thinking about her again. Raine was like all the rest. The concern and worry had been from her near death experience, not because he was shot. If he hadn't pushed her out of the way, she'd be six feet under. That was why she'd hovered over him. She felt guilty.

He made a concentrated effort to put her out of his mind, and wiggled his thumb again. He should pay more attention to what he was doing and stop thinking about mortals. They always got him into more trouble than they were worth.

"Maybe you should use that hammer on your head," a deep voice spoke from behind him.

Dillon swung around, blinking from the sudden glare of bright light. It took a moment for the glowing image to come into focus and the brightness to fade.

A man sat on a pure white horse. The saddle was white and trimmed in silver, as was the bridle. He wore a white hat, white shirt, white jeans, and white chaps; even his boots were white. He didn't look at Dillon but rather the countryside as he drew in a deep breath of air. "I love the country," he said.

"Who are you?" Dillon asked with more than a touch of suspicion. A demon in disguise? He braced himself. Kicking a demon's ass sounded pretty good right now.

The man stared. Dillon took a step back, gut twisting. *I know him!* It was a gut feeling, nothing else.

"I'm your father Tobiah," he said.

Shock ran through him, but quickly died. He was surprised, that was all. *My father.* The words kept repeating inside his head, but the connection wasn't there. He'd never even met the man.

When Dillon was a kid he dreamed of coming face-to-face with his father, the angel who sired him. But as time passed, he grew tired of dreaming and he stopped wondering and waiting.

And he didn't care now. He strode to where his hammer lay and picked it up. "I have a father? I would never have guessed." He marched past Tobiah and began the journey back to the cabin. He didn't say a word for the next mile, but he could hear the steady clop-clop of his father's horse following him.

What did the angel want? Dillon doubted Tobiah suddenly had a yearning to meet his son. Too much time stood between them. Sure, he knew Tobiah had authority over him and, when he went too far, the angel would block Dillon's powers. That was the only time he knew Tobiah existed.

And when Dillon needed his father most, Tobiah hadn't been there. It was the same for the other nephilim.

Until recently.

Chance met his father. The angel saved his life.

Ryder's father almost fried his son with a lightning bolt. Yeah, that was a heartwarming reunion. They hadn't actually met, but that was the closest Ryder came to seeing him.

Now Tobiah showed up. Why?

The steady clop-clop continued. The sound was getting on his nerves. He should've ridden his horse, but this morning when he started out, Dillon hoped the walk would blow off some of the energy inside him. It hadn't. Pounding on posts most of the day didn't make much of a difference either. Raine was in his thoughts the entire time.

Still the steady clop-clop was behind him. His mood didn't improve by the time he stopped in front of the tool shed. If anything, he was more pissed. He unlatched the door and swung it open so hard that when it hit the building, the top hinge popped loose and the door dropped down like an arthritic old man. Something else for him to fix. He tossed the hammer and leather tool belt into the shed and swung around.

Tobiah sat on his horse, leaning against the saddle horn as casual and unconcerned as though they knew each other well and he was there for a visit. The fury inside Dillon exploded.

"Why now? Just answer me that. Why not after I ran away from home? I was eleven years old and alone. I called out to you. Where were you then?" Time passed; he should've been over the rejection. He thought he was, but apparently it had only been dormant, waiting for this moment.

Dillon always felt as though pieces were missing from his life. After his mother died in an accident, his jealous aunt raised him. Once she found out an angel chose her younger sister rather than her, his life became a nightmare. So he ran away.

He met his father's unwavering gaze and asked again, "Where were you when I needed you most?"

"I was nearby, watching over you."

"You saw my pain, and still chose to let me suffer? Angels are supposed to protect the innocent, not toss them out to fend for themselves."

"You were never alone. I protected you the best way I could, by helping you learn how to survive."

Pain gripped him. "Some nephilim didn't survive the demon warriors who hunted them."

"Yes," Tobiah agreed. "They came home. Their souls were never in jeopardy."

"In other words, you let them die. Would you have let me die too?"

"Your existence wasn't my choice to make."

"Yet, you're my father. What? Did you see my mother and

decide to sleep with her because you were bored? A mortal would never be able to resist your charms. You took what you wanted, then walked away without giving a damn about what might happen to her."

A dark light shone in Tobiah's eyes, telling Dillon he pushed too hard, but he didn't care. He wanted his father to feel some measure of the ache Dillon carried every day. As quickly as Tobiah's anger flared, it died.

"I loved your mother very much."

He didn't really care what Tobiah felt. "Why have you waited so long to show yourself?"

Tobiah's smile was gentle. "Hours and seconds pass differently for us. A day is but a speck of time."

"Why are you here?"

"Along with immortality, the nephilim inherited certain abilities. The angels look the other way when you bend the rules. There is more good inside our children than bad."

Dillon cocked an eyebrow. "Are you reprimanding me for something? You may be watching over me, but I think I'm a little old to scold." He snorted. "You might have fathered me, but you lost the right to tell me what to do. Time might not mean much to you, but it damn well did to me when I was a kid. I don't care what your reasons were for sleeping with my mother and creating a child, but as far as I'm concerned, you're a sperm donor, nothing more."

He turned to walk away, but his feet suddenly went out from under him and his ass landed with a thud on the hard-packed ground. For a moment, he sat there in stunned silence, then slowly came to his feet, brushing off the dirt. He faced Tobiah. "You want to fight, then fight like a man." He raised his fists, ready to relieve years of frustration.

Tobiah merely smiled, then glanced up at the sky. Dillon waited for him to get off the horse and take him up on the challenge. So what if Tobiah won; Dillon would still feel a hell of a lot better. Except Tobiah still looked at the sky. Dillon wondered what game he played. He finally lowered his fists and looked up.

A dark cloud hovered above him. What the hell? It burst open, pouring buckets of ice-cold water on top of his head. He jumped back, but he was already soaked. Deep, rumbling laughter followed.

"You think that's funny?" he yelled. He doubled his fists.

"That's what I like about the nephilim. You have the ability to feel so much emotion. You know how to live."

"Step off your horse and I'll show you how we fight, too!"

"I can't stay. Unfortunately, we have strict rules that must be obeyed." He suddenly smiled and Dillon felt as though he watched a commercial for whitening toothpaste. "You should meet my boss."

Dillon couldn't stop the disappointment flowing through him. He shouldn't let the guy get under his skin. Even as he tried to tell himself that, he still wanted to know more about him. "Then why are you here?"

"Raine McCandless."

He only thought the rain was cold as an arctic blast shot through his veins. Tobiah's words froze him in place. "What about her? She's okay, isn't she?"

"You changed her fate."

"I kept her from dying. What was I supposed to do? Let her get shot?"

He shook his head. "She wouldn't have died."

Dillon's eyes narrowed. "I felt pain in my chest."

"You warned her. She isn't stupid. She wore her vest. The

bullet wouldn't have killed her, only knocked her down from the force. She would have captured the bank robbers and been lauded as saving the day. You took all that away."

He squared his shoulders. "Okay, so either way, she wouldn't have died. The outcome is the same."

"Not quite."

"What do you mean?"

"When she hit her head, the blow momentarily stunned her. The bank robbers escaped. She saw you lying on the floor with blood pouring from your chest and called for help. She told them a man was shot. When they asked who the man was, she was still feeling the effects of her injury and told them an angel saved her. When no one could find the *angel*, people began to question if it was all an elaborate hoax. They wondered if Raine and her grandfather had planned everything. Her grandfather is close to financial ruin, after all."

"That's bull and they should know it. Raine and her grandfather would never rob the bank."

"We know that, but the people living in town don't. She was forced into taking a temporary leave of absence until the case can be investigated."

"It'll blow over. Everyone will realize their assumptions are ridiculous." He stared at his father and saw a flicker of something he couldn't name. Regret, maybe? Then everything came together and Dillon understood what his father wasn't telling him. "You know what's going to happen, don't you?"

"The investigation will go against Raine and her grandfather. They'll be arrested. Her grandfather's heart won't be able to take the stress and he'll have a heart attack and die. Raine will be found guilty and sent to prison, where she will die. Other lives they touched will suffer."

Frustration filled him. "I was answering an old man's prayer. What was I supposed to do? I thought she was going to be killed." He wouldn't have done anything differently. He had to warn Raine about the robbery. Before Tobiah could say anything, Dillon continued. "Why didn't he ask for my help when they became suspects?"

"He did, but you blocked his prayers."

"And Raine?"

His father grimaced, but his expression changed so fast, Dillon wondered if he might have been mistaken.

Tobiah's eyes softened. "Go to her, my son. She needs your help. Be gentle with her."

Why did he feel there was something Tobiah wasn't telling him? Before he could ask, a blinding light surrounded him, then in a flash, the brightness was gone and Dillon was alone.

But not for long. Raine needed him.

Chapter 8

RAINE'S HEAD POUNDED WORSE than hail hitting a tin roof. She reached up and ran her hand across her forehead. When her fingers brushed near her ear, she flinched. Her head was still tender. Doc had run some tests but they were negative. She had a feeling stress played a major role in why she had a headache. She hadn't been sleeping well since the night of the robbery.

Sitting at the sheriff's office most of the afternoon was not helping to get rid of the pain. What was taking the sheriff so long? He'd told her to be there around noon. She looked at the clock on his wall. It was fifteen after.

She felt as though she was living in a damn bubble and any moment it was going to pop. They still had her on a leave of absence until they finished with their investigation. Not working was driving her up a wall.

Her gaze roamed around his office—again—looking at the same travel posters that had been there since Sheriff Barnes took office: Rome, Paris, Venice, Switzerland. All the places he said he would go someday. That day hadn't come yet. He once told her people either had time or they had money. He'd laughed and said he had neither. That made two of them.

And now she might soon be doing time for a crime she didn't commit. No, if Sheriff Barnes thought she was guilty, she would already be sitting in jail. This was normal procedure. If she hadn't mentioned an angel she probably wouldn't be here.

Was she crazy? Had she only imagined a man getting shot? No, he'd felt real. He'd kissed real. Warmth spread over her. She crossed her legs, then uncrossed them. She'd only kissed him because she thought he was dying and that was his last wish.

He wasn't an angel, he was a manipulator. Dillon convinced Grandpa he was an angel. Maybe Dillon was the crazy one and really believed he was an angel. That would explain why he attempted to save her life. She sighed with frustration. But it didn't explain where he'd gone after being shot.

She came to her feet, legs cramping. She was tired of thinking and wanted to go home. Except no one was home. Grandpa was staying with Tilly so he would be nearby in case they wanted to question him. It was *suggested* they only have supervised contact. Were they afraid she and Grandpa would make a run for the border?

How could they be suspects? She shook her head. This all seemed unreal.

Tilly would make sure Grandpa was taken care of. Him and his new stray. It was a good thing Tilly had a fenced yard. She should be grateful Sheriff Barnes was giving them that much. He'd promised the informal investigation would only take a few days.

Her lip curled. Ethan was pushing for a trip to the mental ward so Grandpa could be watched. He said Grandpa was unstable. He was one to talk. Ethan might be lead deputy but he wasn't sheriff. The sheriff would never go for that. Grandpa was the main reason he won the election.

That might not mean a thing to him now. Sheriff Barnes had what he wanted and would probably keep getting elected until he decided to retire. She twined her fingers together. But the sheriff agreed with Ethan that Grandpa needed to stay nearby. What was going through the sheriff's mind? Did he think she was the mastermind? That Grandpa would be safer with Tilly? A sob tore from her throat as tears welled in her eyes.

Great, the last thing she needed was someone to walk in and see her crying. She rarely cried. Stay strong, stay in charge, that was her motto. Tears were a luxury she couldn't afford. Besides, it would be damned embarrassing. She turned toward the desk to grab some tissues out of the box and ran into a hard chest. Strong arms steadied her.

"Ow." She rubbed her nose. Her eyes watered more. Where the hell had he come from? Her eyes traveled up. She blinked, her vision blurry. It couldn't be. She scrubbed the backs of her hands over her eyes. But it was.

Dillon! Anger boiled inside her. He was the reason she was in this mess. "You! What are you doing here?" She must have really been lost in thought not to hear him enter the room.

He frowned. When people frowned they usually didn't look their best, but not this guy. A frown looked way too sexy on him. That pissed her off even more. He had no right to look that damned good when she was such a mess.

"I'm here to help," he said. "I'll make everything right."

"Good, you can tell them you were the one shot when the bank was robbed, then maybe everyone will stop badgering me and Grandpa." He was still holding her arms and his touch felt a little too warm, a little too comfortable. She wiggled loose and stepped back, her gaze sweeping over him.

The deep blue shirt molded to his chest while his jeans hugged his lower half. For a brief moment, she forgot what she was about to say as she stared at him. Her senses quickly returned when she remembered why she was there in the first place. "Why aren't you dead? I know you were shot. I saw the blood."

"I heal quickly."

The guy actually sounded genuine. She wasn't buying his tall tale this time. "You're one of the bank robbers. This is all an elaborate scam to make everyone think me and Grandpa robbed the bank. The gun was probably loaded with blanks. Fake blood, right?" Why didn't she think of this sooner? That was the only explanation. A short bitter laugh escaped. "I have to admit, you fooled me into thinking you might be a good guy."

"I really am an angel."

One eyebrow shot up. "I wasn't born yesterday." She studied him. "If you're an angel, where are your wings?"

He didn't say anything, just stared. She was right, the guy was loony. But he had the most beautiful eyes—hypnotic blue eyes. Very intense and… She drew in a deep breath and tried to remain focused, but he made it almost impossible to concentrate. "Stop staring at me."

"You're so damned beautiful," he said, but broke eye contact long enough for her to regain her senses.

"You say you're an angel, but you don't sound very angelic." With a physique like his it was a damn shame Dillon would end up locked away in a mental ward for the rest of his life.

She turned as Sheriff Barnes opened the door. A tall blonde Raine didn't recognize stepped into the office behind him.

"Sorry that took so long. Now we can talk," he said. "This is Emily Gearson, an agent with the Texas Rangers. She'll have a few questions of her own. Don't worry. This is an informal discussion. We're not accusing you or your grandfather of anything."

His smile was kind. He wasn't that old, only thirty-seven, but he always seemed so much more mature to her. He'd been her dad's lead deputy and worked at the sheriff's office since he was eighteen—too young to buy his own bullets. He was teased, but never seemed to mind.

Raine's gaze shifted. There wasn't one thing that stood out about the woman. Short blond hair, maybe five-eight. She wore a dark jacket and black pants with a light blue shirt. Texas Ranger? She didn't look as if she would hurt a fly—until Raine met her hard blue eyes. There was nothing soft about this woman. Raine had a feeling anyone she interrogated would be in for a shock.

Ethan Miles stepped inside. "You wanted something?"

"Can you make sure we're not disturbed?" Sheriff Barnes told him rather than asked.

Raine almost smiled. Ethan being in the room made her good news all the better. "That's the man who was shot," she said before Ethan could leave. "It was a setup." Her smile was wide.

Sheriff Barnes looked around the room until his gaze landed on his lead deputy. "Ethan?"

The agent studied Ethan as though looking at him in a new light.

"Like hell! I was picking up some papers from Joe and I can prove it."

"They can't see or hear me," Dillon quickly told her. "Cover up the blunder or you'll be in the state hospital before nightfall."

"But…" she began.

"Look at their faces," Dillon said. "They're not looking at me, but Ethan. They think he's the man you're talking about. If they can see me, why would they look at him?"

This wasn't happening. It couldn't be. Of course they could see him.

"Are you feeling okay, Raine?" Sheriff Barnes turned his attention back to her. The way he looked at her was as though he was seeing *her* for the first time.

No, she wasn't feeling well at all. She drew in a deep breath. "Yes, of course, and I certainly didn't mean Ethan. He's a very… uh…good deputy."

"Then who were you talking about?" Emily asked softly, but the glint in her eyes got a little sharper.

Fear trickled down Raine's spine. She was right about not underestimating the woman. Oh hell, she was losing her mind. Dillon was right, they would have immediately looked at him, not Ethan. Dillon couldn't be an angel! Demon, maybe, but he certainly wasn't angelic.

"I'm a nephilim," Dillon said, sensing her turmoil. "Half angel, half man. An immortal."

The mental institution she'd toured during her training was cold and bleak. White walls, drab brown furniture that looked like it came from a secondhand store. She rubbed her arms when cold chills popped up. She didn't want to be committed so doctors could prod and probe her.

Now everyone thought she was crazy. This was great. Just freakin' great! She drew in a deep breath and frantically searched for a way to get out of this new mess. "I didn't mean he's here at this very moment," Raine's words stumbled out. She scrambled to find the right thing to say that would make them stop looking at her like she'd lost her marbles.

"What *did* you mean?" Ethan questioned, eyes narrowing suspiciously.

She cast a look in his direction that should've fried him on the spot but it didn't even make him uncomfortably warm. She was losing her touch.

"We can handle everything from here," Sheriff Barnes said, then added, "Close the door on your way out."

Ethan frowned, looked at her once more as if he always knew there was something wrong with her, then left the room.

She breathed a sigh of relief until her attention returned to Emily and the sheriff. They still wanted answers. What was she going to do? She didn't want to be locked away.

"Tell them you were thinking about the bank robbery and trying to figure it all out," Dillon quickly said. "When they came into the room it was still on your mind."

What did she have to lose? "I was thinking about the bank robbery and trying to figure it all out. I guess when everyone came into the room I was still lost in thought."

"Good," Dillon told her. "Now say that you put two and two together and you figured out it was all a setup to make people think you robbed the bank. The robber who fired the gun probably used blanks and the man who pushed you out of the way had fake blood."

Really? She'd told him that very same thing before the others came into the room. It was her idea, not his.

"Just say it. You can tell me later the idea was yours."

Later? Yeah, she would certainly do that and then some, but she wasn't off the hook yet. "This is my theory." She put emphasis on *my* and went on to explain.

"Why would someone try to set you up?" Emily asked when Raine finished.

"So you would look at me and Grandpa and spend less time looking for the real perpetrators."

Silence filled the room. Raine studied their faces as they digested her theory. They didn't believe her. It was a far-fetched idea to begin with. If she lied and said she planned the whole thing, would they leave Grandpa alone?

"It's plausible," Emily finally said.

Raine's heart skipped a beat.

Emily turned to Sheriff Barnes. "We have been more focused on Raine and her grandfather." Her gaze swung back to Raine. "But how would they know you wouldn't have backup with you?"

"They probably knew what was going to happen before they

robbed the bank. Ethan was only on call, not on duty. That night he was at the south end of the county. It's no secret he plays cards every Wednesday. There's no way he could get back into town before the bank robbers finished the job, and isn't it odd Leo had a flat on that night? Everyone was delayed getting to the bank."

"She's right," Sheriff Barnes said.

Raine could feel some of her tension easing.

"Like you say, it's one theory." Emily's gaze met Raine's.

"You at least have them thinking about it," Dillon said. "Nice work."

"Of course," Raine countered, then realized they still didn't see or hear him. She cleared her throat. "Of course that's only one theory, but it makes more sense than me taking the money."

"Do you regret leaving Fort Worth?" Emily asked, changing the subject.

It took a moment for her brain to switch gears. "I miss a lot of things, but regret?" She shook her head. "No, I don't regret coming home. I would do anything for my grandfather." Loyalty meant something to her. She met Emily's gaze head-on and refused to look away.

Emily finally broke the connection when she sat in the chair next to the sheriff's desk. Raine felt a brief moment of victory, but it quickly disappeared. She longed to go back to the ranch but she had a feeling Emily wasn't finished. More questions. Raine knew she should be thankful they were still at this stage and they hadn't locked her in a cell, but she wasn't feeling generous. They should have put her at the bottom of the list of suspects, not the top.

Sheriff Barnes sat in the oak chair behind the desk. The same chair her father sat in when he was sheriff. The chair was on rollers and the seat swiveled. Hank called it his lazy man's chair because he could reach just about anything he needed without getting up.

There was a familiar squeak when Sheriff Barnes turned slightly. Raine gritted her teeth as a flood of memories rushed back. Her father would lean back in the chair and cross his arms in front of him and they would talk about everything under the sun. If they were going fishing that weekend, or maybe they needed to ride the perimeter checking fences.

You never know when a fence will be down, Raine. Always take care of what belongs to you. If you don't, someday you might look around and it'll be gone.

"Sheriff Barnes tells me your father used to be the sheriff," Emily said.

Her thoughts seemed so real that it was a shock to glance around the room and not see her father. He wasn't there. Dillon wasn't either. Maybe he never had been.

She sat in the chair facing them and raised her chin. "Until right before he died."

"Do you resent someone taking his place?" Emily crossed her legs, leaning slightly forward.

She looked at the sheriff. "You mean Sheriff Barnes?"

He glanced down at the papers on his desk. Was he trying to stay neutral? Her father would never have taken a back seat at any interrogation.

"The thought never crossed my mind," she told Emily. "Sheriff Barnes was Dad's lead deputy. He liked and respected my father. I wish my father was here, but he's not. No one will ever take his place, but if I had to choose someone to fill the slot he left open, I couldn't choose a better man than the one sitting behind that desk right now."

Sheriff Barnes raised his eyes; a slight smile played at the corners of his mouth. "Your father was a good man, one of the best." He leaned back in his chair, looking anything but casual. "I think we can leave Raine's father out of this inquiry."

Emily shrugged as if to say she'd only been testing the waters. Raine had a feeling Emily wouldn't cut her much slack. She would do the same thing if their positions were reversed. She could respect the other woman for doing her job.

Emily reached into her pocket and brought out a piece of paper. She carefully unfolded then flattened it with the palm of her hand. "You're not very old to have garnered so much praise from your superiors." She glanced up.

"I imagine we're close to the same age," Raine said.

For a brief moment, Raine thought she caught a glimmer of humor in the woman's eyes, but Emily quickly looked down at the paper so Raine couldn't be sure. Not that it would matter. The agent would still do her job.

"You also have a list of reprimands." She raised her gaze to meet Raine's. "You've taken a lot of chances at the risk of your own life."

"I did what I had to do at the time."

"Like what happened on the drug raid last December?"

How could someone not remove a crying child from a house where a drug deal was going down? If they stormed the place, bullets would fly. The child was in a room by herself. Easy in, easy out. Until one of the drug dealers opened the door to get his stash of drugs out of the closet.

"I removed the child from a hazardous situation."

"The man sued for police brutality and almost won. The trial still cost the taxpayers, though."

Raine cocked an eyebrow. "He tripped." Could she help it if his windpipe landed against her fist? He hadn't been able to call out a warning and she'd removed the baby from the house unharmed.

The questioning continued until Raine thought her head would explode. After an hour had passed, Sheriff Barnes cleared his throat. "I think that's all we'll need for today."

Emily looked as though she might protest, but she nodded instead. "Of course, you won't leave the area."

Where would she go? "I won't go farther than the ranch." She came to her feet.

"Oh, just one more question," Emily said.

Raine was about ready to scream. "Whatever I can do to help." Yes, her words sounded sharp, but Raine didn't care. Her head hurt and she was tired.

"You said you would do anything for your grandfather. Would you rob a bank for him?"

"Of course not!"

"Why was he there that night?"

"He wasn't."

"Yet his handkerchief was found at the scene."

"No." Raine shook her head.

"Your grandfather's brand isn't an M with a leaning C beside it?"

"Yes, but…"

"The cleaning lady discovered the handkerchief in a corner near the vault, along with your notepad, but in your statement you said you were nowhere near the vault. Now, I'll ask you again, was your grandfather at the bank that night?"

Chapter 9

RAINE SAW THE LOOKS as she left the sheriff's office. The kind where you turn and catch someone watching you as though you've sprouted two heads. When they realize you've caught them staring, they quickly turn away. As she strode toward the door she encountered more than one of those looks.

Except one person didn't turn away. Ethan. He acted as though he knew something she didn't. She met his stare head on. There was no way in hell she'd back down.

Another deputy spoke to him. Ethan turned away. A draw. So be it. She held her head high as she walked toward the door, but on the inside she shook like a leaf during a windstorm because the truth was starting to sink in. Dillon was an immortal. An angel. Half angel. If he was a freakin' angel why did he look at her as though he wanted to carry her to bed? And where the hell were his wings? She shoved on the door and marched out of the sheriff's office.

Weren't angels supposed to make a person's life better? Dillon had only screwed hers up. What little respect she'd gained from the other deputies was lost. She and Grandpa were suspects. They might as well have the plague.

"I was better off without him," she muttered.

She stumbled. Dillon *really* was an angel, an immortal. No, half angel, half man. A nephilim. This wasn't really happening. She didn't believe in any other world except the one she lived in right now. Immortals didn't exist. But if Dillon didn't exist, that would make her and Grandpa both crazy. She needed to talk with Grandpa.

She climbed into the pickup and slammed the door closed, then tested to make sure it was secure. Everything was falling apart. The pickup, the ranch, her job. She'd like nothing more than to tell everyone to kiss her ass, but she didn't have that luxury. Quitting wasn't an option. They needed the money. She only hoped they cleared her as soon as possible. She shoved the stick shift into reverse and backed out of the parking space. If she and Grandpa had a guardian angel, then why the hell didn't he at least fix something?

Tilly's place was on the edge of town. A little country, a little city. She'd bought the big rambling Victorian not long after her husband passed away. The house was practically falling down. Her friends told her she was crazy when she used what was left of her husband's life insurance to restore it, turning it into a B&B.

"We're not suspects," Raine told her grandfather after she went inside. "It's a formality." Then she explained to Grandpa how it would look better if he stayed with Tilly. She didn't mention that his handkerchief and her notepad were later discovered near the vault. Raine told him she would take care of the stock. He finally agreed to stay put for now.

Tilly didn't seem to mind that Grandpa had picked up another stray. The golden retriever was beautiful. When Raine thought about it, other than her bandaged paw which was on the mend, the dog was well-groomed for an animal living off the streets. They should put an ad in the Lost and Found, she supposed, or they would be accused of stealing dogs next, even though the dog apparently didn't have a collar or tags. She was getting paranoid.

"Tilly, I don't suppose you have any of your peach tea. I'm really thirsty," Raine said.

"Where are my manners? Of course I do."

As soon as Tilly left the room, Raine turned to Grandpa. "Tell me everything you know about Dillon."

Grandpa wore a grim expression. "I should've never asked him to watch over you. He's caused us a whole heap of trouble. I couldn't very well ask for references, though." His eyes narrowed. "I 'spect he's been back if you're asking about him."

She studied his face. "You really did see him?"

"Seen him, talked to him. He seemed nice enough. He's not too good at answering prayers, though. I caused you more problems. I'm real sorry 'bout that."

She hugged him close. "Don't you be sorry about anything, Grandpa. We'll get through this."

He patted her back. "That we will. And if Dillon bothers you, just send him to me and I'll set him straight. And next time I pray, I'll ask for a real angel."

"Maybe you should let me handle things from now on," she gently told him.

"I suppose you're right. You always take care of everyone. I wanted to help, but I…"

She stepped back and looked him in the eyes. "You did what you thought was best. Dillon is the one who messed up, not you. We'll get through this like we've gotten through everything. Okay?"

He paused, then nodded, but his smile wobbled.

Before she'd left, Tilly pulled her aside and warned her some of the town was starting to come to the wrong conclusion about her involvement in the robbery. On the drive back to the ranch, she wondered how someone could go about killing an immortal. Dillon had screwed up her and Grandpa's life and it looked as if Tilly was next on his list. When Raine mentioned asking the sheriff once more if Grandpa could go home so Tilly's reputation wouldn't be ruined, Tilly would hear none of that kind of talk. She didn't give a hoot what people thought.

Neither did Raine, but it added another mark against Dillon and there were already plenty of marks. From the moment she met him. There was something about his eyes. She was certain he'd used some sort of magic. How else could he get her gun?

A pothole that almost swallowed the truck jarred her out of her thoughts. She paid more attention to the road and missed the next ones. By the time she pulled up in front of the ranch and went inside, she was in a pissy mood.

"Dillon!" She slammed the door closed. "I know you can hear me!" She stopped in the hallway and listened. Nothing. "What? Do you only show up when you decide it might be fun to screw with a mortal's life?"

She strode into the living room, flipping on the light switch. The room was empty. That figured. He wasn't about to show himself because he might have to answer for all the problems he'd caused her. She whirled around and stopped, her breath catching in her throat. Dillon casually leaned against the door frame. For a moment she couldn't say anything.

"Did you need something?" he drawled.

"Yes, I need you to get the hell out of my life!"

"Okay." He closed his eyes and vanished. One minute he was standing in front of her, and in the next, he was gone.

She opened her mouth, but nothing came out. He'd left. Disappeared. Vanished. Poof. She resisted the urge to reach up and rub her eyes.

Dammit! She hadn't told him what she thought about him screwing up her life. "Dillon!"

"Did you miss me?" he asked, once again leaning against the door frame. His grin was slow and disarming.

At least it would be if she wasn't ticked off. "No, I didn't miss you. I wanted to tell you how much I despise you. Grandpa and I were making it just fine before you showed up."

"He asked for my help," he reminded her. "You weren't doing as well as you think."

"We were doing a lot better than we are now."

"True, but you did bring some of this on yourself."

"Me!"

"I warned you there would be a robbery, but you didn't believe me."

"Why should I believe a stranger?"

"Because I don't lie."

She caught a slight hesitation and pounced. "Never?"

He shrugged. "Almost never."

"And you call yourself an angel."

"Nephilim. I'm only half angel."

She glared at him, trying to think of something else she could accuse him of doing. She finally blurted, "You kissed me."

He shook his head. "No, *you* kissed *me*."

Her body stiffened. "I did not!"

He straightened. A moment of panic washed over her as he sauntered closer, but she refused to back off and merely raised her chin. He stopped barely a foot away from her. He didn't say anything.

"I thought you were dying." She crossed her arms. "You'd taken a bullet meant for me. It was all a lie."

"I did take a bullet."

Her eyes narrowed. Was he laughing at her? "You're an immortal."

"I can still feel pain, and nephilim can die."

"But not from a bullet," she countered.

He shook his head. He wasn't wearing his hat and a lock of hair fell forward. She tried to think of something to say but couldn't. He confused her, and he was standing too damn close. "But you weren't dying," she finally stuttered.

"No."

"Then why did you ask me to kiss you?" Let him explain that! "You let me think I was granting your last wish!"

"I think you're beautiful and I wanted to feel your lips against mine. I wanted to see if you tasted as sexy as you look. I wasn't disappointed."

"You screwed up my life."

"I'll fix it." He brushed her cheek with the back of his knuckles. His fingers lingered, massaging her earlobe. "Tell me you enjoyed the kiss as much as I did."

Her eyes met his. She couldn't look away. He had the most beautiful eyes. She thought they were blue, but now she could see they were more a deep purple, fathomless. She could get lost in them.

From somewhere far off she heard his voice. "Tell me you don't want me to kiss you right now."

Before she could lie and say that was the last thing on her mind, his lips lightly brushed across hers. She jumped. His hand slipped to the back of her neck and began to massage.

"Shh. I won't do anything you don't want me to."

That was the problem: right now she wanted him to do a lot more. It had been a long time since she'd had sex. For a while she'd sworn off men. Too many complications. They always wanted more than she was willing to give. Like a relationship. She didn't want the problems that came with something more permanent than a few dates. But this was different.

His tongue slipped inside her mouth and caressed. A shiver of excitement trembled over her body. His hand moved lower, kneading the tense muscles that knotted her back. She sighed. Pure relaxation began to consume her. Her hands wound around his neck and pulled him nearer.

His hands glided beneath her shirt, unhooking her bra with one snap of his fingers. She gasped, but before she could move away his fingers brushed across her nipples, then lightly squeezed. Heat shot downward, causing an ache to settle between her legs.

When he ended the kiss, she could barely catch her breath. "You'll leave after you fix the mess you made out of my life, right?"

He hesitated, then said, "I won't have a choice."

"No strings attached?"

"This will never be permanent. I'm sorry I can't give you more."

He started to step away, but she pulled him back. "I'm not."

Dillon wasn't a real man. He was a nephilim. There wouldn't be any strings attached. As soon as her name was cleared, he would leave. Sex without worrying about making a relationship work was exactly what she needed right now. Besides, he owed her.

She kissed him long and hard. He tasted wonderful, musky and like the woods after a rain, and hot, like a fire out of control. She tugged at his shirt until she was pulling it over his head. He was all tanned, hard, sinewy muscles and sexy ridges. She ran her fingers over his abdomen. He drew in a deep breath. Her hands scraped upward, thumbs pressing against his nipples. He groaned. She liked the way she made him feel. It was all about control with her. She enjoyed taking it and keeping it, and she wasn't about to give it up now.

She reached for the buttons on her shirt. He stopped her from pushing the first one through the hole. "Wait."

"What?" she cried with frustration.

"I have a gift."

"I don't need candy or flowers."

"You don't understand. It's something I do. I can mesmerize you with my eyes. It usually doesn't last this long and most of the time I don't realize I'm doing it. What you're feeling might not be real."

"I know exactly what you did with your eyes. It was obvious the second time."

He frowned. "It was?"

"Yes, but that's not why I want to have sex with you. I want it because I need it." She quickly unbuttoned her shirt and let it fall to the floor along with her bra. "Do you understand?"

His fingers trailed between her breasts, circling one nipple, then the other before moving downward. "I'm getting an idea." He swirled his finger around her navel, fingers tickling, moving back and forth.

He definitely understood what she wanted. She slid her fingers beneath the waistband of his jeans. He unsnapped hers, then tugged the zipper downward, pushing them over her hips until they slid the rest of the way to the floor and she kicked out of them. When she would've unbuttoned his, he took her hands and moved them back to her sides, shaking his head.

"I fantasized about what you would look like without clothes."

He met her eyes and she could feel the warm tingles begin from that one mesmerizing look, but this time was different. She knew the power he had, but rather than run from it, she let his gaze sweep slowly over her, relishing the warmth of his stare as it touched her breasts, grazed her ribs, and slid over her abdomen. She gasped when the waves of heat began to build between her legs, the flames licking over the pale blue silk of her bikini panties. Her breathing was labored short little puffs. If he could do that with his eyes, she could only imagine what he would be able to do with his hands.

"You look better than I could imagine," he said and pushed the first button through the hole of his jeans.

Raine couldn't look away as he pushed another one through, then another and then the last. He toed off his boots. The material of his jeans parted and she saw a trail of dark hair until it disappeared. Her mouth watered.

He bent and removed his socks, then straightened. In one swift motion, he shoved his jeans and boxers down, unleashing the man. His erection was thick. Her hand itched to take him, to guide him inside her. When he sauntered nearer, she couldn't resist and ran her finger over the soft tip, massaging the drop of moisture across the head of his penis. He jerked, sucking air.

Empowered, she stroked over his length, sliding the foreskin downward. He rocked against her hand. That was what she liked. A man who let her take charge. She was in control.

She closed the space between them, running her tongue across his magnificent pecs. "I want you buried deep inside me. I want to feel you pumping hard." She slid her hand up and down. "I want the friction, the heat, to consume us."

She pushed her panties down, then kicked them away from her, pressing against him. It was what she'd longed for. Total release. She closed her eyes, only wanting to feel him against her, letting the fire build inside her.

He moved before she could protest, picking her up.

"What are you doing?"

"Taking you somewhere more comfortable."

"You're going to carry me up the stairs?" She raised her eyebrows.

"Yeah, I am."

"Well, glory be, Rhett, you're positively sending a thrill down my body."

He chuckled. She held tight around his neck, but she knew he wouldn't drop her. He was an immortal with strength that went beyond a normal man's. She was right. He wasn't even breathing hard when he reached the top. He continued down the hallway and nudged open the door to her bedroom with his foot.

He laid her gently in the middle of the bed, moving in beside her. His warm breath fanned her cheek. She inhaled his earthy scent as her body went into overdrive. He nibbled her earlobe before dipping his tongue inside. She groaned, turning her head so he had better access. He trailed a heated path with his tongue until he circled one nipple. She arched her back, pulling his head closer to her breast when he made no move to take the nipple inside his mouth. And then he was running his tongue back and forth across the tight nub and all the time his fingers stroked downward, moving closer to her secret spot.

The tension inside her continued to build until she couldn't stand it anymore. She suddenly pushed on his shoulders, throwing him off guard. In one swift movement she straddled him, her body nestled against his cock. She closed her eyes and stretched her arms above her head as she gently moved her hot sex over his hard length. This was nice. She grew damp from the friction each time she slid up, then down his length. She needed and craved penetration.

He moaned. She looked down, her eyes colliding with the passion in his. "Do you like this?" she asked, but she already knew the answer. His eyes were filled with his desire.

"Yeah, I like it. Do you?" His hand slid over her bare butt cheek and didn't stop until it rested against the crack of her bottom. One finger nudged her as though it sought more warmth.

She didn't move, afraid of what might happen if she did.

"I would never hurt you," he said and began to lightly swirl his finger.

New sensations spiraled downward. She drew in a sharp breath, then exhaled in a whoosh as he pulled her closer to his heat. This new move excited her.

"I love watching the emotions cross your face. You're more passionate than I could have imagined."

His words excited her more. He didn't stop there. He moved his hand from behind and brushed through the curls between her legs, rubbing his thumb over the fleshy part of her sex. She arched her back, loving every second of the sensations he created, but only for a moment. She wiggled against him. When she had him exactly where she wanted him, she raised herself.

He moved his hands until he gripped her hips, bringing her back down until she was resting against his cock. "Better," he said, holding her in place. He drew in a ragged breath as if breathing was too difficult. "Do you always take control?" he finally managed to ask.

He knew exactly what she was doing, but she didn't care. She was having too much fun. She laughed. "Always. And what about you? Are you enjoying me straddling your cock?" She wiggled for added emphasis.

A low growl came from deep in his throat. "You know I am."

"Then you'll like this even more." She leaned forward, taunting him with her breasts. He was so intent on watching them that she knew he didn't realize her main purpose until he was sliding inside her. He drew in a sharp breath.

She rocked her body against him, lowering herself on his cock inch by incredible inch. She'd never had a man so large and thick, but then he wasn't just any man. She didn't care what he was as long as she got release. She closed her eyes, losing herself in the sensation of her body closing around his hot erection. Dillon no longer existed. It was only her and the passion.

His hips shot upward, burying himself inside her, startling her. She opened her eyes and looked down at him.

"Oh no you don't," he said. "If you want to have sex by yourself, then you can buy a vibrator."

Anger fused through her. "I already own a couple. A woman can't always find a warm breathing man to have fun with." She frowned at him. "I don't know what you're so concerned about. I've never heard any complaints before," she said and started to move.

He held her in place. "Lady, I'm not complaining. It's sexy as hell staring at your breasts as they bounce, and watching my cock sliding in and out of your body. It's a hell of a turn-on. I bet the men you've been with loved every minute of you on top and never realized you couldn't care less who was under you."

She clamped her lips together as anger began to build inside her. "You're the one who started this game with your mesmerizing eyes. If you don't like having sex with me, then get the hell out of my bed."

"That's exactly what I mean. I don't want to have sex with you."

Raine couldn't believe the disappointment that swept over her, but she glared down at him rather than let him know how much his words affected her. "Then go."

He shook his head. "I'm just getting started."

She frowned, not understanding what he was trying to say. The guy was definitely crazy. He wanted to have sex, then he didn't. He was probably trying to make her crazy. He was succeeding!

"I want to make love with you." His words were husky with passion, caressing her, filling her with need. "We're going to have the sweetest, hottest sex you've ever experienced, but we're going to do it my way. I'm in charge."

A moment passed before his words sank in. Sex was sex. She wanted release, nothing more. She thought he understood that. The first inkling of doubt weaved through her. "What exactly do you mean?"

Chapter 10

DILLON MOVED SO FAST Raine didn't have time to protest. One minute she straddled him and the next she was tucked beneath him and he was staring down into her startled eyes. This was better. He wanted her to know who was in control.

Her eyes narrowed. "I don't like being on the bottom," she said between gritted teeth.

God, she was sexy when she was pissed off. Her chest rose and fell from the storm brewing inside, while silver sparks danced in her eyes. Even with her lips pressed mutinously together, they were still deliciously pouty and kissable and tempting and…

He lowered his mouth, running his tongue across her bottom lip. She stilled as the battle to give in warred with her natural instinct for dominance. She'd taken care of people almost her whole life and didn't know how to relinquish control. He planned to teach her—and he would fix the mess he'd made of her life. There was a time and a place for everything, and at that particular moment, he needed to be in Raine's bed with her naked body pressed against his.

As soon as her lips relaxed, he slipped his tongue inside, catching her sigh. He almost smiled but knew she wouldn't appreciate gloating. The victory was his. They both knew it. There was no need to rub it in. And then it didn't matter who the winner was as he lost himself in the kiss, tasting, his tongue teasing, darting inside only to pull back before thrusting again, then gently caressing.

He caught her sigh, her surrender, as her arms wrapped around his neck and pulled him closer. Her body was soft in all the right places. Her fingers trailed up and down his back, stroking. He lost himself in the sensations she created, his cock nudging Raine to open her legs and let him in. But she didn't. She drew out the game; her hands trailed farther down. Nice, he thought as he closed his eyes, letting the heat swirl around him. She squeezed his ass, massaging.

"I want to touch you," she said, heated breath fluttering against his chest. "Please."

Her voice quivered on the last word and he knew how much it cost her to beg. Raine, who was always in control, had relinquished and crowned him the victor. He wouldn't humiliate her. He moved partially to his side, sucking air when her fingers circled his cock.

"You're so thick and so big," she said, her fingers running the length.

Did she know how close he was to exploding? Apparently not, because she circled around him, sliding his foreskin down, then moving her thumb over the tip.

"I bet you taste good, too." She ran her tongue over his nipple.

He jerked. "I don't know how long I can hold back."

"I know." She released his cock and shoved against his shoulder, catching him off balance so that he fell onto his back against the mattress with an *oomph*. Before he could recover from the shock that she'd manipulated him, she straddled him, positioning his cock so that it slid into the heat of her body with ease.

He struggled to regain control, but she wiggled her tight little ass against him, then raised herself before plunging downward. Thoughts of gaining control quickly fled. He grasped her hips and rose to meet her the next time she lowered her body. He was gratified to hear her gasp of pleasure.

"Oh, yes, this is fucking good," she said. "I want more." Leaning down, she ran her tongue up his chest, stopping when she came to his nipple, teasing with her tongue. "Tell me you don't enjoy me being on top," she said with a wicked grin.

He couldn't.

He couldn't say a damn word as he raised his hips again and again, sinking deeper and deeper into Raine, her hot juices lubricating his cock as she slid up and down his shaft until his world exploded with lights and colors. He vaguely heard her cry when she came, her nails sinking into his flesh.

As the room came back into focus, Dillon knew he'd been played, that he'd never been in control. He opened his eyes and watched her. Raine's hands rested on her thighs, her breasts jutted forward as the last tremble of her orgasm rippled over her. She lazily opened her eyes and smiled down on him.

"Don't frown," she scolded. "You know you enjoyed yourself." She leaned down and ran her tongue across his bottom lip, nipples scraping his chest. "In the bedroom, I never lose." She climbed out of bed and walked out the door.

Had he really thought she was fragile?

He leaned on one elbow and stretched until he could see her cute little bottom as she sauntered down the hall. Nice. Very nice. He leaned a little farther, lost his balance, and landed on the hardwood floor with a heavy thud. She laughed as she closed the door to the bathroom.

He sat up, rubbing his hip. She beat him at his own game. He shook his head, marveling that a little slip of a woman had won. He frowned. No, that wasn't an accurate description of Raine. She was curvy in all the right places. The loose clothes she wore hid a lot.

"What the hell are you doing?" Chance asked.

"Son of a …" Dillon jumped to his feet. "Popping in unannounced like that could give a guy a heart attack!" His friend had really bad timing.

"Yeah, well, better me than your father," Chance said. His gaze swept over Dillon. "Put some clothes on."

"You're the one who showed up uninvited, and my clothes happen to be downstairs."

Chance snapped his fingers, and Dillon's clothes were suddenly in a pile on the bed. Dillon grabbed his briefs and pulled them on. "What does Tobiah have to do with any of this?"

Chance quirked an eyebrow. "You have to ask?"

"I'm only doing what he wanted."

"The damn door is stuck!" Raine's voice echoed down the hall, doorknob rattling as she tried to open the door.

Dillon looked at Chance. "You?"

"Of course."

"So unstick it."

"I will, but first we need to talk."

"What else is there to talk about? I'm cleaning up the mess," Dillon grated.

"No, you're not. You're fucking her."

"It's no one's business, but if you need to know why, Raine was too tense. I gave her release."

One eyebrow shot upward. "That's your story?"

Dillon frowned. Yeah, he wouldn't buy that either.

"Tobiah isn't happy," Chance continued.

Dillon snorted. "We never even met our fathers until recently and they're not happy?"

"Tobiah has his orders."

Dillon hesitated, unable to ignore the cold chill sweeping

over him. Why would the Powers get involved with the nephilim after all this time? And who was giving them orders?

"I said I would fix everything and I will."

"By going to bed with her?"

"It's complicated." He jerked his jeans on, then fastened them, refusing to meet Chance's gaze. The guy could practically read minds. Dillon grabbed his shirt and tugged it over his head. Hell, maybe he couldn't explain what he was thinking when he made love to Raine because he wasn't quite sure. He'd known he wanted her from the moment she pulled her gun on him. Leaving had been pure torture. It was almost a relief when Tobiah ordered him to fix her life.

"And you've complicated the situation even more," Chance said. "You were supposed to repair the damage, not add to her problems."

Was that what he was doing? Making her life worse? He glanced down the hall as the pounding on the door grew louder.

"Dillon! Open the damn door!"

"No, you're wrong. She was nearing the meltdown stage."

Chance looked undecided, so Dillon located his socks and boots. "How could I fix anything when she was wired tighter than a newly strung bow? If one more person looked at her cross-eyed she might have shot them. Then where would she be?"

Chance started to sit on the bed, frowned, then pulled out the chair in front of the mirrored dresser. He straddled the seat and rested his arms on the back. "Now that you've kept her from shooting half the population of Randolph, what are your plans?"

How the hell should he know? He was winging his way through his fabricated story—no pun intended. The truth was that he'd wanted to hold Raine, to pull her against him. He didn't really have any plan beyond that.

"She'll catch the bank robbers," he blurted. That was even more lame than the reason he'd made love with her. How the hell was she going to catch the culprits when she hadn't seen their faces? They were probably long gone.

Chance was thoughtful, then nodded. "Good plan. That should satisfy Tobiah." He came to his feet.

He bought that? Dillon relaxed.

"I didn't think you had it in you to think up a lie that quickly," Chance said.

He should've known better. Chance could always see through him. There was something unnatural about him. He never backed down. Chance had taken on one of the most powerful demons, knowing he would probably die, but he faced him anyway. The guy always won, be it a horse race or killing demons.

A competitive streak that Dillon buried long ago rose inside him. Maybe he wanted to win this time. "Are you so sure I'm lying?"

Chance opened his mouth, then snapped it closed, frowning. "Are you?"

"Why, don't you think I have what it takes to fix Raine's life?"

Chance studied him. "A long time ago I would never have hesitated to say you could do anything you set your mind to do. Now, not so much."

He couldn't meet Chance's gaze. Dillon knew he was right. He didn't want a repeat performance of what happened with Lily. Even now, his gut clenched at the thought of what she went through when she fell victim to a demon's promises. When she emerged, the Lily he'd known ceased to exist.

"You have to let her go," Chance said. They both knew he wasn't talking about Raine.

Dillon raised his eyes and saw the sympathy in Chance's.

All the nephilim knew what it was like to lose a soul. Not one of them had been left unscarred by the cruelties of fate. Chance was right, though.

"Yeah, I know." As soon as Dillon spoke the words, it felt as though a heavy weight lifted from his shoulders.

A dull thudding noise came from the end of the hall, as though Raine had found something other than her fist to pound on the door.

Chance laughed. "You tangled with a wild mustang this time. You think you can tame her?"

"Nope," Dillon said.

Chance's expression was puzzled.

"I don't want to break her spirit. I only want to gentle her."

"I don't know. She seems pretty determined. You might be the one who gets broken."

"Not going to happen," Dillon said, shaking his head. "I've been coming in second for a long time now. I let it happen. It's time I started fighting for what I want."

"Took you long enough to figure that out. It's good to have the old Dillon back."

"Are you sure? I won't let you win again."

Chance's grin was cocky. "You never *let* me win in the past. I beat you fair and square."

"I'll take that as a challenge to race again."

"You're on."

"As soon as I fix Raine's life."

"You know you can't stay long," Chance reminded him. "Will you have time to put everything right?"

Dillon wasn't sure. The nephilim's powers only extended so far, and Chance was right. The longer mortals were around nephilim, the more they picked up on the otherworld. If he stayed too long, he could do more harm than good. A mortal's intuitiveness would grow stronger. Some could speak with the dead or foretell the future after an angel's lengthy visit.

Nostradamus was one. He was almost burned at the stake because people thought he was a witch when he spoke of things that would come to pass. Today, people called them psychics and fortune tellers. People thought they wanted to be like them, to know their destiny, but they never saw the other side, the dark one. These people also saw the shadowy figures of demons. Their dreams would be haunted with things they couldn't explain. Sometimes it drove them crazy.

"Dillon?"

Chance was still in the room, still waiting for an answer. Dillon cleared his mind. He didn't want to dwell on what might happen. "Yes, I'll have time," he said with more confidence than he felt.

Chance expelled a long breath. "Good. I'll pass that along to Tobiah."

A sour taste formed in Dillon's mouth.

"He's still your father," Chance said.

"So he tells me."

"Dillonnnnn!" Raine's voice echoed down the hall.

"So, she doesn't like giving up control." Chance looked as though he was trying not to grin but couldn't quite manage.

"I'll teach her." There wasn't a damn thing funny about the situation as far as he could see.

"You might have a battle on your hands."

Dillon suddenly relaxed and returned his friend's smile. "I hope so."

"I almost pity her."

"You should. Raine can't win against me."

"I don't know, I have a feeling she won the first round."

Again he wondered if Chance could read minds. "Maybe I let her," he said defensively.

Chance shook his head. "Not buying it."

Why fight the truth? "You're right. But winning the war is what counts, not the skirmishes."

Chance was still grinning when he closed his eyes and disappeared.

The pounding on the bathroom door increased. Dillon strolled down the hall, stopping in front of the closed door. He could hear the very colorful words Raine mumbled on the other side. He liked when she talked dirty. He touched the doorknob and the lock clicked. He casually leaned his shoulder against the frame and pushed on the wood. He crossed his arms as the door swung open.

She was stunning. Raine reminded him of a tiny Amazon warrior with her eyes closed, her hands squeezed around the wooden handle of the plunger she held above her head. She was still as naked as when she'd sauntered down the hall.

His eyes swept over her, from her high, pointed breasts to her small waist, and over her hips. His gaze came to a screeching halt on the thatch of dark curls covering her femininity. He wanted to caress her, to watch her come alive with desire. He wanted her to beg for more…

The plunger came down hard and fast, banging against his forehead. Pain exploded inside his head. The last thing he remembered thinking before he toppled over like a giant oak was that he should've seen it coming.

Chapter 11

RAINE STOOD IN STUNNED silence as a strange look crossed Dillon's face right before his eyes rolled and he stumbled back against the wall with a loud groan. Oh God, she killed an angel. She'd fry for all eternity. No, wait. He was immortal. Hitting him with a plunger probably didn't kill him, but he did say he could feel pain.

She threw the plunger away from her. It landed with a dull thud against the claw-footed bathtub and bounced across the floor a couple of times before coming to a rolling stop. Yeah right, as if that was going to get rid of the evidence. She quickly knelt beside him, pulling his head onto her lap. "Dillon, I'm so sorry. Are you okay? Please talk to me."

Was that laughter? She frowned as she looked up and around. They were the only ones in the house, though. Maybe all her yelling for Dillon to help her get out of the bathroom affected her ears.

"Dillon, talk to me." She ran her hands through his hair. No bleeding, no bumps. His hair felt like silk, it was so soft. Her body began to tingle. She realized that checking his head for an injury had taken on a whole new meaning. Good Lord, the guy was unconscious and all she could think about was having her way with his body. She was immediately filled with guilt.

She cleared her mind and tried not to think about what touching him was making her feel. He was injured and that should be the only thing on her mind. She cleared her throat and rested her hand against his chest. It was a shame he was dressed. She liked him better naked.

Sex had been fantastic. The best she'd ever had and she'd still ended up with complete control. It was the perfect solution to making love without the responsibility of maintaining a relationship.

His chest rose and fell evenly beneath her palm. She slipped her hand beneath his shirt so she could make absolutely sure his breathing was okay. His chest was smooth with only a slight sprinkling of hair. Dillon said he healed fast. She ran her fingers over his upper body. Amazing. She didn't even feel a scar from when he was shot. She pushed his shirt up and examined his chest a little closer. Nope, not one scar.

But she'd seen blood pouring from the wound. She frowned. If he healed that fast from a gunshot wound, then a plunger would be like a mosquito bite. Her gaze returned to his face. Did his eyes flutter? He was lying way too still. Her gaze drifted down. He sported a major hard-on. *Really?* She shoved with all her strength at the same time she jumped to her feet. Dillon's head hit the hardwood floor with a loud crack.

"Ow, what the hell did you do that for?" he asked, rubbing the back of his head.

"You let me think I'd hurt you," she said as she stepped across him.

He groaned again but she had a feeling it was for an entirely different reason since she was giving him a freebie look. Good. She wanted him hurting in more than one area. It served him right for taking advantage of her.

"You're the one who clobbered me," he yelled at her retreating back.

She turned at the door. "Don't worry. You heal fast, and I

still have chores to do!" She slammed the door hard enough the wood rattled. He might be an angel, but he was still part man and that was coming through loud and clear! That was the reason she used sex purely for release. Emotional entanglements caused more problems than she wanted.

Even short-term, this affair might be more trouble than it was worth. She grabbed a pair of panties out of the dresser drawer and tugged them on. Now that she could think a little straighter, she probably shouldn't even be having a fake relationship. Not until after hers and Grandpa's names were cleared. Jeans followed, then a faded green shirt. She didn't bother with a bra.

She paused while buttoning her shirt. Darn, he was sort of starting to grow on her. He'd answered Grandpa's prayer. That made him a nice guy in her book, and they weren't easy to come by. He took a bullet meant for her, too. He saved her life. Maybe the bullet didn't kill him, but must have hurt a hell of a lot. His pain was clear that night. How many people would go through that for her?

She sighed. Not that it mattered. There were still chores to be done. She didn't have time to play sex games with an angel. His naked body filled her mind, and she pictured him below her as she moved to the sweet song of passion. She sighed, then quickly shook her head to clear her fantasy.

Later.

It was time to return to the land of the living. She flung the door open, half expecting Dillon to be standing in the doorway. She should've grabbed something sturdier than a plunger! A niggle of guilt twisted through her. She didn't normally wish pain on anyone and only used violence if she had to. Why the hell had he locked the bathroom door anyway?

The hall was empty. She hated the disappointment that filled her and told herself she was glad he wasn't on the other side of the door. There was too much work to do and it would take her a good two or three hours to get all the chores on the ranch finished. She stomped down the stairs. Having an orgasm used to make her feel relaxed, but she was more tense now than she was before the sex.

She grabbed the flashlight out of the hall closet, hating that it was already dark. She would have to juggle the light and do the chores at the same time. The blasted chickens were probably already down for the night, too. She cringed at the thought of sticking her hand under them to gather the eggs. They always pecked her. Grandpa said she didn't do it right. They sensed her fear, or some such bullshit. If she wasn't afraid to walk the streets of Fort Worth at night, then a hen wasn't going to scare her.

Of course, she also carried a loaded gun when she was on patrol. That was an idea. If a chicken pecked her, she'd have chicken and dumplings for supper.

She came to a sudden stop and sniffed as a delectable scent tickled her nose and started her stomach growling. She realized how many hours had passed since she last ate.

Had Grandpa returned after she specifically told him Sheriff Barnes wanted them to keep their distance? Didn't he know how much trouble that would cause? Her shoulders slumped as she walked toward the dining room. She really appreciated the effort, but what was she going to do with him?

"I thought you might be hungry." Dillon stood near the dining room table, a cart next to him as he lit the last of three candles. A warm glow spread across the table. Her grandmother's best china was laid out. The delicate blue rose pattern was her favorite of all her grandmother's pieces. She used to take it out of the china cabinet when she was having a particularly bad day and wash each piece, then carefully dry them one by one.

She looked up and met his gaze. "I don't use my grandmother's dishes."

"Why not?" he asked as he took the platter off the cart and placed it on the table. A perfectly roasted hen was surrounded by quartered red potatoes sitting on a bed of greens.

Had he been pecked recently?

Her stomach rumbled.

"I don't use them because they mean something to me. I don't want to break anything."

"They're sturdier than you realize." He added a bowl of corn and one of brown rice, then a basket covered by a crisp white dish towel. He moved the towel back halfway and revealed golden rolls.

"Yeast rolls?" she asked before she could stop herself.

"Of course."

"Did you cook all of this?"

He shook his head. A lock of dark blond hair fell forward, grazing his forehead. "I'm probably the worst cook in the world."

"Take out?" She didn't know of any place in town where you could get take out like this.

"A place called Mama Paula's. You've never tasted food as good as hers."

She couldn't remember how long it had been since she ate a meal that wasn't thrown together or one Grandpa had fixed. Bologna sandwiches were his idea of a complete and nutritious meal. If it was cold outside, he'd fry the bologna and add a can of tomato soup.

The only thing going through her mind was filling her stomach. Dammit, she didn't want to think about food. She forced her eyes away from the stupid roasted hen and the other food and stared at him. He looked none the worse for having gotten bonked on the noggin. "I guess you've healed," she said, not even attempting to keep the sarcasm out of her voice.

His smile was slow and started her heart beating faster. "Yeah, nephilim heal fast." He motioned toward a side chair. "Have a seat before this gets cold."

"Can't you warm it up with your eyes or something? You know, zap it with fire?" She was feeling prickly.

He laughed. She liked the sound. It came from way down deep. "No, only demons do that."

"Great. Something else I'll have to worry about."

He frowned. "Not as long as I'm around."

But he wouldn't hang around even if he could. She never let anyone stay very long in her life. Well, except Grandpa. They were family, and family should stick together. He was good to her and he raised her the best way he could. He was always there if she needed him. He was the one who'd taught her about being strong.

And she was strong. When her mother left, she saw what it did to her father. Raine vowed she would never give anyone that much power. The easiest way to keep her promise to herself was not let anyone get too close. It worked.

She watched Dillon open a bottle of wine and pour some into two long-stemmed glasses. He didn't belong in her world any more than her past lovers. Even less. The whole town thought she and Grandpa robbed the stupid bank all because she mentioned an angel was shot saving her life.

But he had saved her life. That counted for a lot.

Her stomach rumbled again. Odd how no matter what went on in someone's life, their body still had needs that had to be met. She was hungry. The emptiness inside her was a hollow ache. She sauntered to the table but rather than take the side chair he motioned toward, she pulled out the one on the end. She always sat at the head of the table and she wasn't about to change. Her choice didn't seem to bother him. She didn't have any idea why that should irritate her, but it did.

"I still have chores I need to do," she told him.

He pulled out a chair at the side of the table and sat. "They're done." He raised his glass of wine and took a drink.

She frowned. They were her chores, not his. As soon as the thought crossed her mind, she realized how ungrateful it sounded. "Thank you. It wasn't necessary, though."

"I know, but I want to make love to you again and I didn't want to wait that long."

Her body trembled. She grabbed her glass of wine and downed half of it before setting the glass back on the table. He was trying to take control again. "*If* we make love." He had his nerve thinking she would fall into his arms whenever he snapped his fingers. "You came back to fix my life, remember."

"You know we will, so don't pretend otherwise." He carved a slice off the roasted hen and placed it on her plate.

Now he was telling her what she would do! He hadn't stopped, if she thought about it. He even wanted control in the bedroom. Not that she let him have it. A few more minutes and she might have given in, though. That bothered her.

"You're overthinking it," he said, breaking into her thoughts.

Startled, she met his eyes. "What?"

He added potatoes and a roll to her plate. "I'll make your life right again." He took her hand in his. "I'll make everything better."

For a moment, his gaze held hers and she found it impossible to look away. The heat began to build inside her as her body ached for his touch. It took all the willpower she could muster to drag her eyes away. As soon as she did, she jerked her hand out of his.

"You're doing it again!" she accused. "It isn't natural."

"What?"

She met his gaze then quickly looked away. "You know exactly what I mean. You hypnotized me."

He chuckled. She frowned.

"There's not a thing funny about it."

"Eat," he said softly and picked up his fork. "Sometimes I don't even realize I'm doing it."

"Don't do it again."

"I didn't mean to do it that time."

She didn't like the idea of him being able to control her for even a few minutes.

"But we will make love again and it won't be because I've mesmerized you with my eyes. You'll want to make love because you won't be able to deny yourself."

She stabbed her fork into the piece of meat and grabbed the knife sitting beside her plate. She sawed off a piece harder than she needed. The meat was so tender she could have cut it with just the fork, but it felt good to wield the utensil. Probably because she knew he was right. They *would* make love again.

"So you think you know everything, huh?"

"No, not everything. But that was a no-brainer."

"How do you figure that?"

"I don't have to figure anything. You're a passionate woman. I doubt you can go without sex for very long."

"You're wrong. I can go without sex for a very long time."

"The reason you don't have a bra on is because you love the way the material rubs against your nipples every time you move. Your body craves a man's touch."

Heat spiraled down her body. She crossed her legs and shoved the meat on her fork into her mouth. She chewed without thinking, then swallowed and stabbed another piece. He didn't know what he was saying. He was guessing.

She shifted in her chair and the material of her shirt tightened across her chest for a brief second, but enough that a thrill ran down her body. Oh hell, he was right. She'd never realized what she was doing.

She slowed her chewing and actually tasted the meat for the first time. The flavors sent her senses into overdrive. She closed her eyes. Dillon was right about something else: she had never tasted anything cooked this well. She savored the bite before opening her eyes and looking at him. She was even passionate about food!

She raised her chin. "So what? I love sex, and I'm a master at the game. You can't win."

He leaned back in his chair and studied her long enough she began to fidget. "You think not?"

A flicker of uncertainty trickled through her as some of her confidence slipped, but with determination drawn from depending on herself, she squared her shoulders and met his eyes without fear he would ever have power over her. She knew his game. "I'm sure."

He suddenly leaned forward, startling her. "I wouldn't be if I were you. Someday soon you'll beg me to tie you up and do what I please with you. And I will. The day will come when I have you bound. I'll take my time stripping off your clothes layer by layer. You'll be naked in front of me, squirming with anticipation. You'll do anything I say."

She drew in a sharp breath as tantalizing images materialized in her mind. It wasn't as though she never thought about domination but when she did, she was always the dominant partner. But her body betrayed her when her nipples grew taut. She ached for release.

No! What was she thinking? She jumped to her feet. "I will never let anyone have that much control over me!"

"You will, and you'll enjoy every minute." He watched her, as though he waited for her to admit that she had entertained his idea, even briefly.

"Go! Leave my house!"

"What scares you the most?" he asked. "Giving up control or knowing how much the thought of being tied up turns you on?"

"Get out," she said between gritted teeth.

"Is that what you really want?"

"Yes."

He nodded, then closed his eyes. She took a step back when he disappeared right in front of her. This wasn't happening. It couldn't be. None of it was real. He wasn't real. She only believed in what she could touch.

But she had touched him. She dropped back into the chair, massaging her temples as her head began to pound. "I'm not a control freak. I enjoy giving pleasure. Big difference." Then in a louder voice, "So screw you."

But why did heat spiral through her at the thought of Dillon taking complete control? The thought of having sex again? She reached forward and picked up her glass, downing the rest of the wine.

She stood and walked over to where he'd left the bottle. It was good wine, though. She poured a full glass, then set the bottle down. And good food. She tore off a piece of meat and shoved it into her mouth. Then another. And another.

Damn him! Damn him for putting thoughts in her head. She refused to be submissive to anyone.

When she was beyond feeling full and tipsy, she grabbed the bottle of wine and the flashlight and headed toward the front door. One last check of the animals and then she might watch a movie or something. Since she'd been forced to take a leave of absence, she had more time on her hands. A movie would be great. She couldn't remember the last time she'd watched one.

She stopped long enough to take a long drink from the bottle. The liquid slid smoothly down her throat and settled in her stomach, spreading warmth down her arms. There was a bit of a breeze rustling the leaves in the trees and it carried the slightest chill. So she took another drink, letting the wine warm her blood, then headed toward the barn. The beam of light bounced on the ground like a crazed kangaroo that had overdosed on drugs. That was enough to make anyone drunk, she thought. She stopped, steadied the light, and continued on her way. Better.

The barn was two stories and painted red. She'd chosen the color when she was ten. Very ingenious of her, she thought, although the paint faded over time. The dull red color gave the old building character.

Once she was standing inside the barn, she found the light switch and flipped it on. The stalls were finally clean and the sweet aroma of hay hung in the air. She refused to feel grateful to someone who had people telling angel jokes all over town at her expense. She sighed.

She drained the last of the wine from the bottle and tossed it in the barrel near the door. The bottle thumped against the bottom. A chicken squawked her anger, the horses whinnied their disapproval, and something scurried beneath the bags of feed stacked in the corner. She wouldn't be investigating.

"Excuse me for wanting to make sure you'd been fed," she mumbled.

The three stalls were clean and fresh hay was scattered about. Dillon told the truth. The chores were done. She shrugged. He owed her for making her look crazy. Until her life was back in order, he would continue to owe her.

Since there was nothing to do, she started toward the door, but something sparkled, catching her eye. It didn't move when she stepped closer so she wasn't too worried it might be the beady eyes of some varmint. The object was partially covered, but it was black and looked like some sort of handle studded with diamonds. Not that she thought they were real.

She squatted down and brushed the hay away. Her heart skipped a beat. The diamonds probably were real. Her fingers wrapped around the handle as she came to her feet. Knotted black velvet cords dangled from the end of the whip. Her thighs clenched as she imagined herself naked, Dillon wielding the whip across her bare buttocks, sending shivers of desire over her body.

"You've never known pleasure like I can give you," he whispered close to her ear.

She didn't move as he ran his hand down her arm and covered her fingers. If not for that, she would've dropped the whip. Instead, he moved her hand so the cords swung back and forth. Like a hypnotist with a watch, the cords were captivating. She swallowed hard.

"It won't happen. I'm not the submissive type," she told him, but she couldn't force her feet to move.

"Are you sure you don't want me to bind your hands, then unbutton your shirt?" With his free hand, he unbuttoned the top button. Her breasts ached for his touch.

She sucked in a deep breath as he reached for the second button and tugged it through the hole. This was crazy! She had to tell him to stop. After the third one, he reached inside her shirt, running his hand across her abdomen.

She jumped, but the movement only put her in closer contact

with him. His erection bumped her bottom. Her thighs clenched and it was all she could do to stifle her moan. She wanted him, but on her terms.

"No," she said, lacking the conviction she wanted to convey. She cleared her throat and tried again. "I want you to stop right—" He tweaked her nipple, sending heat down her body. "—now." She leaned against him.

"Liar," he whispered.

Yes, she was a liar, because what he was doing to her body felt right and good and she never wanted him to stop.

He cupped her breast, massaging and kneading before sliding his hand lower, tugging the belt until he could slide it out of the loops. Without the belt to hold her pants up, they slid down to her knees. Instead of dropping her belt, he moved one end across her stomach. His implication was clear.

Some sanity returned. "I will not be a submissive."

"You can't control everything."

"But I can control my sex life."

"Can you?" He dropped the belt, moving his hand down, tickling across the silky material of her panties.

A shiver swept over her. She'd never wanted a man like she wanted Dillon. Her body was on fire. She would have exactly what she wanted, too. She never lost. She toed off her sneakers and kicked out of her jeans. In one swift movement, she turned in his arms.

"Yes. I can control every bit of it." She pressed her lips against his chest and was gratified to hear his sharp intake of air.

He leaned down and raised her chin. His lips covered hers. She wasn't quite sure when he gained control. One second her tongue gently caressed his, and then he was the one doing the teasing. They were his hands sliding inside her panties and pulling her tighter against his erection. She was the one breathing harder, pressing even closer. When the kiss ended, she was panting.

"Do you want me to bind your wrists? Will you give me the freedom to do anything I want?"

A few seconds passed before she realized what he asked. A cold chill passed over her. She shook her head. "I can't."

"You might as well give in. You will eventually."

She squared her shoulders and took a step back. "No, I won't."

His gaze drifted over her. "It's a shame to cause both of us this much pain." He closed his eyes and disappeared.

For a moment she couldn't say anything, then she exploded. "Damn you!" The chicken fell off her nest and began to flap her wings and run around as though the barn was on fire. The horses whinnied and stomped the ground. And Raine discovered what had scurried behind the stacked bags of dry feed—a rat. She screamed and ran toward the house, not bothering to grab her clothes. She hated rats almost as much as she hated a certain nephilim!

Chapter 12

DILLON KNEW WHAT HE was doing. Knowing didn't make him hurt any less. He wanted nothing more than to let Raine take control, to feel her naked body pressed against his, to make sweet love all night long. But that wouldn't help her. She needed to learn that giving up control didn't mean it would make her vulnerable.

He leaned back in the chair, raising the cup of coffee to his lips. For a moment, he closed his eyes and savored the strong flavor. There was something to be said about early morning, sitting on the porch watching the sun come up, casting hues of orange and yellow across the land.

"What the hell are you doing here?" Raine asked.

Dillon winced at the sharpness of her tone. Her eyes were rimmed with dark circles as if she hadn't slept well. She was dressed in her usual attire when she was at the ranch: baggy jeans and shirt, scuffed boots, and a stained hat. She still looked good to him. Maybe because he knew what was under the ugly clothes.

"I *was* enjoying the start of a new day and a cup of coffee."

"That's my coffee you're drinking."

"Technically, no. I used your coffeepot, but I brought my own coffee. Try it. I think you'll like it." She opened her mouth. He held up a hand. "Go pour yourself a cup and join me. Then we'll talk." He turned his attention back to his cup. "That's if you still want me to fix your life."

She opened her mouth, then snapped it closed, eyes

narrowing. "You're an ass," she finally said and turned on her heel. The screen door slammed behind her.

Dillon wondered if she would return. He didn't relax until the door opened again. She carried a cup of coffee, but didn't speak to him. She didn't take the chair near him, either, but chose a rocker two spaces away. He watched out of the corner of his eye as she took a drink, then lightly pushed with the toe of one foot, setting the rocker into gentle motion. She brought the cup to her lips, blew across the top, then took a drink, closing her eyes for a moment.

She liked it. He knew she would. The coffee was strong but not bitter and with just a pinch of cinnamon. He learned that trick a long time ago. A pinch of spice or a bit of chocolate made a nice change.

"It's okay," she finally said, words stiff as her back.

He smiled because he knew the coffee was better than okay, but he quickly made his expression bland when she looked his way.

"I'm still pissed about last night. I hope you get blue balls and your dick rots off."

"Yeah, I knew you'd still be angry."

"You've got that right. When you start something, you're supposed to finish it."

"You made your choice."

"And I won't change my mind."

"Then you'll never know what you're missing."

Her smile didn't reach her eyes. "Then I won't miss it, will I?"

"You will, because I've put the idea of being a submissive in your head. You probably dreamed about it last night. Did you dream about what I would do if I had you under my complete control?"

Something close to a growl came from low in her throat. Rather than admit to anything, she gulped down the rest of her coffee and set the cup on the floor with a resounding thunk. He was surprised she didn't break the handle off. Rather than admit to anything, she asked, "How exactly do you plan to fix my life?"

He drained his cup, then set it on the side table beside his chair. The sun squeezed the rest of the way above the horizon and a burst of color spread out in all directions. A rooster crowed, signaling the start of a new day.

"You're going to catch the bank robbers." He crossed his legs at the ankles and sighed. It was a damn good plan. Putting the thieves behind bars would certainly clear her name.

"That's your plan?" she asked incredulously. "Well hell, why didn't I think of that?" Sarcasm dripped from her words.

He frowned. So maybe she had thought about it. The plan was a good one, though, and she couldn't fault him for thinking that was the best way to clear her name.

"And exactly how do you plan to go about catching the criminals when they're probably long gone?"

"I've been thinking," he began.

She crossed her arms in front of her and shifted slightly in her chair, giving him her full attention. One eyebrow rose.

He wasn't sure he liked her attitude. "I'm trying to help," he said.

"Okay. What's your plan?" When he didn't answer, she continued. "You do have a plan, don't you?"

He had to quit winging this and come up with something concrete. Except he didn't have a plan, only an idea. It was lame at best. She would know he hadn't thought anything through. The way she sat there staring at him with that haughty look was as if she expected whatever he said to be a joke at best. People had no faith, Raine least of all. Not that he could blame her, and she didn't look as though she was going to cut him any slack.

"You heard them talking," he began.

"Yeah." She didn't look impressed.

"We need to pick everything apart. Isn't that what you do at a crime scene? Go over every detail to see if you might have missed something?"

Her shoulders slumped as the fight suddenly drained from her. He wanted to pull her into his arms and tell her not to worry. Tell her that everything would be okay and he would make it right, but he didn't know for sure that would happen.

She pushed with her toe again and set the rocker in motion. Her gaze moved to the horizon. "Don't you think I've already done that? I've gone over everything in my mind a thousand times and still come up with nothing. I told Sheriff Barnes all I know and I still don't have a solid clue. Now they say they found one of Grandpa's handkerchiefs. His brand is embroidered in one corner. Also my notepad was near the vault." Tears sparkled in her eyes before she quickly blinked away the moisture and squared her shoulders. She turned her attention back to him. "Your plan sucks."

"Thanks for the confidence."

"Do you screw up everyone's life? Or were you just bored the day you decided to interfere in mine?"

"I'm only half angel. I still make mistakes." She really had an attitude problem.

"Oh yeah, I forgot. You're half man. That explains a lot."

"You didn't seem to mind when we were making love."

She gripped the arms of the rocker, shifting in her seat. He knew she was remembering what they'd experienced. She opened her mouth, but no words came out. When she drew in a deep breath, his gaze lowered. Was she wearing a bra today?

An ache began to build inside him. He'd never wanted a

woman as much as he wanted Raine. Even Lily hadn't made him feel this almost overpowering need. He waited for the pain, the regret that always followed when he thought about Lily. It didn't come. For the first time in a very long time, he felt at peace.

He studied Raine as she stared off into the distance. If he failed her, would it destroy him? The thought shook him to his core. Everything inside him said run. Protect himself. Raine was Lily all over again.

No, it wasn't the same. There were no demons this time, and Raine was nothing like Lily. Raine was a fighter. She would never fall for the lies of a demon. There was a strength in Raine that Lily never had. Lily wanted everything handed to her on a silver platter. Raine was willing to work hard for what she wanted.

Raine's gaze suddenly met his. "What's your plan?"

He came to his feet, walking to the edge of the porch. "You had the right idea at the sheriff's office," he said. "Everything adds up. You were on duty the night of the robbery and the robbers knew it."

"But why would they try to kill me?"

"I don't think they did. You probably weren't supposed to even show up. They planned to rob the bank, drop a handkerchief with your grandfather's brand on it, and your notepad."

She shook her head. "But I might have dropped my notepad."

"Did you?"

She shook her head again as she tried to remember. Finally, she reached up and massaged her temples. "I'm not sure about anything. And I don't know why Grandpa's handkerchief was there. That night is still a blur."

"The people investigating the robbery see your notepad near the vault, along with your grandfather's handkerchief, and the fingers begin to point to the two most likely."

"How could they even think it was us? My father was the sheriff. He swore to protect and serve, and I've done the same thing."

"And the ranch is in trouble. A property that has been in the family since your grandfather was a young man. Without a cash flow, you might be forced to sell it."

She faced him, eyes blazing. "I'd never let that happen! This place means too much to Grandpa."

"My point exactly," he said quietly. The more he thought about it, he was almost certain that was what happened. Raine and her grandfather were perfect to take the fall.

"How do I find them?" she finally asked, but with the fire of determination in her eyes. Yeah, she was a fighter. Nothing would get her down very long.

But this was where his plan became tricky. "I'm not sure."

Her eyebrow shot up again. "You're half angel. Don't you have a magic ball or something?"

"Half is right. The other half makes mistakes like other men. I can't see the future."

She stared at him, not saying a word. Damn it, she could be aggravating as hell at times. "I see glimpses," he finally told her. "Or I feel as though something will happen. I'm not one hundred percent accurate."

"Ya think?"

Raine went beyond aggravating. "Would you rather I leave?" Not that he would, but she didn't know that for sure.

The fight went out of her. "No. I don't want Grandpa to suffer."

Guilt flooded him. He was supposed to be helping her, not sparring with her. "I'm sorry this turned out the way it did."

"I'll fix it." She didn't look very confident, and the vulnerability was back in her eyes.

"*We* will fix it. You're not in this alone."

Her expression said she didn't think he could pull it off. "Then don't screw up again." Her determination was back in full force. She reached down and picked up her coffee cup off the floor. "I think I'm going to need lots more coffee."

Chapter 13

RAINE SCANNED HER LIST of suspects. Some of them bordered on the ridiculous, but Dillon insisted she write down everyone she knew or might have talked to in the days before the robbery and they would eliminate them one by one. She studied the names. This was crazy. Sheriff Barnes did not rob the bank. She flipped the pencil to the eraser side and pressed it against the paper. Before she could remove his name, Dillon pulled the pencil out of her hand.

"What are you doing?" he asked.

"Sheriff Barnes did not rob the bank."

"You know that for a fact?"

"No, but my gut tells me he didn't do it. My gut is very seldom wrong."

"But you didn't say it was never wrong." He tossed the pencil onto the table. "He's a suspect until we eliminate him." He flipped one of the dining room chairs around, then straddled the seat, resting his arms casually against the back. She couldn't keep from staring at his biceps. The guy had some serious muscles. He made her whole body ache for his touch, to have him wrap his arms around her and pull her close.

Dillon barely noticed her. And why should he, she argued. They were trying to catch the men who robbed the bank, not have hot sex. She clenched her legs together. But that was all she could think about.

He suddenly came to his feet, as though he was the one feeling restless, and paced the floor. His forehead puckered. Then he strode back to the table and leaned over her. Her thought processing abilities came to a grinding halt when his warm breath tickled her neck. He leaned in a little closer to read the names on her paper. His scent filled her space. Sandalwood and sage, maybe? A hint of leather. She closed her eyes and inhaled. Yes, definitely leather. The aroma weaved its way around her, caressed with a light playful touch.

"Raine?"

His voice penetrated the fog of desire. She snapped out of it and met his gaze. "What? Did you say something?"

Dillon picked up the paper and studied it. "Why not Sheriff Barnes?" he asked, meeting her gaze.

She shook her head. "No, he wouldn't do it. He's a good man, not a criminal."

"But you put his name on the list."

She jumped to her feet, feeling a need to put space between them. "Because you told me to write down the names of people I was in contact with before the robbery. He's my boss. It was inevitable that I speak to him before the robbery."

"Does he like his job?"

"Of course he does."

"How well do you know him?"

"Very well. He was lead deputy for my father, and before that, deputy. He's been with the department since I was nine years old and he was twenty. Why would he rob a bank?"

"What's with all the posters on the walls of his office?"

She opened her mouth, then snapped it closed. "First the sheriff is a suspect and now you want to know about his office decor?"

"Humor me."

"They've been up since he took office." Not long after her father died, she dropped by the sheriff's office to collect a box he'd found in the far corner of the closet. She'd called him by his first name back then—Glen. As soon as she stepped into the office and saw the changes Glen made, Raine knew she would never think of it as her father's office. Glen had made the space his. He was the sheriff and due the respect that went with the office. That's when she started calling him Sheriff Barnes.

He balked at first, but she wouldn't budge. He finally got used to it. She frowned. He'd told her she was stubborn. Dillon said the same thing. She pulled out a chair at the far end of the table rather than taking the one closer to Dillon. Was *stubborn* a nice way of saying she was a control freak? She dismissed that notion. She didn't always need to be in charge.

She glanced up. "He told me he was going to travel someday. He put up posters of places he wanted to go. What's your point?"

"That maybe with the money from the bank heist he can go sooner than he planned. Take early retirement."

No, it couldn't be! But even as she told herself that Glen would never break the law, she had to wonder if he was getting tired of small-town life. For as long as she'd known him, all he ever wanted to be was an officer of the law. Her father was the same way.

Except she'd heard her father grumble about the low pay and the lack of respect he got from some people. He threatened more than once to get into another line of work, anything that would pay more money. Raine's mother had eagerly agreed, but after the first few times he mentioned changing his profession, then not following through, she knew he would never quit.

Glen had once voiced the same complaint, but then he would start talking about a case he'd handled and his eyes would have the same sparkle that had been in her father's. Glen wouldn't leave. He loved his job too much, and he wouldn't do anything to jeopardize his career.

"Scratch his name off," she said.

"You're sure?"

"Positive." But she wasn't. Not one hundred percent. She hated all the doubts Dillon created inside her.

Dillon picked up the pencil and drew a line through Sheriff Barnes's name. "Then let's move on."

"Good." But she knew she wouldn't feel any kind of relief until the bank robbers were captured.

He set the paper on the table in front of her, but it wasn't the paper she looked at. Dillon was way too distracting.

"What about Ethan? His name is on your list." He raised his head.

Dillon's eyes were so blue, so vibrant. She could get lost in them if she wasn't careful. They were mesmerizing.

Mesmerizing? Dammit, he was doing it to her again. "I know what you're up to," she said, dragging her gaze back to the paper, but it didn't really help. She still felt his nearness.

"Up to?" He wore a confused expression. "I thought we were trying to catch the bank robbers."

Yeah, right. This was a maneuver she used all the time. The seductive scent, leaning in closer to look at something, warm breath tickling. Her poor victims never knew what hit them.

Dillon was trying to seduce her. Losing was not in her vocabulary, even if he did have otherworldly powers. "You can't fool me."

His eyebrows veed.

"That cologne you're wearing." She would admit his tactics were pretty good. Not good enough, though. "You're also mesmerizing me with your eyes. You would love to seduce me. To make me your submissive, but it isn't going to work. I'm on to you."

"I'm not trying to seduce you," he said. "When you said you weren't into playing sex games, I took you at your word and backed off."

His smile was slow and sexy. She could feel herself begin to melt on the inside. Could she have misread the signals he sent? He looked truthful. It wouldn't be the first time she was wrong about something. Sincerity practically oozed from his pores. He was an angel—at least half. Had she misread him? Her gut feeling wasn't *always* right. Great. Now she questioned herself.

"I didn't say I wasn't into sex games," she finally muttered.

"As long as we play by your rules." His gaze dropped lower.

Raine's body responded to his heated look. She could almost feel him touching her, tweaking her nipples, flicking his finger across them right before he lowered his mouth. It took a moment for his words to sink in.

She drew in a deep breath, pushing away from the table. "What's wrong with my rules?" She put distance between them, walking to the window. She stared out at nothing in particular. A male redbird landed on one of the branches in the oak tree at the front of the house, looked around, then swooped down to the bird feeder. Grandpa always made sure there was wild bird seed in the feeder. She doled out fifteen dollars a month to feed the damn birds. He always asked if she had filled the feeder and she always did—for him. She couldn't care less about the stupid birds. Most of the time they built their nests in the rain gutter, and she would have to drag out the ladder and move the nests to one of the trees. It was a pain in the butt.

The redbird grabbed a black sunflower seed before swooping

away. She wondered if he was taking it back to the female. The he-man. He would probably get laid for his efforts. Not a bad idea. She could feed Dillon, then maybe he would have sex with her. Only one problem with that idea—she was a terrible cook. Worse than Grandpa.

"It wouldn't be as bad as you think," he said, breaking into her thoughts.

She glanced over her shoulder. "Why can't we just have sex and leave it at that? Why does there have to be games? We would both have release, satisfaction."

He shook his head. "All or nothing."

She gritted her teeth. The man was stubborn! "Then nothing." She hugged her waist, glaring at him. She could be just as stubborn.

He shrugged as if to say that was fine, he would abide by her decision, and turned back to the paper she'd scribbled names on. "Why did you put Ethan at the top of your list?"

Just like that he switched gears. They'd been talking about sex; now they were back to the bank robbers. Sure, she knew what was at stake. They had to catch them so she could clear the McCandless name. But it took her a minute longer to stop thinking about Dillon and sex and concentrate on bank robbers.

"Because I don't like him," she grated out.

"That's not a good enough reason."

She knew that, but she was pissed. Deep breath. Inhale. Exhale. She really had to get her emotions under control.

"He was the first one on the scene," she finally said when she could think more clearly. "Him and Leo. They're tight. I don't trust either one of them."

"Still not good enough."

The man was infuriating. Worse than a detective. "My gut tells me there's more going on than either one is letting on."

"Do you think they might have robbed the bank?"

She sat on the edge of the windowsill, planting the palms of her hands on either side. Her anger evaporated. "I honestly can't say," she finally admitted. "I definitely feel like there's more going on than meets the eye."

"What do you know about them?"

"Not a lot. Ethan's from the Galveston area. He's thirty-three. I don't think he's ever been married. He's never mentioned an ex-wife or kids, so he probably isn't strapped paying child support." She was thoughtful for a moment. He did have one passion. "He's into old cars. From what I've heard, he's restoring several."

"A hefty investment."

He and Leo had been putting their heads together a lot recently. Things she'd forgotten began to take on new meaning. "Darla mentioned something once, that Ethan was trying to buy the old Chevy showroom and garage. It's been vacant for a couple of years, but she said he didn't have enough money yet."

"Maybe he decided to borrow from the bank and make it a no interest loan. Leo could've helped."

She shook her head. "They're still cops. They wouldn't rob a bank." As much as she would like to point the finger in their direction, she didn't think Ethan and Leo would turn to crime to finance their business.

"Are you positive?"

Again, she wasn't sure. She wasn't sure about anything. "There were three bank robbers, though. Who was the third man?"

"It could be anyone they brought in."

"Ethan and his gang." It sounded more insane when she said the words out loud. "No, I don't think so."

"Why did he take so long to get to the bank? Wasn't he on call that night? He might have been stashing the money."

She thought back to something Ethan said. "When I was at the sheriff's office for questioning, he said that he had been picking up some papers."

But where? She closed her eyes and thought back. Sheriff Barnes and the Ranger had just entered his office. She'd blurted "this is the man who was shot." No one had been able to see Dillon and she'd had to cover her blunder. She practically accused Ethan of being the guilty one. He'd hurried to defend himself by saying he was picking up papers from…

Her eyes flew open. "Joe," she said as though she just answered the million dollar question. "He was picking up papers from Joe." She breathed a sigh of relief. The bump on her head and not being able to remember everything had scared her. The doctor said her memory would gradually return, but she wasn't good at being patient.

"Easy enough to check out if he's lying. Or maybe this is the third man. He would make a convenient alibi, and they would know that."

Her elation fizzled. Now she was even more confused, because Dillon might be right. Ethan, Leo, and this guy called Joe might have robbed the bank. Ethan would know exactly where she would be that night. He even wanted her to go to the other side of town. His plan backfired when she saw the light flash inside the bank. But would he rob the bank?

"What about Leo?" Dillon asked.

"He's an idiot."

"Do you have anything more to go on?"

She knew her observation wasn't what she would call being a good detective, but it was the truth. "He's married. His wife is sweet but she doesn't have a clue he flirts with every female in town."

"Affairs?"

She was thoughtful, then shook her head. "No, I think he likes the chase. It makes him feel more important than he is.

"He buys the women presents," she continued, thinking aloud. "He would need money. I know he's invested in a few wild schemes in the past that fell through and cost him. He's not much of a salesman."

"Anything else?"

No, she couldn't think of anything. But Leo? Nothing he ever did turned out well. He was gullible, too. Ethan might have talked him into robbing the bank with him. "Maybe," she said.

"We'll keep them on top of the list."

Her head was starting to throb. She reached up and massaged her temples as Dillon scribbled something on the paper.

"Whose name did you write?"

"Your grandfather's. You forgot to write his name down." He scribbled something else. "And Tilly's."

Chapter 14

"That's not funny," Raine said.

"I didn't mean for it to be." Dillon knew she would be angry at him for putting her grandfather on the list, but he couldn't rule out Sock or Tilly.

"That's totally ridiculous. Tilly and my grandfather did not rob the bank. Think about what you're saying. There's no way they could pull it off without me knowing."

"You know that for a fact?"

"Yes," she said without hesitation.

Always the protector, even though it might clear her name. If her grandfather was guilty, Raine would do whatever it took to keep him out of trouble, even go so far as taking the blame herself.

"Sock would do anything to save the ranch," he said to explain his way of thinking. "You're exhausted from trying to keep everything together. You work the graveyard shift, then come home and do the chores. He knows you were close to the breaking point. Being financially stable would fix everything. No more long hours for you. He could hire someone to do repairs. All his problems would be gone."

She was shaking her head, still not seeing the big picture, so he continued. "You gave up everything for him. A job you loved, an apartment in the city. You even traded in your car to help pay bills. The least he could do is rob a bank for you."

She strode toward him, fire shooting from her eyes. "My

grandfather would never rob a bank. Not for me or anyone else."
She stopped in front of him, fists doubled. "He would rather lose
everything than break the law."

"Yet he steals animals."

Her eyes grew round. "That's a lie."

"Isn't that one of the reasons you came home? He was accused
of stealing a horse?"

"He didn't steal the horse. The owners were letting the poor
animal starve to death because they couldn't afford the feed. He
rescued the mare."

"And they filed a complaint."

"Which was dropped."

"He stole a horse."

"Rescued!"

"Stole."

Her cheeks turned red and her mouth puckered. "Rescued!"

She drew back her arm. Before she connected with his chin, his
hand closed over her fist and he pulled her forward. She was so intent
on throwing a punch that she lost her balance and fell into him.

Her gaze collided with his. "I hate you," she said between
gritted teeth.

He drew in a breath as the warmth of her body surrounded
him. Yeah, he pushed her. He wanted her to lose her temper
because he couldn't stand not holding her one second longer.

"Liar," he said.

Raine attempted to squirm away, but she only managed
to ignite the fire inside him, and apparently inside herself, too,
because her arms suddenly went around his neck and she pulled
him closer, her body melting against his. He'd been an idiot to
think he could go much longer without taking her into his arms,
without making love to her.

"I do hate you." But her words were soft and lacked conviction. "Grandpa and Tilly didn't rob the bank."

"Shh, it'll be okay."

"Say it." She pulled away enough to look into his eyes.

"They didn't rob the bank." In his heart, Dillon knew Sock wouldn't commit a felony. Not even to save his ranch.

She raised her lips to his. He leaned down, tasted her. The kiss deepened. He wanted her so damn bad it made his knees weak. He tugged her shirt out of her pants, then pulled the sides apart, ignoring the sound of ripping material. She pushed his T-shirt up. A sigh shuddered through her body as naked flesh pressed against naked flesh.

He broke the kiss long enough to toss his hat to the side. He grabbed the hem of the cotton material and yanked it over his head before he pulled her back into his arms. When he looked into her eyes he saw victory shining in hers.

"You think you've won."

Her smile was slow and oozed confidence. "I know I've won." She rubbed her breasts against his chest.

He gritted his teeth as pleasure filled him. Her nipples scraped back and forth. Before he could recover, she slipped her hands under his waistband. The first button was undone before he could think of anything to say. Her knuckles scraped across his erection. Fire shot through him. He wanted more.

"Let me stop the ache," she said.

He barely heard her words right before she shoved his jeans down. His briefs went with them. The scraping of material across his already swollen member had him grasping her shoulders so he wouldn't fall over.

"Nice," she murmured as her gaze dropped. She caressed the tip of his erection.

He jerked.

"I'm going to make love to you and you'll enjoy every minute," she said.

Dillon fought to regain control of his emotions. There would be new rules to the game. He wasn't about to let her win this time.

"That feels good," he said.

Her laugh was light. "I knew you were hurting. We both want the same thing. Why deny it?" She had the look of a woman already picking up her first place trophy.

"Take off your pants," he told her.

Her forehead furrowed as though she questioned if that was a good idea or not. He could see the wheels turning inside her head as she wondered how vulnerable that would make her. Dillon didn't want her to think too long or too hard about what she should do.

"Please," he pretended to beg. "I can't stand another minute not seeing you naked."

She relaxed, thinking she still had control. "I'll please you in ways you've never thought about." She unfastened her jeans and pushed them over her hips.

"Better?" she teased as she lightly rested her hands on her hips. "Or would you like me to take off more?" She snapped the waistband of her silky blue panties.

His dick jerked. "More," he barely managed to say. Okay, so this wasn't going to be easy. But did he really want it easy?

"Then you take them off." She turned and walked a short distance away. When she faced him again, she stood with her feet slightly apart. "Come over here and remove them," she demanded.

Always the dominatrix. His eyes swept over her. He wouldn't mind playing the game her way, but he wanted her to experience more. To do that, she had to give up control.

He strolled toward her but didn't stop in front. He continued until he stood behind her. When she would have turned, he put his hands on her shoulders. "Not this time, lady. We're going to play the game by my rules." He lightly rested his hands on her shoulders.

She stiffened. "I refuse to…"

He slid his hands down until they covered her breasts, then lightly squeezed.

"This isn't…"

"Isn't what?" He spoke close to her ear.

"I won't let any man dominate me."

"I don't want to dominate you."

"But you said…"

"It's only a game. Let me take you somewhere you've never been. What are you afraid of?"

"Losing control," she finally whispered.

"Don't be." He would have to prove to her that losing control would make her stronger, not weaker. "Close your eyes."

A tremble swept over her.

"I'm only going to take you somewhere."

"What about my clothes?"

"You won't need them. Now close your eyes."

Dillon hoped she was ready for this. He closed his eyes. The ground beneath their feet disappeared. She gasped and clung to his arm. Her backside pressed against his front, creating a sweet ache inside him.

"What's happening?" she cried.

"Shh, I'll keep you safe."

Over the centuries Dillon had gotten used to traveling through space. The air rushing past, the whirring sounds, and flashing lights didn't bother him. He supposed anyone could get used to anything over time.

He opened his eyes and watched the lights swirl around them. They never ceased to amaze him. Shades of brilliant blue, red, and green, flashing and turning as though he was on the inside of a kaleidoscope. Then the lights faded and the sounds ebbed to a whisper. Raine's nail-biting grip loosened when their feet settled on solid ground once again.

"Where are we?" she asked without releasing his arm.

"The House of Ecstasy."

"It's dark."

"Would you like to see?"

"I'm not sure. Why did you bring me here?"

"The house is a place where all sexual inhibitions are left at the door. It's a place where you can experience incredible delights." He lightly brushed his fingers back and forth across her nipples. "I can make it lighter so you can see. If you're not scared, that is."

She stiffened. "Did you think I would be?"

"Are you?"

"Of course I'm not frightened. But I still won't let you dominate me."

He smiled, knowing she was curious. He sensed from the very beginning she had a strong sexual appetite but was afraid to let go. To her, that would be a sign of weakness. She had to be strong for everyone around her. To do less was unthinkable. He planned to show her that losing control wouldn't destroy who she was.

"I doubt anyone will ever dominate you completely. Are you ready to explore?"

"Why not? Okay, show me the house. I'll let you know if I'm impressed."

He waved his arm and the dim light began to grow brighter. The room was large with fine silk in pale blue covering the walls. A multi-tiered chandelier hung from the ceiling, dripping with royal blue teardrop crystals with diamonds looped between them. The white carpet was thick and plush beneath his bare feet. There was no furniture. Fountains poured into a small pool at the end of the room.

"It's beautiful," she whispered.

He slid his hand down her arm and grasped her hand. "Come with me. There's more to show you."

"What is this room used for?" she asked as he led her toward the door on the far side.

"It's called the orgy room."

She stumbled to a stop. "Say what?" Her eyes grew large and her mouth dropped open.

Her reaction didn't surprise him. Dillon remembered the first time he came here, but the room wasn't empty then. There were quite a few people. Men and women in various stages of undress. Some were making love, others were talking and laughing. It didn't seem to matter if they were the same sex or the opposite as long as the main goal was to experience pleasure in all its forms. He'd been shocked and aroused at the same time.

"You mean like naked people having sex?"

"Exactly."

"How does someone like you come across a place like this?"

"Stereotyping?"

She raised her eyebrows.

He laughed. "I dated a fairy once."

Now Dillon could see he'd shocked her. "Fairies are very sensual creatures. She was no exception."

"She?"

"Yes, a female. What did you think I meant?" She didn't have to answer. He enjoyed teasing her. "Love comes in all forms," he said, turning serious. "Don't let preconceived notions cloud your mind."

"I didn't say anything," she said defensively. "Is this all you were going to show me?"

She was getting testy again. He enjoyed arguing with her because he knew she couldn't win. He took her hand again and they moved toward the door. "Fairies have houses similar to this one all over the universe. The fairies' powers fade if they don't feed their sexual appetites. These are safe houses, you might say."

He tapped on the door. A window opened and a scanner swept over their bodies. The blue light warmed his skin like a caress. Raine gasped. This was just the beginning of her tour.

"I assumed the house was empty. I only have on my panties, and you're naked!" she whispered. But when she looked at him, desire rose in her eyes before she could tamp it down.

Dillon almost pulled her into his arms and said to hell with the rest of the tour. The only thing going through his mind was making love to Raine. Before he could act on his impulse, the window closed and the door swung open.

He told himself what Raine experienced would make the wait worthwhile. He stepped over the threshold, then held out his hand. There was only the briefest hesitation before she took it and stepped into the other room.

Dillon loved the fact that Raine was up for any challenge. This was only the first one.

Chapter 15

THE ROOM WAS DARK. Raine wondered what exactly she'd gotten herself into by telling Dillon she wasn't scared. House of Ecstasy? Sex? Orgies? Besides the fact that she was naked except for her panties. Of course she was scared! She was terrified.

No you're not.

Yes I am, she told the voice inside her head, but she knew she felt anything but terrified. Dillon made her feel vibrant and alive.

Excited trembles ran up and down her body, much like the blue scanner right before the door swung open. Not wearing much didn't concern her at this point. She wanted to see what Dillon was going to show her. Her curiosity wasn't the only thing aroused. But she couldn't see a damn thing. Only shadows.

"What's happening?" she finally gave in and asked. She knew Dillon wanted her to make the first move.

He stepped behind her and squeezed her breasts as he pulled her closer. That was nice. Her eyelids drooped as she leaned against him. She enjoyed being snuggled against his chest; knowing he was ready for sex added to her pleasure.

Were they in the middle of another orgy room? She didn't hear anyone else, but the thought of being surrounded by naked bodies in the throes of passion turned her on. When Dillon waved his arm, she was a little disappointed to see they were the only ones in the room.

As her eyes adjusted, Raine saw they stood behind a picture

window, so it was almost as though they were looking into the neighbors' living room. The room was stylishly decorated with a beige sofa and two dark brown chairs. There was a brown fur rug on the hardwood floor. Two end tables and a glass coffee table. Artwork on the wall. Nothing fancy. Modern but generic. This was what he wanted to show her? "No one is home," she said.

"Wait."

A door opened and two men and a woman entered. They were dressed well, like they were just getting home from a party. The woman wore a white silk top tucked into a black-and-white polka-dot skirt that came to just above her knees, and black heels. Both men wore dark gray slacks. One wore a pale yellow shirt and the other a red one. They all looked happy and relaxed as they came inside.

One of the men went to a cart in the corner of the room and mixed drinks while the couple made themselves comfortable on the sofa. Raine couldn't help wondering what would happen next, if they would have their drinks, say good night, and go to bed.

The man brought three drinks over and gave one to the woman and the other to the second man before making himself comfortable on the other side of the woman. The woman said something Raine couldn't hear, but the men both laughed.

"Is this legal? Watching them, I mean," she asked, but couldn't drag her eyes away from the scene unfolding in front of her. She knew something was going to happen between them. Why else would Dillon bring her here?

"They know someone is watching. That's why they chose this room. It heightens their experience."

She swallowed. What experience? Her mouth grew dry and she found it hard to swallow. Dillon's fingers trailing over her breasts and abdomen were only making her imagination more vivid.

The man in the red shirt casually placed his hand on the woman's knee. Raine couldn't drag her gaze away when he began to run his fingers back and forth across her knee. The man said something, but Raine couldn't hear his words.

Again, Dillon waved his arm.

"That feels nice, Scott," the woman said.

Raine stepped back, except Dillon's body directly behind her made it impossible to go far.

"Don't worry," he said. "We can hear them, but they can't hear us."

She nodded, taking his word for it, but knowing something about this had to be wrong. Still, she couldn't force herself to look away.

The other man finished his drink and set his glass on the coffee table in front of him. He shifted his position, then placed his hand on the woman's other knee.

Raine's thighs clenched. She could almost feel the men touching the woman. She wanted them to move their hands higher.

"Intense, isn't it?" Dillon asked.

"Yes." Her voice cracked and she couldn't say more.

The woman smiled, then finished her drink, fanning herself as though the alcohol had made her overly warm. "It's getting a little hot."

The other man set his glass down, then took hers. He laughed and picked up a magazine, waving it in front of her. "Maybe you have on too many clothes, Kara."

"You're such a bad boy, Nick." She wagged her finger at both men, but began to unbutton her blouse. When she had the buttons undone she pushed open the sides of her shirt. The lacy pale pink bra cupped her breasts and pushed them up, but didn't cover her rosy nipples. They were bared for both men to enjoy.

Raine's body grew warm. She knew it was wrong to watch but she couldn't stop. The scene playing out in front of her was so damned erotic, like she watched a live porn movie. Dillon didn't make matters any better by lightly tracing his finger around her nipple, then moving to her other breast and repeating the movement. Her nipples already ached to the point that they were painful.

"That's better," Scott said.

"I dreamed about looking at your tits the whole time we were at the party," Nick told her. "That, and touching your pussy."

Raine drew in a sharp breath when Nick reached beneath Kara's skirt. The woman gasped, then wiggled farther down on the sofa so Nick could have better access. Her hips began to raise and lower.

Raine found herself moving her own hips to the same rhythm. She moaned. Dillon slid his hand over her abdomen and beneath her panties. When he touched her, she cried out, then quickly stifled the sound.

"It doesn't matter. Remember, they can't hear you. Do you like watching them?"

"Yes." Did that make her sick and perverted? She'd never watched anyone having sex.

"Then keep watching." Dillon's breath fanned her cheek, causing ripples of pleasure to tingle over her body. He didn't have to tell her. She couldn't look anywhere else.

"I want to see you touching her," Scott said, then pushed the woman's skirt up so that her sheer white panties showed. Nick's hand was inside and he was moving it back and forth. "Fucking sweet," he breathed. "But let's take them off."

Scott tugged on her panties. Nick hooked his finger in the waistband and began to help. Kara's panties slid down her thighs, over her knees, and dropped to the rug. They each took one of her legs and draped it across their own.

Kara glanced down, then covered her mouth as though she might be shocked. "Oh my, what are you two going to do now that I'm so exposed?"

"We'll think of something." Nick laughed.

The men began to rub their fingers over her clit. Scott took an ice cube from his glass and ran it over her nipples while Nick rubbed an ice cube between her legs. The woman arched her back.

"Oh yes, that feels so fucking good."

Dillon slid his fingers down lower. "You're damp."

Raine's nerves were raw. She was almost to her breaking point. "I want you," she gasped.

"Not yet. Soon," he whispered, then dipped his tongue inside her ear. "Watch."

Raine nibbled her bottom lip, barely able to stand the exquisite pleasure he created inside her. But she watched, just as he asked. She didn't think.

Nick eased the woman's leg from across his thighs and stood. While Scott caressed her, Nick began to remove his clothes. The couple on the sofa watched him strip. Nick's shirt fell to the floor. He took his time sliding his zipper down.

Raine held her breath. Waiting. Just like Kara and Scott.

Nick's pants slid to the floor. He hooked one finger in the waistband of his gray boxers, then paused. The woman reached toward him, silently pleading. He didn't keep her waiting. He lowered his boxers far enough that he exposed the red, glistening tip of his penis.

"I want to touch you." Kara's words were husky with need.

Raine held her breath, afraid the sound of her breathing might cause her to miss hearing something. The man pushed his boxers lower. Raine stared.

"Beautiful." Scott openly stared.

Nick reached out and took Kara's hand, closing it around the tip of his penis. Then he took Scott's hand and pulled it against the shaft. "Yes," he breathed as he rocked against their hands.

Raine had never seen men touch each other, but it was beautiful, it was sexy. Scott fondled Nick as though he admired something that had been created so perfectly that he couldn't help but caress it.

Nick moved to the sofa. He stroked the other man's face, then kissed the woman. Scott stood and began to remove his clothes. When his pants slid to the floor, Kara sat forward and licked up the length of his erection before taking him into her mouth.

Scott groaned and closed his eyes, hips rocking forward. Nick pulled Kara's shirt down her arms and tossed it away from them before unhooking her bra. He leaned his head against her back, placing tiny kisses on her pale skin as he took her breasts in his hands and massaged.

"Fuck her, Nick," Scott said. "I want to see your dick sliding in and out of her."

"Yes, fuck me," Kara moaned.

Nick didn't need any more encouragement. He unhooked her skirt and tugged the zipper down. Kara stopped sucking Scott's dick long enough to stand and wiggle out of her skirt. All three were naked. Nick sat back on the sofa, patting his thighs. Kara backed up to him, straddling his legs as she lowered her body onto him. His dick slid inside her wetness.

"Oh yeah, right there. Damn, that feels fucking great. Your pussy is so tight," Nick said.

Scott moved so that Kara could take him in her mouth again. As she began to suck Scott's dick, Nick slid his hand down to Scott's balls and began to fondle him. Kara rocked her body back and forth.

Dillon slid his fingers up Raine's clit, then pressed them against her pussy. She couldn't think straight. Her thoughts were jumbled as she watched the threesome, her body on fire. Nick fucking Kara, Kara sucking Scott's dick.

Raine grasped Dillon's thighs, pulling him closer, tighter against her. His erection pressed against her. She ached to feel him buried deep inside.

Nick pulled out of Kara. She moved to her back. "You make me so fucking hot," she said as her hands slid over her breasts, squeezing and massaging. Scott and Nick were on their knees on each side, watching her fondle herself. Her hands moved lower until she touched between her legs.

"Don't stop," Scott said as he moved between her legs and entered. "I want to watch you masturbate while I'm fucking you." His dick slid in, out, then back in with slow, deep strokes.

With her free hand, Kara guided Nick's dick toward her mouth. He drew in a sharp breath when she sucked him inside.

Raine moved against Dillon's hand and struggled to breathe as a wave of desire overwhelmed her. She wanted relief at the same time she wanted this moment to last forever. Exquisite torture.

Nick closed his eyes as he lost himself in the pleasure Kara's mouth gave him as she sucked his dick. "Your mouth is fucking hot. Suck it, baby." His breathing became ragged. "Ah, damn," he groaned and moved away just enough so he slipped out of Kara's mouth. She replaced her mouth with her hand, not willing to end the game so soon, and began to slide her hand up and down his dick. "Oh yes, like that," he groaned. He moved against her hand, raising his hips until his body jerked and he came.

Raine whimpered as the ache inside her grew. Kara continued to massage her clit, moving faster and faster. Raine nudged closer to Dillon's hand, but his movements stayed slow.

"Oh God, this feels so…" Kara cried out. Her back arched. Her expression became one of intense delight.

"Dillon, I can't stand it. Please fuck me." Raine's body was on fire.

Scott drove into Kara's body, then pulled out almost all the way. Raine watched as he plunged again. Deeper, harder. Hips rocking until he cried out.

Raine could barely take a breath when Dillon waved his hand in front of her and the threesome faded from sight. The room around her lit with a soft violet glow. In the center of the room was a bed.

"I want you," she said, feeling as though she would shatter into a million pieces if he didn't make love to her.

He didn't say a word as he picked her up and carried her to the bed. Dillon laid her down and nudged her legs open. She didn't care that she wasn't on top. She only wanted him inside her, stroking her.

One look at his face and she knew he wanted the same thing. His lips were clamped; beads of sweat dotted his forehead, his tight jaw. Watching the three lovers was a test of endurance for both of them. She knew Dillon held back for her. No one ever thought of her pleasure before their own. She didn't wonder about the novelty as Dillon entered her, filling her. A shudder of pleasure rippled over her.

He moaned as though he'd waited a lifetime for this moment. Her body closed around him. She tightened her inner muscles, feeling the rush of pleasure spiral through her. She'd never felt like this before and the sensations flooded in from every side, overwhelming her.

"Shh, easy now," Dillon said.

She opened her eyes and stared up at him, realizing her

breathing was erratic, ragged, as the rawness of so many emotions hit her all at once.

"Relax. Just feel me deep inside you."

She exhaled, then inhaled as calmness stole over her.

For a moment, neither one moved. She savored this sweet torture, testing the limits their bodies could endure. Then as one, they began to move. He slid deep. She rose to meet his stroke. Then back down. Her body trembled as heat spread over her, building in intensity until she couldn't stand another moment without release.

"Dillon," she whispered. "Now. Please, now."

He began to move faster, stroking her long and hard. She strained, letting the friction of their bodies carry her over the edge. Little earthquakes erupted inside her. She cried out. Her body clenched. She grabbed his shoulders.

He plunged inside her once, twice, then sucked in a deep breath. She watched through half closed eyes and saw the pleasure she had given him. It didn't matter that she hadn't been on top. It didn't matter at all. She still accomplished what she needed to.

She wrapped her arms around his neck, but a thread of fear weaved its way through her. Had she let a little piece of herself go? What would she give up next? No, it was only this one time, she told herself, but the feeling that she'd been weak was still with her.

"Don't analyze it," Dillon told her.

Being on top might not mean much to him. It was only sex, after all, but to her it meant she was in control of the situation. If she was vulnerable, she opened herself to hurt.

A shudder wracked her body. He rolled to his side, taking her with him, holding her close. She drew her knees closer to her chest. "I'm tired. I want to rest," she said. His lips brushed her forehead as she closed her eyes. His warmth wrapped around her like the sun bursting from behind a dark cloud.

It won't last, the voice inside her head warned.

I know.

Chapter 16

WHEN RAINE WOKE THE next morning, she was in her own bed. She sat up and looked around, feeling as if she'd tied one on the night before. If she weren't so sore she'd think she'd dreamed the whole thing.

No dream had ever been that vivid, that real.

She eased to the side of the bed and sat there for a moment. Dillon had controlled the night and she let him. In the light of day, her fixation about being the one on top seemed silly. Had it killed her to let go? No.

She got up, grimacing at the throbbing between her legs. Sore, yes, but the pleasure had been worth the pain. She'd never been so out of control. So what did that say about her sex life?

Once she was under the gentle spray of the shower she couldn't help reliving the previous night. Would voyeurism be considered a crime if the persons involved knew they were being watched? Dillon said the threesome had known there might be people on the other side of the window. They hoped someone would be watching.

She squirted a large dollop of bath gel onto the palm of her hand. The apricot scent filled the shower cubicle. For a moment, she closed her eyes and let all her troubles drift away. As she slid the orange gel down her arm, her senses came alive. Erotic images filled her mind. Scott and Nick touching Kara, fondling her breasts, their fingers probing between her legs.

A shiver of need swirled over her as an ache began to build. Just as suddenly, the water coming from the showerhead began to cool. She shivered and quickly washed away the soap. Damned hot water heater. They needed a new one. Three and a half minutes was not enough time to take a shower.

She stepped out and grabbed the threadbare towel. They needed new linens, too. It was always something. More repairs than she could keep up with. With all the added problems, they were going to be in a real bind if they didn't find the bank robbers. Dillon said he would help, but would he only cause her more trouble?

She dried off the best she could before she tossed the damp towel over the shower rod and opened the door. She padded down the hall and stepped into the bedroom, but came to an abrupt stop when she saw Dillon sprawled on her bed.

He glanced up. His heated gaze slowly moved over her body, touching the side of her neck, skimming her breasts, her waist, the damp curls between her legs, then slowly made the trek back to her eyes. "I love it when you're naked."

She exhaled, not realizing she'd held her breath. Damn it, how could one hungry look send her sexual appetite into over-drive? She forgot about everything she needed to do. The only thing going through her mind was making love with him, but that would only solve her initial problem of needing physical release.

"You're beautiful," he said, then closed his eyes and inhaled. "Apricot. Nectar of the gods."

She cocked an eyebrow, then strolled to the dresser. "Bath gel. Thrifty Market on the corner of Main Street. Dollar twenty-nine, unless I have a coupon." She opened the bottom drawer, ignoring his quick indrawn breath as she dug around for a pair of panties. That was a dumb move, she thought to herself. She grabbed a lace-edged pair of sage green panties and quickly pulled them on, then shoved the drawer shut.

With her back still toward him, she opened the top drawer and dug around for a bra. Her hand scraped across her .22 pistol as she hunted for a T-shirt, but she quickly dismissed the idea of removing one of her problems by shooting him. He might be able to help her. She didn't know for sure. Besides, he was immortal. He would heal. She slammed the drawer closed, opting not to wear a bra.

"Are you angry about something?" he asked.

"No." The one word came out clipped, betraying her emotional upheaval.

He was beside her in an instant, pulling her against him. She inhaled his rugged scent, letting it wrap around her. She didn't want to relax around him.

"Tell me what's bothering you," he said.

"Nothing. Everything."

"Last night?"

She pushed out of his arms, needing to put a little space between them. She went to the closet and grabbed a pair of her jeans that were nicer than the jeans she usually wore to do chores. She didn't try to figure out why she wanted to wear the black jeans that fit snug against her body. She pulled them on, sliding them up until they rested low on her hips. She wouldn't try to figure out why she grabbed an olive green T-shirt that she knew looked good on her, and poked her arms through the armholes, tugging it over her head. When she turned around he was leaning against her dresser, staring. "What?" she finally asked.

"You look hot."

"I have chores to do," she mumbled and started past him. She must be losing her mind. Why else would she want to wear her good clothes to do chores? She grabbed her boots and a pair of socks. She had to move around him to get to the door. She breathed a sigh of relief when she was almost there, but he moved fast and blocked her from leaving the room.

"What?" she asked again with more than a touch of exasperation, but she couldn't meet his eyes.

He lightly ran his fingers down her arm. She shivered.

"What did I do?"

She swallowed hard. What had he done? She couldn't think straight when he was so close. She moved to the bed and sat on the edge as she pulled on her socks. The act of pulling on socks and boots worked to ground her in the reality of her life.

"You took me to a place and made me watch those people," she finally spat out, and knew that wasn't what bothered her.

"I didn't force you."

"You should've asked before you took me there." She clamped her lips together and tugged the first boot on with more force than she needed.

"Would you have gone if I had?"

"No," she blurted.

"But you enjoyed watching them have sex. The way the men touched her, touched each other."

Her movements slowed as images danced across her mind. Her stomach began to churn because she knew he was right. She'd enjoyed every second of it.

"There's nothing wrong with having needs."

She grabbed her other boot and glanced up at him. "Even perverted ones?"

"It was consensual sex between three adults. Where was the perversion?"

She yanked her boot on and jumped to her feet. "I don't

know! But you told me to watch, and I did. You told me to feel, and I did. You were on top, and I let you." Her chest heaved as she tried to draw her emotions back under control.

"That's your problem? That you gave up control for a brief moment?"

She marched toward him, but stopped when she was only a foot away. "Yes, that's what pisses me off," she snarled. "I never give up control. Never. You won't trick me again." She stormed past him.

"But you enjoyed it, so why was it wrong?"

She pretended she didn't hear him. She kept walking until she was in the kitchen preparing the coffee pot. She dumped a scoop of coffee into the brew basket. She started to replace it, but at the last second dumped another scoop inside. She only hoped Dillon was gone when she turned around. She didn't want to discuss last night with him. She gripped the counter, her knees growing weak just thinking about the way she'd responded.

"Oh, for Christ's sake!" she muttered, pushing away from the counter and striding out the back door. She let it slam behind her. Once outside, she continued down the steps and toward the barn. Visions filled her mind when she remembered what had taken place the last time she was inside.

"Is no place safe?" She turned and went to the chicken coop. She hated chickens. They always pecked her. After opening the gate, she grabbed the basket and went inside. The first chicken glared at her. Raine glared back and reached beneath the feathery creature and grabbed the two eggs the fat hen was sitting on. She almost dared the hen to peck. The hen looked put out that Raine took her eggs, but she didn't peck. Raine gathered twenty eggs from the sitting birds without a single injury. Maybe they knew she would have chicken and dumplings if they pecked her.

She strode back toward the house and through the back door. She quickly scanned the room. No Dillon. Good. Maybe he would leave her alone for a while. The coffee was ready so she poured some into a cup and took a long swallow. She almost choked. Two scoops might have been a little too much. Definitely an eye opener.

Someone knocked on the front door. She jumped, almost spilling coffee down her shirt. Some of the hot liquid sloshed onto her hand. "Damn it," she muttered and turned the cold water on. The water cooled her hot skin. She let it run for a few seconds then inspected her hand. A little red but nothing more.

The knocking started again. If that was Dillon she'd castrate him. She grabbed a dish towel and patted her hands dry. Her forehead wrinkled. Maybe she wouldn't castrate him, but she could think about it!

The knocking grew louder. "I'm coming!" She tossed the towel and hurried to the front door. She glanced at the clock as she hurried past. It was still early. Only eight. Who the hell dropped by at this time? She unlocked the door and flung it open. Her answer was standing on the front porch, eyes just as cold as when she first interrogated Raine. Now what?

"I thought we could talk some more." Emily Gearson smiled.

Raine raised her eyebrows. "A girl-to-girl chat?"

"You could say that. May I come in?"

"Texas Rangers don't have chats. They fish for answers and they keep baiting the hook until they find out everything they need to know. Come in if you want."

Emily opened the door and stepped inside. "I have a job to do. You can't fault me for that." She sniffed. "Is that coffee? The coffee at the café was pretty awful."

Those were the first genuine words that came out of the

woman's mouth, and Raine had to agree with her. The café in town had the worst coffee. She had a feeling they reused the coffee filters until they petrified. "I hope you like it strong." She turned and walked toward the kitchen.

Once in the kitchen, Raine brought down another cup. It didn't match. The cups were gifts throughout the years. A birthday present from one of his cronies when Grandpa turned sixty that had Old Fart plastered more than a dozen times in different fonts and sizes. Raine's fingers brushed against it, but she brought out a plain dark blue cup instead. She poured coffee into the cup and looked at the ranger. "Cream? Sugar?"

Emily shook her head. "Straight up. Too many years on stakeouts. We always had coffee but never enough cream or sugar. I got used to drinking it black."

"Back porch?"

Emily nodded.

It just seemed the safer thing to do. The ranger had been covertly looking around when they were in the house.

"This is good coffee," Emily said as she sat down. She took another drink and crossed her legs as she leaned back.

They could've been two friends sharing the start of a new day. But they weren't. The ranger might look relaxed, but Raine figured it was all an act. Two could play that game.

"Why did you become a ranger?"

Emily looked surprised that Raine had asked a question. "I grew up with tales of my great-great-grandfather the Texas Ranger," she said after a moment's hesitation. "He lived in Tokeen for a while. The town doesn't exist anymore, but the stories found their way down through the generations. I thought it would be cool if I followed in his footsteps."

Raine was surprised the other woman had opened up. Maybe

Emily was a little surprised too, because she sat a little straighter and wore a grim look as though she might have somehow failed in her duties. Raine's father once said never make an enemy out of someone if they'll make a better ally down the road. Raine had a feeling she might need the other woman's help someday.

"It was the same for me." Raine sat in the other rocker. "One of my favorite times growing up was stopping by my dad's office when he was sheriff. He'd discuss case files—"

Emily raised her eyebrows.

"Nothing specific. Generic stuff. Usually cold files. Then he would ask me to solve the case."

"Did you?"

She shrugged. "Sometimes. Sometimes not."

"What about the robbery? Are you going to solve that one?"

"I don't have much to go on. Everyone seems to think it was me and Grandpa."

"Was it?"

"What do you think?" Raine countered, meeting the woman's gaze.

Emily studied her. "I'll reserve judgment for now."

"That was noncommittal."

"I don't like to accuse unjustly. I'm more of a know-all-the-facts type of person." She leaned back in her chair again. "If I find out you're guilty, I'll prosecute you to the full extent of the law."

"I would expect no less."

Emily's gaze slowly scanned the area. "It's nice out here. Peaceful. I would think it would be hard to let go of this ranch."

"I don't plan on letting the property go. We may not be rich, but we get by. My grandfather is an honest man. There's not a criminal bone in his body."

"Yet he was accused of stealing a horse," she spoke almost to herself.

Raine tensed. Of course she would know about that. "The charges were dropped." She pronounced each word slowly and distinctly, forcing herself to keep her temper under control. Why did everyone keep bringing up the damn horse?

"Just the same, it was a criminal act." Emily brought the cup to her lips and drained the last of her coffee.

"The owners were the real criminals for letting the poor horse starve. You could count the creature's ribs."

Emily didn't say anything as she got up, still staring at the landscape as though she found something of particular interest. "I can't say what he did was right. He broke the law. But I can't say I wouldn't have done the same thing, either," she murmured.

Raine stood. "Right or wrong, he's not a criminal."

"I know," she admitted. "But all the evidence points toward the two of you."

Surprise left Raine speechless. She never expected Emily to make a declaration like that.

"What? I'm not stupid. I've read the files on your years as a police officer. I read back as far as when you went to high school. You might be a little unorthodox at times, but you're honest." She handed her empty cup to Raine. "Don't prove me wrong. I really hate when I'm wrong."

Raine came to her feet, taking her cup. "You're not wrong this time."

"I hope not." She studied Raine for a moment. "You know, in another situation we might be friends."

Raine began to relax. Emily was down to earth, and against her better judgment, Raine was starting to like her. The woman had to have grit to be a Texas Ranger. She admired that.

"You're dressed differently," Emily observed. "One might think there was a man you wanted to impress. But then, you're not dating anyone around here, are you?" Her expression was puzzled.

Raine couldn't think of anything to say. She could argue the point, but Emily was already going down the steps and around the side of the house. A few minutes later, Raine heard her car start. Lying never sat well with her, and she was afraid that telling Emily she wasn't trying to impress anyone, especially a man, would be a bald-faced lie and the other woman would know it. Sometimes it was better to keep her mouth closed. "I think she likes you," Dillon said as he came out the back door.

Raine whirled and threw the cup toward him. It hit him square in the chest. With a loud oomph, he doubled over.

"Your reactions haven't slowed since you've been on leave," he gasped.

"Damn it, don't you know not to startle someone like that? If I'd had a gun I might have shot you!"

"I'm immortal," he said as he weaved his way to the chair and sat in it.

"But you still feel pain."

He nodded. "For a bit." He rubbed his chest.

"Then you would think you'd learn not to scare people." She hadn't meant to throw the empty cup at him. "Are you okay?"

He stretched his shoulders and rubbed his chest. "Did anyone ever mention you'd make a great pitcher?"

She grimaced. "I took my softball team to state my senior year in high school. I was the pitcher. I had more strikeouts than any other team that year."

"I believe it."

"Does it still hurt?"

His eyes met hers. "Not really."

She breathed a sigh of relief. Dillon continued to stare. She began to fidget.

"What?" she finally asked.

"You're so beautiful."

She rolled her eyes. "So you've told me."

"Because you are."

"Why are you here?" she asked, changing the subject. He made her uncomfortable talking like that.

"I'm going to help you find the men who robbed the bank, remember?"

"Like you helped me find them last night?" As soon as the words were out of her mouth, she wanted to call them back. She didn't want to think about last night.

"You're blushing," he said.

"I am not. The sun's up. It's getting warm."

"You enjoyed yourself last night. Why are you so afraid to admit it?"

Because then she would have to face the fact that she'd let him take charge for just a little while. He said watch, and she watched. He moved on top when they made love, and she let him. For just a little while last night, he was the one in control and it scared the hell out of her because she'd enjoyed herself. What would she give up next time? No, she didn't want to think about it.

She marched to the edge of the porch, but stopped before going down the steps and sat on the top one instead. "I don't want to talk about last night."

"What happened last night?" Grandpa asked.

Chapter 17

RAINE WHIRLED AROUND. GRANDPA pushed open the screen door and joined her on the porch. Her heart was beating so fast she was afraid it might jump out of her chest.

"Grandpa, you scared me!" She caught her breath, then stood on trembling legs. "What are you doing here? Did Emily see you?" And where was Dillon? He wasn't sitting in the rocking chair. She frowned. He could've warned her someone was coming. And why didn't he warn her about Emily? Some guardian angel he was. Or was he? No, now that she thought about it, she didn't think he was much of a guardian.

"That Ranger lady was here?"

"She just left."

He shook his head. "Nope, she didn't see me. Just in case they have the ranch staked out, I came in from the back side. I wasn't born yesterday."

Lady barked as she ran around the side of the house. She jumped up the steps and stopped beside Raine, resting her head on Raine's knees.

"She likes you." Grandpa beamed.

Raine patted the dog's head, marveling at the beauty of her golden yellow coat. Then it hit her. "This dog isn't a stray, Grandpa." Grandpa looked down at his feet, refusing to meet her eyes.

"I found her limping down the road," he mumbled. "Sort of. Her foot was hurt real bad. I just made sure she got better."

"Grandpa, how could you?" If anyone got wind of this, they'd be in so much trouble.

"I was real careful this time."

Her expression must have shown her shock because he back-tracked fast enough.

"I mean when I loaded her in the truck. No one saw me. I didn't dog-nap her. She *was* hurt and she *was* going down the road, sort of."

"And she didn't have tags?" she asked.

Grandpa looked at his feet.

"Oh, Grandpa." They were going to jail. Sheriff Barnes would have no choice but to arrest them. He'd fold like a bad poker hand when they questioned him. It wouldn't matter if they were abused or not. If he would steal an animal, why wouldn't he go a step further and rob a bank?

Something rattled in the kitchen. Raine froze. Had Emily returned? Maybe she'd only been trying to catch her and Grandpa together. Would she lock them up this time? She could feel the color draining from her face.

"It's okay, Raine." He nodded toward the kitchen. "Tilly came with me. She brought over a breakfast casserole. Figured you were living off peanut butter and jelly sandwiches and could use some decent grub. Brought stuff you could put in the microwave, too. I told her 'bout the angel helping you out, but I don't think she believed me."

Why did her life always have to be so complicated? "You're not supposed to be here. It'll look bad if anyone catches you at the ranch."

"Then I won't get caught."

Something in the way his words came out made her pause. It was almost as if he was talking about something else. She closed her eyes and took a calming breath. Of course he didn't rob the bank. The idea was preposterous.

"So what happened last night?" he asked.

She'd lost the thread of his conversation and had no idea what he was talking about. "Nothing happened. Why?"

"Right before I came outside you said something about not wanting to talk about last night." He glanced around. "Was Dillon here?"

"Yes."

He smiled.

"I mean no," she quickly amended.

He frowned. "Well, which is it, girl? Either he was here or he wasn't."

She was so bad at lying. "He was here," she finally admitted. "We're trying to find the men who robbed the bank."

"Good, then he's watching over you."

She silently pleaded for him not to ask any more questions.

"I have breakfast on the table," Tilly said as she stepped to the screen door, wiping her hands on the red apron tied to her ample waist. "Come eat before it gets cold."

Did neither one of them realize she and Grandpa were suspects in a bank robbery? They acted like today was just another day. Raine's head was starting to pound as she walked back inside. An aspirin would be nice. Did she have any downstairs?

"By the way, there's leftover roasted hen in the refrigerator," Tilly said as they took a seat at the table. "I hope you don't mind but I stole a tiny bite." She closed her eyes for a moment as though she savored the taste again. "Absolutely heavenly. I know you don't cook any better than Sock, no offense, and there's not a restaurant nearby that has a cook who could have roasted a hen that would taste that good. Where did you get it, dear?"

Raine looked at Tilly, then Grandpa, then back at Tilly. She was right. Dillon created more problems than he solved. Now what was she supposed to say?

"It was Dillon," Grandpa finally spoke for her.

Tilly's eyebrows drew together and her eyes turned sad. "Your angel?" She reached over and patted his hand as though she could take away his fanciful ideas.

Grandpa nodded. "The one I prayed for."

Tilly sniffed.

Grandpa shook his head. "I promise I'm not losing my mind, woman."

"Of course you're not, dear."

Raine silently watched the exchange between them. Everything was tumbling down around her and there wasn't anything she could do to stop it.

Grandpa finally turned toward her and said, "You tell her I'm as sane as you are."

Maybe they would have cells next to each other. They could play cards all day long. Go Fish or Old Maid. Something simple.

Dillon suddenly appeared, sitting at the opposite end of the table from Raine.

"About time you showed yourself," Grandpa scolded.

Raine didn't know whether to laugh or cry. "Tilly can't see him, Grandpa."

"That's the craziest thing I've ever heard. Of course she can see him. He's sitting right there. You need your eyes checked?"

"Excuse me," Tilly said. "Who are you?"

Raine drew in a sharp breath and choked. Her eyes watered and everything blurred, but she could still see Dillon at the end of the table. What was he doing here? And why could Tilly see him?

"That's the angel I've been telling you about," Grandpa explained.

Tilly chuckled. "Of course he's not an angel. Stop ribbing an old woman."

Dillon closed his eyes and disappeared. A second later he reappeared in the chair beside Tilly. "I'm Dillon. The angel." He smiled.

Tilly looked at the end of the table where Dillon had been sitting, then where he was sitting now. "Oh, you weren't lying," she mumbled right before her eyes rolled to the back of her head. Dillon caught her before she tumbled out of her chair.

"Great, you've killed her," Raine said as she hurried to Tilly's side.

"Tilly!" Grandpa pushed out of his chair.

"She's not dead. I just startled her," Dillon said.

"Carry her to the sofa." Good Lord, what else was going to happen? No, she didn't want to know. As Dillon laid Tilly on the sofa, her eyes fluttered open. Raine breathed a sigh of relief. Tilly had been awfully still, and she didn't know if she trusted Dillon's medical savvy. She supposed he would know if someone died or not, though. He might see their soul rise or something.

Tilly's eyes narrowed as she studied Dillon. "Are you really an angel?"

Dillon's smile was kind. "Yes."

She squeezed his arm. "You feel like a real man."

Grandpa cleared his throat a little too loudly. Tilly frowned when she looked his way. "I wanted to be sure." Her gaze returned to Dillon.

"I'm a nephilim, to be exact," he started to explain.

"I told you about that already," Grandpa interrupted. "He's part angel 'cause that's what his daddy was, but his momma was mortal so the other half is man."

"Yes, I remember now." She smiled like an infatuated teenager.

Raine looked between Grandpa and Tilly. He was in love with her. Did he realize it? The pieces of the puzzle began to fall in place. She remembered the salesman that rented one of Tilly's rooms. Grandpa had been really ticked about that and left the B&B and returned to the ranch. The next morning Dillon was there to warn Raine about the bank robbery.

"Isn't breakfast getting cold?" Grandpa snarled and stomped back to the kitchen.

Tilly winked at Raine. "I love it when he's jealous. Makes me feel young again." She quickly sat up. "But he's right. My casserole is getting cold."

Tilly acted as though she met angels every day. Raine's world was crumbling around her and no one seemed overly concerned.

"You brought the roasted hen." Tilly took the hand Dillon offered and let him assist her to stand. Before he could answer, she continued. "I knew it wasn't prepared around here. No one can cook that wonderfully. I took a small bite. Absolutely divine. Was it made by angels?"

"Mama Paula's. A little place in the middle of nowhere. Best home cooking you'll ever eat."

Raine followed behind them, shaking her head. Anyone would think Tilly and Dillon had known each other forever, the way they acted.

"You're not even going to question that he's an angel?" Raine asked as they sat back down at the table.

"Not when I can see him with my own eyes, dear."

"But we could all be lying."

"You forget I saw him move from the end of the table to the chair beside me."

"I thought you were supposed to be helping my granddaughter, not making more problems." Grandpa set his elbows on the table and glared at Dillon. For the first time since he spoke about the angel, Grandpa didn't look quite as happy to have him in their lives.

"Sock, mind your manners. We're entertaining an angel."

"Half angel," he groused. "And he's the reason we're in this fix. They think we robbed the bank."

"Well of course you didn't," Tilly scoffed. "Soon everyone will see the truth." Tilly must've seen Raine cringe. "Is something the matter?"

"They might think you were involved, too."

Tilly chuckled. "That's priceless." Her voice tinkled like tiny wind chimes moving in the breeze. As suddenly as her humor appeared, it disappeared. "You're serious."

"We'll find the real bank robbers," Dillon reassured her.

Tilly turned slightly in her chair to cast a doubtful eye in his direction. Raine watched as her anger slowly rose to the surface. "You're damn right you'll find them. I do not plan to spend my golden years in a jail cell." She sat a little straighter. "Those orange jumpsuits do nothing for my figure."

"I like your figure," Grandpa said with a wink.

"Hush, Sock!" she whispered, then dabbed at the corner of her mouth with her linen napkin, her cheeks turning rosy. "Here, eat some of my casserole before it does get cold. I don't like that you haven't been eating as well since this whole mess began."

"I've gained five pounds," he said.

"You could stand to gain a little more."

"See how bossy she is?" Grandpa was smiling when he looked across the table. Just as quickly, he cleared his throat. "Now, what are we going to do about catching these bank robbers?"

"Nothing," Raine quickly told him. "You're going to let me handle this." The last thing she needed was Grandpa's help.

"Well, *I* can certainly assist in some way. I have friends who will help, too."

Raine groaned.

Tilly frowned. "I wouldn't tell them how they'd be helping me, and I'm just offering. It's not as though I'd actually be chasing down the bank robbers. Goodness me, I'm not sure I would even be able to fire a gun."

"Gun!" Raine exploded. "I don't want you to go near any guns."

Tilly jumped. Grandpa's chair wobbled, then righted itself. Dillon gave her a warning look. What the hell was she supposed to do? Tell Tilly she could borrow one of hers? She raised her hands in supplication.

"I was trying to help," Tilly said in a small voice.

"We know," Dillon quickly reassured her. "You frightened Raine when you mentioned guns."

"I merely pointed out the fact I'm not familiar with the workings of a firearm, not that I have any intention of using one." Tilly raised her chin and pursed her lips.

Raine wanted to crawl beneath the table. "I'm sorry," she apologized. She would never do anything to offend the older woman. Tilly had always been a friend and she didn't mean to hurt her feelings. "You scared me. I'd feel responsible if you were hurt."

"I spoke up because I thought you might need assistance in some other way. Looking up records or some such thing. I'm certainly not in law enforcement and never claimed to be."

"I know, Tilly." Raine finally looked to Dillon for help as much as she hated having him step in and fix everything. It seemed she was depending on him to do that a lot lately.

"Of course Raine meant nothing by her words except to express her concern for your safety," Dillon said.

"She has a funny way of showing it." Tilly spoke to Dillon as though Raine and Grandpa weren't in the room. "It's not good to scare an old woman. Our bodies don't function as well as they used to."

"I understand," Dillon said.

"I understand more." Grandpa frowned.

Tilly preened, enjoying the attention from both men. "All is forgiven. Now, everyone dig in, then we'll all put our heads together and decide how to catch these hoodlums."

"Good idea," Dillon agreed.

"Who's at the top on your list of suspects?" Grandpa asked.

"No one—"

"Ethan and Leo," Dillon supplied. Throughout the meal, the three carried on a lively conversation about how the men could be caught.

This was his idea of smoothing things over? He hadn't helped. Dillon made things worse. Now Tilly and Grandpa were going to be pulled into the thick of everything. The last thing she wanted was to involve them. Apparently it wasn't up to her. She was the only one in the room that had any idea how to catch the bank robbers and no one seemed to care.

Half an hour later the casserole dish was scraped clean. Dillon ate as though he hadn't had a decent meal in…eons, and insisted on carrying some of the dishes to the kitchen. Raine grabbed hers and Grandpa's plates and silverware, following right behind him. As soon as she had him alone, she dropped the dishes on the counter with a loud clatter.

"Why are you encouraging them?"

"What do you mean?" he asked, looking completely dumbfounded.

"You're joking, right? You really want Grandpa and Tilly helping us find the bank robbers?"

"It will keep their minds occupied. This is the most excitement they've had since they dog-napped Lady."

She drew in a deep breath as she took a step backward. "He did steal the dog and now he's dragging Tilly into a life of crime."

His forehead wrinkled. "I thought you knew about the dog."

"Not positively, and not that Tilly helped. Dammit, Grandpa said he wouldn't kidnap another animal. But getting Tilly involved is irresponsible."

"I think he calls it rescuing them. She's the one who encouraged him." He was thoughtful for a moment. "He's right, you know. About it being more a rescue mission than actually stealing the animal. Sock has a good heart. He doesn't like to see an animal abused. If he hadn't helped, Lady's paw would've got infected. She might have lost her leg."

"Okay, okay." She held up her hands. "I get the picture." She didn't want the dog to suffer, but Grandpa needed to go through the proper authorities. He was breaking the law. "I don't like the idea that they're both criminals." She didn't think he could handle going to court again. What if it caused him to have a heart attack? Like being accused of robbing a bank wouldn't.

Dillon came up to her and wrapped her in his arms. She immediately felt safe and secure, as though no harm would come to her as long as he was nearby. She indulged in this feeling for a moment before stepping out of his arms.

"I don't want either one of them getting hurt, Dillon," she warned.

"I'll watch over them."

"That's what I'm afraid of," she mumbled.

Raine went into the other room. She wanted to explain to Grandpa he couldn't go around stealing animals. As soon as she walked inside the dining room, Grandpa and Tilly looked up, guilty expressions on both their faces. What had they been plotting?

Grandpa cleared his throat. "You never did tell me what you were doing last night."

Raine stumbled. "What?"

"When I was about to step out to the back porch this morning, you said that you didn't want to talk about last night. What happened?"

Dillon came in behind her. He was grinning. Grinning? Really? Her mouth turned down. The man half of him would be no help whatsoever. Typical.

"Go ahead and tell them," Dillon said.

He not only wouldn't be any help, he was going to throw her under the train as well. She was so going to kill him. Except she couldn't. He was going to be in a world of hurt when she got through with him, though.

"Yes, tell us." Tilly smiled. "It would be nice to have a bit of fun news for a change."

"I...I...I..." Raine implored Dillon with her eyes to please stop helping her.

Chapter 18

DILLON KNEW HE BETTER let Raine off the hook or she would make him pay dearly. It was kind of nice she turned to him for help. He glanced between Tilly and Sock. They made a nice couple.

"I took Raine out. I thought she could use a night away," he told them.

Raine made a gurgling noise.

"A date with an angel?" Sock's expression was skeptical.

"I didn't know angels dated," Tilly said, smiling. "How interesting."

"It wasn't a date," Raine interjected. "We went...uh..."

"To a friend's house," Dillon finished.

"They were friendly," Raine blurted.

Sock's eyebrows veed. "Then why didn't you want to talk about it?"

"It's not that I didn't want to talk about meeting them." Raine stumbled over her words. "I wanted to work on finding the bank robbers."

"I thought she needed to get away from the ranch for a while," Dillon said. "Take a breather. Then she might be able to concentrate better."

"It looks as though your plan worked." Tilly's gaze meandered over Raine. "At least you're not wearing those grungy pants that are way too big. What you're wearing now will turn a man's head."

Raine's shoulders relaxed.

"Or an angel's," Tilly added with a mischievous smile.

Raine cast a look in Dillon's direction that had him quickly looking the other way. Yeah, she was probably going to make him pay, but she needed to loosen up. She took life way too seriously. And another thing that bothered him: he didn't see the problem in involving Tilly and Sock. Elderly people needed adventure in their lives, and this was a big one for them. He liked the couple. Raine didn't look too happy by the time they left, though.

"Don't worry," he told her. "They won't get hurt, and they might surprise you with the information they dig up."

"You showed yourself to Tilly and now she's investigating the robbery." She closed the door a little harder than necessary and marched past him. "What part of I don't want them involved did you not understand?"

She jumped when she entered the kitchen and he was leaning against the counter. He probably shouldn't pop in and out like that. It always seemed to bother people, especially mortals. She didn't say anything but her expression turned grim.

"She's only going to ask a couple of people she knows if Ethan and Leo might have increased their income. She said she has a friend who works at the bank."

"Do you really think they'll redeposit money they stole? They're not that stupid."

"All at once?" He shook his head. "No, I don't think so, but checking on Ethan and Leo will make Tilly and Sock feel as though they haven't been put out to pasture, and your grandfather will keep Tilly safe."

"I don't know." She nibbled her bottom lip.

Dillon could see she wavered. "What will it hurt?"

"I still owe you for bringing up last night."

He closed the distance between them. "Last night was my pleasure. I'm glad you enjoyed yourself."

She screwed up her mouth. "That's not what I meant."

"I know, but you have to admit you enjoyed the hell out of watching the threesome."

A tremble swept over her as her nipples tightened, pushing against the cotton material. He didn't wonder why he wanted her so much. He just did. He was reaching for her when Chance popped in.

"You're digging yourself deeper and deeper, bro," Chance said as he casually lounged in one of the dining room chairs. The biscuits were still in a basket sitting in the middle of the table, covered with a red-checkered cloth. He flipped a corner of it back and brought one out. As soon as he bit into the flaky bread his eyes closed. "Tilly cooks almost as well as Mama Paula."

"Who the hell is this guy?" Raine asked, hands on her hips.

"This would be Chance." Great. The last thing he needed was his friend interfering. "He's sort of like an older brother. He's a nephilim. Who likes to poke his nose in where it doesn't belong."

"I'm wounded." Chance took another bite, not looking a bit bothered by Dillon's comment.

Chance's gaze drifted over Raine, slow enough that Dillon decided he didn't like his frank appraisal. "Was there something you wanted?"

Chance chewed the last bite, then licked his fingers. He didn't look to be in any hurry to explain his presence. "Tobiah wants to see you. I'm his messenger." Chance reached for another biscuit. "Damn, these are good."

"Who's Tobiah?" Raine asked. "Another nephilim who's going to make my life hell?"

Dillon cringed. "My father."

She weaved just a bit. He put out his hand to steady her.

"Your…what?" she asked, looking a little dazed.

"My father. At least that's his claim. I didn't meet the guy until a few days ago."

"That's when Tobiah told Dillon he had to fix your life and pronto, or your grandfather was going to have a heart attack and die when you went to prison."

Her face lost some of its color. "What's he talking about?" Raine turned to Dillon for answers. "Am I going to be found guilty of the bank robbery and sent to prison? Don't lie to me."

"You didn't tell her?" Chance asked.

"No. I thought it would scare the hell out of her," he ground out. He quickly grabbed a dining room chair and pushed it beneath Raine when she swayed, then guided her into the seat. "Which it has, thank you very much."

"You're telling me that if we don't find the bank robbers, Grandpa will have a heart attack and die and I will spend the rest of my life in prison," she mumbled.

"It won't end like that." Dillon knelt beside her, taking her cold hand in his. He didn't like the lack of color in her face.

"And Tilly. What will happen to her?" She looked to Chance for answers.

Chance shrugged as if to say Dillon might as well tell Raine the rest. When Dillon didn't say anything, Chance continued.

"She'll mourn your grandfather. A drifter will rent one of her rooms and take her for all she's worth because she won't be paying attention to her finances. She'll lose everything she's got when she can't pay her bills."

"And die?" She sucked back a sob, her bottom lip trembling.

"No, she hitches a ride to Fort Worth and ends up living

under one of the bridges in a cardboard box. She survives under the bridge for another three years."

Raine grabbed Dillon's hand and squeezed until he thought his fingers would break off. "Please tell me we can catch the bank robbers."

"We will. I promise. You won't get sent to prison, Sock won't have a heart attack, and Tilly won't be living under a bridge in a cardboard box. None of that will happen. We can catch these men."

"Unless Tobiah pulls the plug on the assignment." Chance started to reach for another biscuit but apparently changed his mind when Dillon cast a thunderous glare in his direction.

"Will he do that? He's an angel. Right? Angels help people." Raine looked between the two of them as she searched their faces. When neither one said anything, she clamped her lips together.

Dillon felt as ill as Raine looked. "He won't do that. He's not heartless."

"Except you hadn't met him until a few days ago so you don't actually know that much about him." She frowned as though some new information had just occurred to her. "If not for him, you wouldn't have returned. I'd be charged with the crime, Grandpa would have a heart attack, and Tilly would end up living under a bridge."

"I thought you were better off without me. I didn't know you were a suspect," he tried to explain. He didn't think she cared as she came to her feet, back ramrod straight.

"You're right about one thing. I would've been a lot better off without you in my life. Now, if you'll excuse me, I have chores to do and bank robbers to catch. I'd rather you weren't here when I return." With those parting words Raine walked out of the dining room. A moment later Dillon heard the back screen door slam. He flinched.

"She's pretty mad at you, bro," Chance casually commented as he reached for another biscuit.

"I'm going to kill you." Dillon started toward Chance.

"Hey, don't kill the messenger." But he apparently decided he'd overstayed his welcome and quickly closed his eyes. A second later he was gone.

This was great, just great. Raine probably hated him. Last night he'd envisioned a different beginning today. Searching for more clues, making love, putting the bank robbery puzzle together a piece at a time, working with Raine, making love with Raine. So much for his plans. Now he would—

Something incredibly strong pulled at him from all sides. He thought his body was going to be ripped to shreds. He grabbed the chair, but caught air instead. The room began to break into a million tiny pieces right before it exploded all around him.

Dillon floated through time and space, wondering if this was some kind of new punishment Tobiah was forcing him to endure. Raine would think the worst when she returned from the barn and he was nowhere to be found. He looked down and saw her filling the horse bins with new grain. She was talking to herself but he couldn't make out her words. The way she frowned, he wasn't sure he wanted to hear.

She was gone an instant later. Dillon's stomach lurched as he began to spin wildly out of control. He clamped his lips together to keep from throwing up. When he thought he could stand no more, he was plopped down onto something hard and uncomfortable. He thought at first it was a big rock, then realized it was a cloud. He'd been brought upstairs. He had a feeling he was in deep trouble.

<center>~~~</center>

Raine finished the chores and trudged wearily into the house. All the life seemed to have been sucked out of her body. She pushed her hair out of her face and looked at the dark clouds hovering low in the sky. Lightning flashed around one angry cloud. Did Dillon live on one of them? She didn't know. Come to think of it, she didn't know a lot about him.

Except that Dillon would've left her high and dry if not for his father ordering him to right his wrongs. That hurt more than anything. Dillon would've let her and Grandpa and Tilly suffer. Her rotting in a prison cell, Grandpa having a heart attack and dying, and Tilly living under a bridge. Some guardian angel he turned out to be.

No, she didn't believe what she was thinking. Dillon wasn't the kind of person who would leave someone hanging. She knew that about him, at least. He answered a prayer sent by an old man to watch over his granddaughter. It wasn't totally his fault, and he had saved her from a bullet. Ninety-two percent his fault, maybe.

She walked up on the porch and stopped at the screen door. There wasn't a sound coming from inside. Had Chance left? Where was Dillon? She'd said some pretty harsh things. When she thought about it, she believed him when he said he hadn't known about her troubles and thought she would be better off without him.

She moved through the house, sensing she was the only one there. It was an eerie feeling to be all alone. In the past, she always preferred her life that way. She had company when she wanted people over and not before. People knew not to drop in on her unexpectedly because she refused to answer her door. Yes, she was anti-social and she liked her life that way. If she needed something, she went out and got it whether it was groceries or sex. There were no entanglements that way. She didn't need to worry about being in a relationship and pretending to enjoy the person she was with when both of them wanted one thing, and it wasn't small talk.

Her cell phone began to ring. She listened, then remembered she left it in her bedroom. She hurried up the stairs and down the hallway. Her phone was still ringing when she jogged into her room and scooped it off the nightstand. Good Lord, she could barely take a deep breath. She used to go for a run every morning. That stopped when she moved back to the ranch and there never seemed to be enough time to exercise. Maybe she should find time. She scooped up her phone, glancing at the screen. Tilly. Raine slid her finger across the bar at the bottom of the screen and brought the phone to her ear. Her heart skipped a beat.

"Yes? Is Grandpa okay?"

There was a pause, and in that moment Raine wondered if Dillon's dire prediction might have come true sooner than he thought. Had Grandpa suffered a heart attack?

"Of course he's okay," Tilly said. "Why would you think he wasn't?"

Any energy Raine had left quickly drained. She grabbed the bedpost as she sat down hard on the side of the bed. "I worry about him," she was finally able to say. "I know the stress can't be good for his health."

"Don't you worry about him. He still has a lot of life left."

Raine certainly hoped so. "Did you need something?"

"I talked to my friend at the bank." Excitement laced her words.

"Oh, that's…uh…nice." Tilly had played detective. Raine stifled her groan. Why did Dillon encourage Tilly and Grandpa? They should be sitting on the porch at her bed and breakfast taking life easy and not adding more tension. Grandpa might not be able to take the strain.

"Don't you want to hear what I found out?" Tilly sounded a little miffed by Raine's lack of excitement.

"Of course, I want to know everything," she said, trying to summon more enthusiasm. Tilly was trying to help. Dillon had been right that a person's age shouldn't matter as long as they felt useful. And the excitement didn't kill them in the process.

"Good, because I have news."

"Really?"

"You sound surprised."

"No, I mean, I'm not at all surprised," she quickly interjected. "It's as you said, you have connections."

"Yes, I do." Some of Tilly's excitement returned. "My friend at the bank is still checking, so nothing yet from her. All hush-hush though, so I can't reveal my source. If I have to take the stand and testify, her name will not leave my lips."

Raine crossed her legs as she tried to make sense of what Tilly was telling her, but she had no idea what the other woman was talking about. "Why would you have to take the stand?"

"I've watched those courtroom shows and the reporter always goes to jail to keep from revealing their source. My friend could get into a lot of hot water if anyone found out she was helping me."

Raine rubbed her hand across her forehead. Dillon did this to her. He'd gotten Tilly stirred up. The pounding in her head increased, but when Tilly began to speak again, Raine attempted to pay attention.

"She owes me a favor, you know. I introduced her son to a very sweet girl. David was twenty-five and still living at home. The boy had no direction in life. Remember that movie where the young man refused to take any responsibilities? Same situation. She was at the end of her rope with that kid. The young lady put him on the right track fast enough."

Heaven help Shirley Cowan if Tilly was ever questioned about a source. She was the only woman who worked at the bank with a twenty-five year old son named David.

The incessant bomp-bomp-bomp inside her head grew steadily louder, and Raine could've sworn there was someone poking little needles at the backs of her eyeballs. She had to end this before her head exploded.

"Tilly? Your news?" Raine redirected her back to the conversation.

Tilly's laughter tinkled. "I do occasionally lose the thread of what I was talking about. Sock is always fussing at me. Just the other day— Oh well, that's not important. What I called you about is that another friend of mine told me Ethan bought the old car dealership. He said Ethan paid cash."

The blood rushed through her veins making it impossible to think, but it didn't matter because only one thought was going through her mind. Ethan was the one who robbed the bank.

Why was she surprised? His name and Leo's were at the top of her list of suspects. But she never really thought they might be the robbers. Ethan always preached, no matter the situation, that a deputy has to abide by the law. The badge would stand behind the deputy. It hadn't, though. Not for her, anyway.

"Are you still there, Raine?"

"Yes, I'm here."

"The finger is pointing right at him. He's not from around here. I heard he was from the Galveston area. I knew there was something fishy about him." She realized what she'd said and laughed at her own humor. "Not that him being from a coastal area or being a criminal is funny," she quickly put in.

Guilty until proven innocent? No matter how damaging the evidence, it proved nothing. "We don't know he bought the building with stolen money. If we accuse him without proof, we're no better than the ones who pointed the finger at me and Grandpa."

There was a moment of silence before Tilly's deep sigh came over the phone. "I much prefer everyone pointing the finger at him than at you and Sock."

So did Raine, but just because he'd bought a building didn't mean he was guilty. "I'll do some more checking."

"I suppose you should." Tilly sounded deflated.

Raine had to give the older woman credit for what she'd discovered so far. "Your information has been a lot of help. We only need to dig a little deeper."

"You think so?"

"Immeasurably. I'll see what I can find out on my end and you do the same, but be careful when you ask questions. I don't want anyone getting hurt. And Tilly…"

"What, dear?"

"Thank you for everything you've done."

"No, thank you. I haven't had this much excitement in a long time."

Raine could do without this kind of excitement, but she didn't voice her thoughts. They said good-bye, but Raine didn't move. All she could think about was that Ethan might be guilty. The thought didn't bring her any relief. Her gut feeling didn't make things any better because it kept telling her that Ethan was innocent. If she couldn't trust her gut, what could she trust?

Chapter 19

"Did you have to be so melodramatic?" Dillon came to his feet. He was right about being on a cloud. He was surrounded by them, but they weren't the soft marshmallow kind. These were dark and ominous with the occasional lightning bolt sending jagged streaks through them.

Tobiah stood a short distance from him looking equally ominous and dangerous. Today he wore all black. Dillon never realized angels were so into drama.

"I can show you theatrical if you like," Tobiah warned as his eyebrows drew into one bushy slash across his forehead.

Damn. He'd fought demons who didn't scare him as much as his father. And that was another thing: he was still having a hard time wrapping his brain around the fact that this angel was his father.

He'd also dumped ice-cold rain on him and Dillon would just as soon not get soaked again. "Was there something you wanted?" he asked with a bit more respect, but he wouldn't apologize for the way he felt.

"Raine's future is still the same," Tobiah fumed. "Nothing has changed except you've shown yourself to another mortal."

If his father knew Raine's future was still the same, then he must be watching them. He wondered what else his father saw. For the first time in his life, Dillon felt a flood of warmth crawl up his face. This was an awkward moment. He might not accept Tobiah as his father, but he didn't want an angel seeing everything he did.

"No, I didn't watch that," Tobiah said as though he read his thoughts. "As soon as you two arrived at that house, I tuned you out. Sometimes the nephilim need to remember what they are," he chastised.

"I'm half man," he defended himself, standing a little straighter.

"I would say more than half. You inherited more of your mother's side than mine," Tobiah complained.

"You were the one who descended to earth and seduced a mortal."

Some day he needed to learn to keep his mouth closed. Pointing out the fact Tobiah impregnated Dillon's mother might not have been wise, since he was already on his shit list. But it was the truth. Angels were as susceptible to sin as anyone. Tobiah was no exception.

"You will do well not to try my patience. And stay away from fairies. They're more trouble than they're worth. Once they reach their twenty-sixth year their sexual appetites are out of control."

"They can't help their nature. Besides, I heard if they don't have sex, the hot flashes they suffer can disintegrate them, so they're not really to blame."

"What are you doing about Raine's future?" Tobiah asked, changing the subject.

Dillon didn't mind Tobiah's redirected line of question. Talking about the birds and bees with his father was one thing. Since his father was an angel, the subject matter took on a whole new meaning.

"We're trying to find the real bank robbers. We have a few leads we're checking. If Raine can expose the real criminals, she'll not only clear her name and anyone else wrongly accused, but she'll gain the recognition she deserves."

"You know what will happen if you stay with her too long?"

"Yes." He didn't want to think about it, though. The danger was always at the back of his mind that he wouldn't be able to completely erase her memory of him. If he stayed too long, the veil separating their worlds could become thin enough that Raine would be able to see what only a few mortals knew existed. Flashes of light and dark, shadowy figures, evil and good.

There was a strong possibility that having second sight would drive her to the brink of madness. A rare few completed the transition and were gifted with the ability to speak to mortals who crossed over and were entering an immortal world. These men and women became psychics and healers, but their gift carried a high price. They also saw the demons who walked amongst them. The things that went bump in the night.

"I'll leave before that happens," Dillon told him.

"See that you do."

"Was that all you wanted? To remind me about the amount of time I have?"

"Don't push your luck, boy."

Dillon wanted to remind Tobiah he wasn't a boy, but decided to do as Tobiah warned.

"And stop fooling around with the girl."

That was the kettle calling the pot black. "When we do find the real bank robbers and Raine is exonerated, she'll still have deep-rooted problems she needs to face. I'm trying to help her work through them before I leave. Where's the good of fixing the outside if she still has issues she refuses to face?"

Tobiah only glared at Dillon as though he didn't believe everything he said. He was right not to buy every word. Yeah, what he said was the truth, but even Dillon knew there was more to it than his wanting to help Raine deal with the past. He wanted to stay as long as possible and didn't like the thought of leaving.

Tobiah waved his arm. "Then go, and be quick about it. I haven't got all day."

"I thought time didn't mean the same to you. At least that's what you said." He couldn't help throwing Tobiah's words back at him.

"And I don't like insolence, either!" Tobiah raised both arms, then dropped them back down with a fury that caused the cloud beneath Dillon's feet to open. He fell, going faster and faster, spinning out of control.

He was headed toward the ground at an extremely high speed. This wasn't good. He was traveling so fast that when he crashed there'd be nothing left of him except a spot on the ground. He gritted his teeth, waiting for the impact as the ground came closer and closer, the whistle of air the only thing he heard.

But at the last second, his rapid descent came to a jarring halt. He exhaled a deep breath until there wasn't any air left in his lungs. The grass directly below his face waved back and forth, as if to mock him.

"Yeah, that was real angelic of you," he muttered.

He was jerked back up as if he was attached to an invisible bungee cord. *He just had to open his mouth again.* If Tobiah didn't stop, Dillon would lose his breakfast. There was only one way he could see to make him stop. "Okay, you win. I'm sorry!"

His body flew toward the ground again, but this time he stopped about two feet from it. As soon as he caught his breath, the invisible bungee cord broke. He landed with a loud thump. Stars exploded all around him.

"Thanks for—"

Thunder boomed across the sky, causing the ground to shake beneath him. He snapped his mouth closed and glared upwards but he didn't say another word. For an angel, Tobiah had a real temper.

———

"Do you think you were a little hard on him?" Michael asked.

Tobiah glanced down. "He has a hard head. Besides, our sons heal fast. They're scrappers." Yeah, he was proud of Dillon and he didn't care who knew it. He glanced toward Michael. "You're just as proud of Chance."

Michael's eyes glowed with warmth. "You're right, I am. He never once backed down from the demon. There for a while he worried me. He crossed more lines than I wanted to count."

"No, Ryder is the one who refused to back down," Abram's voice boomed from the next cloud over. "My son dodged everything I threw his way."

"What'd you expect? You were throwing lightning bolts," Tobiah said with undisguised sarcasm. "I'd dodge them too." They could brag all they wanted, but it was Dillon who would show them all what the nephilim were made of. The kid had been through a lot. Not a kid anymore, he supposed.

And Dillon resented him. All their sons resented their fathers for not being there; some still did. They'd had orders from management. No interfering with the lives of their children. It was the only way they would learn how to fight demons. That's why the nephilim were created in the first place: to protect people.

From their fathers they were gifted with compassion, and from their mothers' side they were given the frailties of man so that they would know suffering. They were thrown out into the world at an early age, too early some would say. Only a few remained. The threat of demons invading the world was less likely because of the nephilim. Some demons still came topside. They created havoc wherever they went, but as soon as they were detected by the nephilim, they quickly went back to Hell.

Tobiah sighed. It was past time the nephilim found happiness of their own, and that their fathers were finally allowed to make a connection with their sons.

"Hunter will show them all up," a booming voice declared.

The other three angels turned at the same time. "It's good to see you, Zachery," Abram said. "When are you going to meet Hunter?"

"Soon. Don't push me. I could ask the same of you," Zachery said.

"I met Ryder."

"No, you threw lightning bolts at him," the other three said in unison.

Abram shook his head. "Why do you have to keep reminding me? It all worked out for the best."

"You were stubborn," Tobiah told him. "Still are."

"Someday soon."

"You always say that," Michael pointed out.

"I have time. All the time in the world." He glanced down. "Will Dillon be able to fix Raine's life?"

"That's the problem," Tobiah said. "We can gently guide them, but nothing more."

The others cleared their throats.

Tobiah frowned. "Okay, maybe shove is a better word. But upper management will only let us do so much. With one wave of my hand I could fix—"

"No!" they spoke again.

"I have faith in my son," he said. "And I don't plan on getting kicked out of Heaven, so don't worry that I would break one of the commandments." He looked with longing down to the Earth below. His son lived the life he longed for. Tobiah was born an angel and, although he loved who he was, he thought it might be nice to stay on Earth for longer periods than they were allowed.

There were so many delights to be tasted, so many adventures he could have.

"You're doing it again," Zachery said.

A moment passed before his words sank in and when they did, Tobiah felt heat rise up his face. But he couldn't help thinking what it would be like to live on earth. "Wouldn't it be fun to—"

"No!"

"I was only saying it would be fun, not that I was going to follow through."

"Good," Michael said.

They were right, of course. If you lived with mortals, you had to take the bad with the good. Life wasn't always a silver-lined cloud. Dillon was a walking testament to that. Speaking of which, his son better be careful or he was going to get into trouble again, not to mention what he would do to Raine's life. He hoped everything would work itself out, but right now he wasn't sure.

Chapter 20

As soon as the door of the beauty shop closed behind Raine, everyone looked up with a smile of greeting, but their smiles slipped. She recognized some of the patrons. Mrs. Weatherspoon was under one of the hair dryers. She had retired after thirty-five years of teaching sixth grade. The elderly woman cocked an eyebrow as she obviously mulled over the accusations thrown at Raine.

Amy, the young waitress at the café, was getting her nails done. She jumped as though she thought Raine would pull her gun out and rob them at any second. Only problem was the manicurist was painting one of the girl's fingernails and ended up leaving a streak of fluorescent orange nail polish down her own hand when Amy moved. The manicurist pursed her lips and grabbed the remover while Amy stuttered an apology.

Two more ladies were under dryers, and two beauticians were cutting hair. Raine could feel the stares of everyone as she walked up to the appointment desk.

"I made an appointment earlier this morning," she said. "For a trim."

Raine knew the woman behind the desk. Cynthia was a stuck-up snob in high school and Raine doubted she'd changed much.

Without looking at the appointment book, she smiled sweetly. "I don't think I have you down. I'm terribly sorry. Maybe you could come back another time."

One of the beauticians was just coming from the back with bottled water. She twisted off the cap and handed the bottle to Mrs. Weatherspoon, who smiled her thanks. The beautician had apparently heard Cynthia because she didn't stop until she was at the desk.

"You called for an appointment?" she asked.

"This morning," Raine said. "My name is Raine McCandless."

There was a moment of surprise in the woman's eyes, but she quickly covered it and glanced down at the book.

"I told her we don't have her down and we're all full." Cynthia's bitchy smile was fixed in place.

"Nonsense. If she said she called, then she called. This isn't the first time you've forgotten to write down a client's appointment. Don't let it happen again."

Cynthia's face turned deep red. "But... But..."

"Did you want to say something else?" The beautician's steady stare never wavered.

Cynthia pursed her lips. "No."

"Good." The beautician met Raine's gaze and smiled. "I'm Jill, what can I do for you today?" She waved Raine toward one of the chairs.

"Just a trim. A wash and blow dry." She didn't add "and to hear all the latest gossip." This was the busiest place in town. In the mornings the coffee shop at the café took center stage, but by nine, the beauty shop began to buzz. Raine had made an afternoon appointment. She hoped by then word would have spread of Ethan's purchase. But it might take longer than she'd expected for everyone to get over their nervousness around her. They'd all clammed up. "Maybe a new style? I'm getting tired of this one."

Jill cut the rubber band around Raine's ponytail. It was like opening the door of an over-filled closet. Everything sprang out.

"You do have a lot of hair," Jill exclaimed with a laugh. "Maybe we need to tame it a little."

"I have a problem with the frizzies."

"I can see that, but it's an easy fix. I'm sure it won't take me long at all."

But Raine didn't want to leave too soon. "I don't suppose I could get a manicure and pedicure too?"

Jill glanced toward the manicurist, who looked up and shrugged. "I don't have anything after Amy. My whole afternoon is free."

"Great." That should give her time to gather any information.

By the time Jill finished with Raine's hair, the patrons had started talking amongst themselves again. Apparently, there were other things going on in town almost as important to them. Like the revival coming to town next week, and the bake sale to raise money for Luther Gaines had been a success. He was in the hospital in Dallas after Gilbert Rutherford tripped and accidentally shot his friend in the leg when they were hunting. It looked as though he'd have a speedy recovery.

The Smith boys were caught riding their bikes across old Mrs. Swan's yard and she had every right to complain when they took the shortcut. They'd already managed to cut a path through her beautifully landscaped yard. It might do them good to spend the next few weeks picking up trash.

RJ, who worked on the ambulance, and his wife were expecting another little one. Their second, and they were hoping for a boy this time. And Cory Bradley wrecked his red 1980 Mustang. He was okay, but his father said the boy would have to save up the money to get it fixed. Raine was glad to hear that his parents finally got a little sense. The other women breathed a collective sigh of relief, too.

"I'm so glad I won't have to listen to his loud muffler at two in the morning," one of the women remarked what they all were thinking. "I told his mother something like this would happen, but she wouldn't listen. About time his father stepped up to the plate. He might have a bat, but Jarod Bradley doesn't have any balls. Nice to know he finally found some."

The other women snickered at her play on words. Raine smiled, glancing in the mirror when Jill swung her chair around.

"Better?"

Raine's usually thick hair was trimmed a few inches shorter and had been thinned. Jill had washed it, applied styling gel, and blew it dry. She followed up with her flat iron. Raine's hair was tamed and shiny. "It looks wonderful." She met Jill's eyes in the mirror and they smiled at each other.

"I think Marsha is ready for you," Jill said.

Raine moved to the chair across from the manicurist. Marsha took her hand and grimaced.

"Ohmigosh, when was your last manicure?"

"I've never had one," Raine admitted.

"Then darlin', you're in for a treat. When you leave here I guarantee you'll be a steady customer."

Raine smiled. She didn't plan on telling Marsha she could barely buy food each week, let alone fritter money away on non-sense like going to the beauty shop. Although Raine had to admit, there was something to be said for feeling pampered.

The door to the shop opened behind her. Raine glanced in the mirror that ran the entire upper half of one wall and recognized the owner of the small boutique on the corner, Ruth Albright. She'd seen the other woman who was with her around town but couldn't remember her name. Mrs. Albright catered to a clientele that was obsessed with anything shabby chic. Raine once heard the woman made most of her money by tripling the price and sending her merchandise up North.

"He bought the dealership," Ms. Albright said as they stopped at the front desk.

Raine's heart jumped to her throat. She dared not breathe in case she might miss what Mrs. Albright might say next.

"Anyone home?" Marsha waved her hand in front of Raine's face.

Raine jumped. She was so intent on listening to the other women she wasn't paying attention to what Marsha was saying. She focused on the manicurist since the two women were checking their appointment times. They'd stopped talking about the dealership being sold. It might not even be the one in town, but that still didn't stop her heart from thudding against her ribs.

"Did you say something?" she asked Marsha.

"You zoned out again. I asked what color."

"What color of what?"

"Polish. Did you forget that you're getting a manicure?"

She quickly glanced at the colors. "Clear."

Marsha casually picked up the clear and shifted slightly in her chair, then dropped the nail polish in the trash. "This is your day to shine, and I don't do clear."

Drama Queen. She glanced toward row after row of nail shades. There were at least fifty to choose from.

Ms. Albright began to talk again as the two women moved to the waiting area where there were a cluster of chairs. As soon as they were seated, Ms. Albright turned to her friend. "He paid a pretty penny for the building."

What did Ms. Albright know and how much would be accurate? It didn't matter. Raine could find out the particulars. Ms.

Albright was confirming what Tilly had told her. This was it, the break she was looking for.

"Color?" Marsha asked again.

"You choose," she absently told her.

"Deep purple it is," Marsha said then smiled.

Raine didn't pay attention to the color. She wanted to hear what Ms. Albright said next.

A woman suddenly leaned out from under a dryer. Raine recognized her as Barb Ware. Recently married for the fifth time. Everything about her was fake. Her husbands liked having a trophy wife, even though she wasn't exactly first place.

"Hey Ruth, did you get that shipment in you were talking about the other day? I've been dying to see the new stuff."

Raine stifled her groan of frustration.

Ms. Albright began a lively discussion about the new merchandise she was about to put on display. Barb promised to drop by the next day and asked if she really was going to open a tea room as well.

Raine counted to fifty before Jill went to the hairdryers and uncurled one of the woman's rollers.

"You're done, Barb. Let's get you combed out or you're going to be late for your own party."

Raine breathed again. Finally, the stupid conversation was over. Except the two women didn't stop their discussion as she hoped. Raine had to think of something to get their attention back on track. Nothing came to mind to redirect their attention back to Ethan purchasing the dealership.

"Are you ready for the chair?" Marsha asked.

"The chair?"

"Yeah, for your pedicure."

Raine knew she was losing it fast. She needed to think about something else before Marsha thought so, too.

Dillon suddenly appeared, leaning casually against the corner of Marsha's desk. Raine jumped, heart once more pounding against her chest. "I hate when you do that!"

Marsha hesitated. "What'd I do?"

Raine looked between Marsha and Dillon.

He grimaced. "Sorry, she can't see or hear me. Only you."

Great. Just great. Even if she was cleared of the bank robbery charges, everyone would probably think she was crazy. She smiled at Marsha. "Oh, not you."

"Then what?" Marsha glanced around.

"I was thinking aloud." Raine gave a weak laugh. "I guess I was lost in thought. I just remembered I forgot to grab a gallon of milk. Don't you hate to buy groceries, then later that night remember you forgot something?"

Marsha didn't look convinced, but before she could come up with another lie, Marsha laughed. "I thought I was the only one who didn't remember to jot down a list! I always say I will, but can never find the time. Well, at least you didn't drive all the way home. You can grab a gallon after you leave here."

"You're right. I'll do that." She moved to the chair, but narrowed her eyes at Dillon. He only shrugged as if his popping in was an accident.

"I'll be right back. Just need to get water for my basin. Can I bring you back a bottle of water?"

Raine smiled and shook her head, willing the other woman to leave.

"You look pretty," Dillon said. "It's about time you did something for yourself."

She couldn't stop the flutter of excitement that went through her, but she quickly tamped it down. She was on a mission, nothing more. "Tilly got a tip that Ethan bought the dealership," she spoke beneath her breath and tried not to move her lips any more than she had to. She gained new respect for ventriloquists. Her jaw ached after one sentence.

She looked at the row of hairdryers with women sitting under them, then over at Ms. Albright and her friend, who were waiting for their appointment. No one paid her any mind.

Dillon wore a confused look. "So you decided to get your nails done?"

"This is the best place to hear the latest gossip. The two women in the waiting area were talking about it when they came into the shop."

Marsha returned carrying a heavy tub filled with water, so Raine didn't say more. When she glanced around the room her gaze skidded to a stop. Jill was looking at her as though Raine had lost her mind. Great, just great. She pointed toward one of the speakers in the corner of the shop. "I love this song." She wasn't sure Jill completely bought her story, but it was the best she could do in the short amount of time. Dillon received another glare.

"This song?" Marsha asked with surprise.

Raine didn't even know what was playing. She listened for a moment. A rap song. She hated rap. This one was particularly bad. She nodded and lied. "It has a catchy beat."

"Not really my cup of tea, but I suppose someone likes it or the artists wouldn't be making so much money." She sat on a small stool in front of Raine, checked the water in the basin, then motioned for Raine to put her feet inside. While Marsha worked, Raine eavesdropped on the two women.

"No, he didn't pay all the purchase price in cash." Ms. Albright said. "On his salary? Just a hefty down payment. He'd have to rob a bank to buy it outright." She laughed as she looked around the room, then started choking when her gaze met Raine's.

Ms. Albright's friend began to beat her on the back and Jill ran to the other room, returning a few minutes later with more bottled water. She twisted the cap off and shoved it toward Ms. Albright, who quickly took a drink.

"I swallowed wrong," she croaked, then cleared her throat. "Thank you for the water, dear. I'm fine now."

Jill nodded before returning to Barb.

Ms. Albright reacted like everyone in town. They'd already tried and convicted her. It didn't matter that she'd lived in Randolph most of her life or that her father had protected the town on very little salary. She looked at her hands, twining her fingers together. It didn't matter that she was an officer of the law, sworn to serve. Disappointment began to weave through her.

Remember, people are only human, Raine, Hank McCandless's words filled her head. *We all make mistakes. You will, too. Sometimes all you can do is hold your head high and make the best of a bad situation. If you're honest and do your best, then you'll always have that to fall back on when times get tough. Be proud of who you are.*

Her father was a smart man when it came to people, except for her mother. He turned a blind eye to all of Lucille's flaws. But before Raine could begin to feel sorry for herself, she raised her head and met Mrs. Albright's gaze without wavering. The other woman cleared her throat and looked away.

"She's right. Ethan wouldn't pay cash," Dillon said, drawing her attention back to him. "Not for the full price."

Raine thought about what he said. Ethan wasn't stupid. If he paid the entire amount he would automatically become a suspect. He could get away with a down payment. Why would he even go that far? Why not wait until she was charged with the crime?

"I wondered if that eyesore would ever sell," Mrs. Albright's friend commented. "The plate glass windows are so grimy they're disgusting."

"You haven't seen it recently, then. The owner washed the windows squeaky clean. He had *two* interested buyers, so there was a little competition. Ethan won the bid."

"How do you know all this?" Her friend regarded her with more than a little skepticism.

"Ethan came to me. He said that he trusted my business acumen. He asked if I would put in a good word with some of my connections regarding his business venture." She sat a little straighter. "He had to explain his plans to me before I would agree, of course. There's a reason why I'm a good businesswoman. I probably shouldn't say a word, though." She nibbled her bottom lip as though she couldn't decide.

Her friend was on the edge of her seat. "You can't leave me hanging! I'm your very best friend and you know I won't breathe a word."

"You can't tell a soul," Mrs. Albright warned, and her friend vigorously nodded. Mrs. Albright leaned in closer, but she was a little hard of hearing so her quiet voice was still just loud enough Raine could hear. "Ethan restores old cars and pickups. He does all the work himself, but the profits have been low. He came up with this idea of making sculptures out of old vehicle parts. A few months ago he showed me pictures of the finished product. They're very good. I was a little surprised. He is only a deputy."

Raine frowned, but quickly cleared her expression and closed her eyes as though she was dozing in the chair.

"The poor boy almost had to scrap the whole venture. The house he's renting finally sold. There aren't any decent houses in town for rent which would have allowed him to continue his restoration and sculpting. A fire hazard, you know, with all the welding he has to do."

"What happened?" her friend asked as though she couldn't wait to hear the ending.

"He inherited some money from an uncle he didn't know he had! It was enough he could put a down payment on the building. Now he'll have plenty of room. Isn't that the most amazing thing you've ever heard?"

Amazing, Raine thought. How fortunate for Ethan.

"I love happy endings." The woman clapped her hands together, then quickly looked around to make sure she hadn't drawn attention to herself.

"Yes, I know. And the best news is that I've been talking to my clients up North and they're practically salivating to buy the sculptures. Some of my clients asked about the restored automobiles, too. Of course, I'll get a small finder's fee."

"You're so smart!"

"I know." Mrs. Albright preened. "It's a win-win business deal for me. Mind you, I won't make that much, but all I had to do was make a couple of phone calls."

"All done. What do you think?"

Raine looked at her feet and hands. Dark purple? She didn't remember choosing the color, but Marsha was waiting for Raine to say something. "I love it."

Marsha smiled.

After paying, Raine left the beauty shop. "The town is so quick to believe Grandpa and I robbed the bank, but Ethan has become Mrs. Albright's golden boy. He has to be the one who robbed the bank."

"We'll find the evidence. It shouldn't be that difficult to discover where the money came from."

"If we don't?"

"We will."

"Ethan's a good cop. He would know how to cover his tracks." Her spirits sank lower. She looked up and saw a long table right outside the drugstore. It was draped in a pretty red-and-white checked tablecloth and there were a dozen or so desserts displayed with white folded cards in front of each that told the name and price. The church bake sale.

Behind the table were four of the biggest gossips in town, along with three potential customers who tried to decide what they would buy. That is until they saw her coming down the street talking to thin air.

"Can my life get any worse?" She turned on Dillon. "Will you please go away and leave me alone? Your help is going to get me a life sentence!" And she didn't care who heard her as she stormed toward her pickup. When she opened the door it almost fell off the hinges and creaked so shrilly that if it were an octave higher, the sound would have shattered windows all over town.

The townspeople would crucify her. By nightfall it would be all over town that she'd gone off the deep end. She better get used to wearing orange. There wouldn't be beauty parlors, either. She only went for information, but getting her hair fixed and her feet massaged was better than she'd expected. She could forget about having that in her future. Gangs, that's what they had in prison. She would end up as some big, ugly, burly woman's bitch.

She stepped on the running board and slid inside the cab. Everything she loved would be gone. She turned the key and, after a couple of weak attempts, the pickup started. She should be grateful. She wasn't. As she drove down the road, the frame vibrated like a jackhammer chipping concrete. Old Red was one of the few things she wouldn't miss. Yeah, Dwayne fixed it, all right. She should've known not to let him come near her pickup.

She *was* grateful Dillon was out of her hair. She was better off without him. Her stomach lurched at the thought of never seeing him again. No, he meant nothing to her. A great sex partner, but nothing more. Unwanted visions crossed her mind. The way he pulled her closer to his naked body. His hands. She sucked in a trembling breath. Her body grew warm thinking about the way he touched her.

She grabbed the steering wheel in a death grip. She needed to think about something other than him. Look at how he'd screwed up her life. "Oh yeah, let's think about how he *screwed* up my life," she mumbled.

As she drove down the street she tried to think about anything *but* Dillon. Her gaze landed on her newly polished nails. That was it. She would think about her nails. They were nicely shaped. Deep purple. Raine didn't think she was the purple type.

It wasn't working! Who the hell cared what color her nails were painted? Maybe the butch inmate who latched onto her would like them. Well, except they would be chipped by then.

Her stomach rumbled, but this time because she was hungry. She made a split-second decision and turned in to the grocery store parking lot. She actually did need milk, and she didn't want to face an empty house. That was a first. She usually preferred being alone.

After snagging a parking place close to the entrance, she turned the key. Old Red came to a teeth-jarring stop, then rattled and sputtered for a good thirty seconds before finally dying with a loud bang. One woman on her way inside almost got whiplash turning to see if there was some kind of natural disaster occurring behind her. A man scooped up his little boy and hurried toward his truck. Three teenage girls stopped to point and giggle.

No, she definitely wouldn't miss the pickup. She hurried inside, grabbing a cart, except when she pulled on the handle, the whole line of carts moved. *Not today*, she silently prayed, then glanced up. "Never mind. I don't want any help."

Placing one foot on the bottom of the cart and taking a firmer grip on the handle, she pulled with all she had. The cart broke free. Victory. She swaggered down the aisle and picked up a gallon of milk. A loaf of bread was next, followed by a small jar of peanut butter. The staples of life. She still had a brand new jar of strawberry preserves at the house.

As she moved toward checkout, she passed the candy aisle. Chocolate sounded therapeutic right then. She grabbed a giant chocolate bar, then tossed in another for good measure. That was it, nothing more, she told herself and veered down the next aisle. Marshmallows. Great big fluffy ones. She tossed in two bags, then added a third. She might as well go for broke. She backtracked and grabbed a box of graham crackers. As she checked out, Raine was pretty sure she would regret her purchases. What the hell, tomorrow was another day. Today, she wasn't going to regret a thing!

Chapter 21

DILLON KNEW THIS MIGHT not be a good time to approach Raine. She was upset because people saw her carrying on a conversation when no one was with her. He doubted she would listen to reason. Not that he could blame her. Every time he tried to fix her life, he made it worse.

He glanced at the clock. She should be home by now. She was probably trying to find a way to nail Ethan. She wouldn't want his help. He didn't blame her.

But all the evidence pointed to the deputy. It looked as though Ethan robbed the bank. Maybe Leo helped. He didn't act as if he had very many working brain cells, but it could be an act to throw off suspicion.

They only needed evidence. Talking to Raine about setting a trap for Ethan sounded like a good reason to see her again. Hell, he didn't need a reason except he missed her. He closed his eyes.

"We're going to the bar," Hunter said. "Want to tag along?"

The sound of another voice was jarring. Dillon caught himself before he could transport, but lost his balance and fell backwards, landing with a hard whack on his ass. Damn, what was it with people knocking him down? "You had to ask when I was about to leave?"

Hunter grinned.

"It's not funny. I think I cracked something."

"Yeah, your ass."

"Now you're a comedian?"

"Have a beer with us. Chance is leaving in the morning."

Chance never stayed long. It was as though he'd finally found what he was looking for. As had Ryder. Dillon started to tell Hunter that he had things to do, but there was something in his friend's expression that made him pause. "Something's wrong."

Hunter shook his head. "No, the ranch is starting to feel deserted, that's all. With Ryder gone, Chance leaving, and you on assignment, the place echoes." He shook his head again. "I guess I wanted to go out like we used to do in the old days."

"You mean when you started barroom fights?" Dillon started to laugh at his joke, but something in Hunter's eyes said he was serious.

"The guy had it coming." He waited, then said, "What do you say? For old times."

When he thought about it, Dillon knew what he meant. The four of them had been together for a long time. They'd fought demons and saved lives. They answered prayers and watched each others' backs. Hell, they were kids when they'd banded together.

Hunter never talked about his past. Once when he'd had too many beers, he mumbled something about his mother trying to save herself. It was an unspoken law between all of them they wouldn't pry into the past but move forward into the future. Over the years they discovered small things about each other—except for Hunter. They still didn't know a lot about him. He liked to watch *Survivor*, even the reruns. He had an affinity for animals. They'd created a place years ago, before they bought the ranch and it became a haven for the strays he rescued. Other than that, he was a mystery. But he was a brother, a friend.

Dillon took the hand Hunter offered and pulled himself up. "Yeah, let's have a beer." He was pretty sure Raine would be okay until he returned, but he wasn't so sure about Hunter.

Chance arrived a few minutes later. He looked from one man to the other. "Brothers," he said and held out his hand.

Hunter grasped it. "Brothers."

Dillon nodded and held tight to the hand his friend gave him. It was as if to say no matter what happened in life, they would always have the bond that was forged so long ago. Dillon couldn't help looking to his left. When he raised his eyes, he knew they all thought the same thing. There was still one missing.

It was much later that night when Dillon transported. There was an eerie silence surrounding him when he opened his eyes. Raine's kitchen resembled a war zone. A box was on its side with graham crackers spilling out. Marshmallows were scattered on the counter, and the wrapping from a chocolate bar was missing but the bar was intact.

Something was wrong. He wondered if Raine might be asleep, but a noise from the living room drew him in that direction. He stopped in the doorway. She was the most beautiful woman he'd ever seen. She'd changed into a purple T-shirt that reached just above her knees. Her legs were curled beneath her on the sofa and she had an album open on her lap.

She turned the page. A whisper of a smile curved her mouth. "My father was a good sheriff. He never ran an ad in the paper when election time came. He didn't need to, since no one ran against him. They wouldn't have stood a chance."

Dillon wondered how she knew he was there. She looked up, met his eyes, and he saw the sheen of tears swimming in hers.

"When you're near, I catch the scent of leather and sage," she explained as if she knew what he'd been thinking. "It's a clean, outdoors kind of aroma. My father taught me to be alert to changes in my surroundings. The strange thing was, he didn't have a clue my mother cheated on him. He loved her so much he looked the other way. Then she left him anyway. But until then, he was a good sheriff." She closed the album and leaned forward to carefully place it on the coffee table in front of her.

"Are you okay?"

"For someone about to go to prison? Sure, I'm fine." She came to her feet. "I was going to make s'mores but changed my mind. They say chocolate makes everything better. I don't know. I've never gotten around to checking it out for myself. Would you like some?"

He shook his head as he walked toward her. "We still have time to catch them."

"If Ethan robbed the bank, then we won't pin him with the crime. We never quite hit it off, but I can't say anything against his skills as an officer. He's good. On the other hand, Sheriff Barnes has enough evidence needed to place the blame at mine and Grandpa's feet. It will happen like your friend predicted. I'll go to prison, Grandpa will have a heart attack, and Tilly's new digs will be under a bridge. I wonder how bad the other inmates will treat me once they discover I'm a cop. Maybe they'll have chocolate in prison and I can finally see if it works to ward off the blues."

He stopped beside her and gathered her in his arms. At first she resisted, but it didn't take much prodding for her to rest her head against his shoulder with a deep sigh. He held her close, breathing in the scents of almond and coconut from her trip to the beauty parlor. She smelled good, and her soft body pressed against his made it difficult to concentrate.

"Make love to me," she whispered, voicing his thoughts.

"You're depressed."

"Make me un-depressed."

"Close your eyes."

He felt the tremble that ran through her. Air rushed past. She tightened her hold around his neck. He kept her close against him so she wouldn't be scared. Like before, air swirled around them, lights flashed. Her hold tightened. Then it was over and they were standing on solid ground again.

"The House of Ecstasy," she said as she looked around the cavernous room. "I don't know if I'm up to watching other people making love."

"We won't be watching anyone this time."

She cocked an eyebrow. "I don't want anyone watching me, either."

He pulled her along with him as they walked to the door. The window opened. The blue light swept over them again, creating the same heat as before. When the door opened, they walked inside.

"Where are you taking me this time?" she asked, curiosity lacing her words.

"We're going swimming," he told her and stopped in front of another door. Before he opened it, Dillon pulled his shirt over his head and tossed it to the side. Raine nibbled her bottom lip. He unfastened his belt, then the top button of his jeans. Her eyes locked on his hands as he tugged the zipper down. He toed off his boots; his socks followed. Then he removed his jeans and boxers. She visibly swallowed. She finally dragged her gaze back up when his hat landed on top of the pile.

"You're magnificent," she breathed, reaching out to run purple painted nails down his chest.

He sucked in a mouthful of air, wondering how her touch had the power to turn his insides to mush. Rather than dwell on the answer, he took the hem of the long shirt she wore and pulled it over her head, adding it to the pile. He'd known she wouldn't be wearing anything else, but his imagination wasn't nearly as good as looking at the real thing. His dick quivered with the need to sink inside her, but it was too soon and he had more pleasure to experience with her.

He opened the door and took her hand. She followed, but he noticed her slight hesitation. She wasn't as tough as she acted. He waited for her reaction, hoping she wouldn't be disappointed.

Her gaze slowly scanned the room. Her eyes opened wide in disbelief. "This is perfect." She began to laugh as she moved the rest of the way inside.

He relaxed. "I thought you'd like it." He glanced around. The pool was filled with chocolate rather than water. There was a chocolate waterfall and a chocolate hot tub. "Are you game?"

"Yes, I am." She walked to the edge of the pool and jumped in. Chocolate came to her shoulders. "It's cold." She laughed.

"But how does it feel?"

"Join me and find out for yourself."

He walked to the edge and jumped in. The chocolate was thin so they could easily move around. And she was right. It was cold. He moved nearer, scooping up a handful and dumping it over her head.

She screamed and jumped back, laughing more. "I can count on one hand the times I've splurged on going to a beauty shop, and you've ruined my new hairdo," she said with a pout.

He was an idiot not to think about that. Women were very particular about their hair and makeup. "Raine, I'm sorry." He didn't pick up the emphasis of the palm of her hand sliding forcefully across the chocolate until a wide stream hit him square in the face. "That was dirty." He wiped the chocolate off his face just in time to see her grin and dive into the pool. He should've known she wouldn't be that concerned with messing up her hair. He dove in after her.

She didn't stop swimming until she was beneath the waterfall, then she moved to her back and floated under it, gasping when the chocolate hit sensitive areas. Her moan of pleasure almost did him in. He should've known it would be harder to hold back when she was floating naked in a pool of chocolate.

But he wanted her to relax and not worry about what was happening back home. There would be enough time for that when they returned. For now, he would enjoy watching her play. When he saw she grew tired, he took her hand and helped her out of the pool.

"I want you," she said.

Her words were almost too much. "I want you, too, but not yet." He led her to the hot tub.

"Hot chocolate?"

"Hot fudge."

The hot tub was even with the tiled surface so all they had to do was go down the steps. He went first, the heat of the chocolate surrounding him, then he reached out his hand. She took it and followed his lead. The thick chocolate moved over her legs, up her thighs. Her eyes drifted partially closed as she moved farther down the steps. She gasped when it rose higher, skimming between her legs.

"It's very warm," she said.

"Too hot?"

She shook her head. "I like it."

He scooped some up and covered her breasts, smearing the thick chocolate over them. Sliding his hand down, then scooping up more, he massaged the warm fudge between her legs. She moved against his hand.

"They were right," she said.

"Who?"

"The ones who said chocolate would make everything all better."

He smiled and pulled her down deeper into the heat. Her expression showed her disappointment that he wasn't going to continue touching her, but he had a feeling she knew there would be more pleasure, so she didn't argue.

"Sit," he told her when they were on the other side of the hot tub. "There are places below the surface to hold."

She sat on the step. The fudge rose to her shoulders. "I have them."

"There are pillows that will rise when you lean back. Rest your head against them and let yourself relax."

She leaned back, her head resting against the pillow that rose beneath the surface. The fudge was thick enough to keep her body below the surface. But the best was yet to come.

"Do you feel relaxed?"

"Very."

"Then spread your legs."

Her eyes opened. The heat inside the hot tub rose. Her teeth scraped across her bottom lip and he knew her legs were opening. With a wave of his hand jets began to vibrate the chocolate. She moaned, eyes closing. He sat down, grabbed the handles, and let his body unwind as the gentle vibrations caressed him. Wave after wave of hot fudge lapped his body, his dick.

He looked at Raine and knew she experienced the same sensations. The same pulsating massage. Her breathing came in tiny little gasps. Her back arched. Her breasts rose above the surface. He pushed himself up until he sat on the side of the hot tub and watched.

"Dillon, oh damn, it feels so fucking good."

He watched the passion on her face. She was at the peak of her desire. Close to the edge. "Spread your legs more," he said. He waved his arm again and the gentle lapping of hot fudge began to ripple faster and faster.

Raine drew in a breath. "Dillon, I'm..."

"What? About to have an orgasm?"

"Yessss."

"Let yourself go. The House of Ecstasy is no place to hold back. It's a house where every sexual pleasure is experienced." He waved his hand again. The sensual vibrations increased.

She cried out, back arching. He stared as she reached the peak of her passion. When he knew her energy was spent he jumped back into the hot tub and slipped his arms beneath her. As he lifted her out, tremors were running through her body.

He carried her past the pool and stepped into what looked like a jungle. She dragged her eyes open and smiled at him.

"That was nice. Thank you."

"I'm not finished." Water sprayed down on them. He set Raine on her feet, holding her until she was steady once again.

"A rain forest." She laughed and raised her arms. Chocolate fudge ran down her body as she swayed to the erotic beat coming from speakers around them. He could only watch as her body undulated beneath the spray, her breasts lightly bouncing, hips swaying to the rhythm. The rain changed to a light mist scented with jasmine and coconut, then to fog that changed colors from hazy blue to red, green, and yellow. He caught glimpses of her naked body as she danced.

She watched him, knowing exactly what she did to his senses. Her eyes told him she teased with her body. The house was a place where you could indulge in every kind of sexual fantasy. When he knew she was ready, he strolled nearer and slid his hands over her shoulders and down her arms. He led her out of the jungle. There was a lot more he wanted to show her. The night had only just begun.

Chapter 22

WHEN DILLON TOOK HER hand and led her from the foggy mist, she was more than ready to have him make love to her, but he apparently had other plans. She wondered what he would show her this time, but he only took her to a bar. There was no one behind the counter. Crystal glasses in all shapes and sizes sat in front of a mirrored wall.

"Would you like something to drink?" he asked as his hands circled her waist and he lifted her to the barstool. She didn't have a chance to enjoy his touch before he moved away.

She was certain he was up to something and decided to play along. "I'd love something to drink." Two long-stemmed glasses with a green frothy liquid were set in front of them. She quickly looked around, but they were still alone.

"Fairies are very fast. Sometimes you don't realize they're even around." He picked up his glass and took a drink. "Try it. I think you'll like the taste."

Being nude when there might be people or fairies about didn't really bother her. She was comfortable in her own skin. Since the drink Dillon took didn't kill him, she figured it probably wouldn't kill her either. She raised the glass to her lips and took a tentative sip.

But then again, he was an immortal.

"I'm not going to start dancing on tables, am I?"

He laughed and she decided she liked the sound. "No. I promise you won't do anything you don't want to do."

She took a longer drink, then set her glass down. The drink actually tasted good.

"What do you think?" he asked.

"I like it. Tropical, but different."

"It has a special ingredient. A spice called carrella that you can only get in a fairy town."

"What's so special about it?" She brought her glass to her lips again and drained it.

"It heightens the senses. When mortals ingest the spice, their awareness increases. They feel things, like touch, more strongly." He brushed the backs of his knuckles over her breasts.

She jumped, then had to brace her arm on the edge of the bar so she wouldn't tumble off the stool as erotic sensations flooded her system. Her nipples tightened, aching for more.

"And smell." He picked up a rose that suddenly appeared on the counter and brought it to her nose. She automatically inhaled. The sweet aroma of the flower filled her space. She wanted to see more, taste more, feel more.

"Why the drug, though? Haven't I been a willing participant?"

"I don't want you to think, only feel. I want you to experience the ultimate orgasm." He trailed the rose between her breasts, over her abdomen, then between her legs.

"But a drug?"

He shook his head. "It's only a spice. There will be no cravings later. No addiction. No aftereffects."

"Nice." She opened for him, wanting more. He didn't disappoint as he brushed the rose back and forth between her legs. She wiggled to the edge of the stool. "More," she demanded.

"And you will have more." He tossed the rose to the side and took her hand.

She willingly followed where he led. Her body tingled as a

soft breeze brushed across her skin. There were plants and trees everywhere. Butterflies and birds flitted about as they sought nectar. Vines grew up trees, the flowers bigger than two large fists put together. She looked down and saw that she walked across mossy ground. It was spongy beneath her feet.

Dillon stopped at two long tables covered in flower petals. He helped her to lie down on her stomach, then he moved to the other. She couldn't help wondering what he planned now. She didn't wonder long. A man and woman stepped from behind a tree, each carrying a silver tray with pretty bottles. They set them down on a stand between the tables. The man came to Raine, the woman to Dillon. She wasn't so sure she liked the turn of events.

Before she could protest, the man drizzled warm oil over her back. The tropical scent of the drink she'd had rose around her. His strokes were smooth as he began to massage the oil into her skin. She sighed and closed her eyes. Maybe she would allow him to touch her for a few minutes more. She'd given her share of massages, but this was the first time she'd received one. It was luxurious, sensual.

The man's hands moved over her bottom, then down her legs. He squeezed and released, inching his way back up. He stayed longer on her bottom this time, massaging her bare flesh. The movement caused her to rub against the bed. The friction started a warm ember glowing inside her. The heat began to spread to other parts of her body.

When he nudged her shoulder, she hesitated. Being around strangers naked was one thing, but facing them would be an entirely different matter. "Dillon?"

"Yes?"

She opened her eyes and stared. He was on his back and the woman was massaging lotion over his chest. He didn't seem to have a problem. She felt rather silly for even questioning what the masseur was doing. She scooted to her back. The man scooped thick creamy lotion out of a jar and began to smear it across her shoulders. She could feel the stress and tension leaving her as she began to completely let go. She sighed, her eyes drifting closed, but not before she looked up.

Her heart skipped a beat. There was a mirror above them. She saw everything the woman was doing to Dillon, her hands massaging his chest, moving lower. Dillon closed his eyes and raised his hips slightly when the woman's nimble fingers stroked his cock. Raine couldn't look away. She didn't want to look away.

Until the man began to knead and massage her breasts. The lotion was cold at first but then it began to heat. He pulled at her nipples, pinching them. He took both her breasts in his hands and squeezed. Everywhere he touched, her body came alive. He scooped more of the thick lotion and smeared it across her abdomen. His hands moved lower and lower until he was spreading her legs apart.

Her eyes moved to the mirror. He spread the lotion over her mound. She could barely breathe as she watched him inch closer and closer until he rubbed the creamy mixture down to her slit. She was so sensitive that she cried out. The man moved to her legs. With long strokes, he massaged the cream into her skin.

The woman left Dillon and moved to Raine's shoulders. She splashed oil on her hands, then rubbed them together. The woman began to massage the oil into Raine's skin. Raine looked into the mirror. Dillon was no longer on his table.

"Shh," said the masseuse. "Just let the oils perform their magic."

There was something soothing about her voice that calmed any reservations Raine might have. She was pretty with blond hair reaching to her waist in soft golden waves. The man was golden too, with pale blond hair. She frowned. And they were no longer wearing clothes. But it didn't matter as the woman's light touch moved over her body. She stroked and caressed. The man moved to her shoulders, the woman to Raine's waist. They massaged at the same time, touching her in places that left her panting.

When she thought she could stand no more, Dillon was suddenly beside her on the table and the couple was gone. His mouth covered her breast, his tongue teasing the nipple while his other hand teased the nipple of her other breast.

"You're doing it again," she said.

He released her breast and looked into her eyes. "Doing what?"

"Taking control. I don't like giving it up."

"But doesn't this feel good?" He slid his hand lower and began to run his fingers through her curls.

She raised her hips. God, yes, it felt so good, but her mouth was so dry she couldn't talk. She desperately needed to have him inside her, stroking her in other places. Before she could say more, he nudged her legs open and scooted between them.

"I love looking at you like this." He met her eyes. "It's not so hard to let go."

No, she would not give in to weakness. "No one will ever control me." She started to rise, but he moved his thumbs over her labia, massaging, and she collapsed back on the table.

"Don't you know how much you're controlling me right now?" he asked with disbelief. "Can't you see how much I want you? How much I need you?"

She moaned as his thumbs pressed against her and began to rotate. All thoughts of demanding to be returned to the ranch vanished as fire began to spread through her. "I need you, Dillon," she said on a dry ragged breath.

"You need what?"

"For you to fill me, to make love to me." She was begging but she didn't care. He made her body come alive. She wanted him so much that she thought she might die if he didn't make love to her soon.

He lowered his head and tasted her. "You're sweet. Like the lotions and oils they massaged onto your body." He tugged lightly with his teeth on the fleshy part of her sex. His tongue scraped across her clit, then he sucked her inside his mouth.

She couldn't think as her vision blurred and heat flooded her body. She tried to take a breath but only small amounts of oxygen entered her lungs. She didn't know when he moved, when his erection nudged against her opening. She became aware when he entered her, when he pressed closer. She circled her legs around his waist and pulled him even closer. She tried to move against him, but he had her pinned to the table. "Please, don't torture me any longer."

"Me torture you? Sweet lady, you still don't know what you do to me. I only stopped so I wouldn't end it all too soon. I want you so much my body burns. You fill a need that no one has ever met. It's you who controls me, not I who controls you." He looked into her eyes.

She saw the truth of his words. The barely unleashed passion that rose inside him. "Then fuck me."

He groaned and began to move inside her. His thrusts were long and deep. She rose to meet him. Their bodies came together, then moved apart. The friction inside her burned with an intensity she'd never felt before.

He cried out. As his seed spilled into her, he continued to stroke. He rose above her then lowered. The heat continued to build inside her until the sky lit with vibrant colors as they exploded across the sky. She cried out, her arms circling his neck.

She didn't need to worry that he might let go because he held her just as tightly.

"I didn't give up control," she finally said.

"No, you didn't."

She nodded. "Good." There was a moment of quiet before she began to talk again. "You understand I can never give up complete control, don't you?"

"Yes, I do. I would never ask you to."

Relief filled her. She believed Dillon spoke the truth. When he rolled to his side, he took her with him. She snuggled against his chest, feeling comforted by the steady beat of his heart. She'd never felt so satiated in her life. Or so exhausted. She closed her eyes. She needed to rest for a little while.

———

When Raine opened her eyes next she was in her bed and sunlight streamed through her window. The scent of a tropical paradise surrounded her. She rolled to her side and found herself staring at Dillon's sleeping form. He'd stayed with her the rest of the night. A warm feeling spread from her stomach to her limbs. She had no idea why the thought of him staying with her should give her so much pleasure, but it did. This was the first time she'd spent all night with a man. It was an odd feeling waking up beside someone.

He stretched and yawned as his eyes came open. When his gaze landed on her, he smiled. "Morning, beautiful."

She smiled. "Morning." Waking up beside him every morning wouldn't be a bad thing. As soon as the thought crossed her mind, she could feel the cold fingers of dread caressing her body. "How long will you stay?" she asked.

"I'll be with you all day."

She shook her head. "I'm talking about after today. If we don't find enough evidence against Ethan, will you go to prison with me? I don't mean sentenced to jail time, but will you be there when I need you?" Even as she warned herself to shut up, the questions rolled off her tongue. And they didn't stop. "Can you close your eyes and make us disappear?"

"They won't let me." He trailed his fingers lightly up and down her arm. "We'll need to find the real bank robbers before my time here is over."

"Or what?"

"I'll make sure if that happens, one of the others will be there for you."

She closed her eyes tight. It wouldn't be the same. She drew in a shuddering breath. "Then you're planning to leave."

"I won't have a choice."

Pain ripped through her. No one ever stayed except Grandpa.

"You knew I couldn't stay," he said quietly.

Raine rolled to her other side, hugging the sheet close. Yes, of course she knew he wouldn't stay. He wasn't like her. He was immortal.

She'd always told herself she wouldn't get married. The thought of a permanent relationship scared the hell out of her. She remembered the countless times her father talked about when he'd first met her mother. His eyes would shine with a special light when he talked about sweeping Lucille off her feet. If her mother heard him talking, she would smile, but the same light didn't shine in her eyes.

After Raine's mother walked out on them, he never spoke her name again. The light dimmed until it went out altogether and the only thing left was an empty shell. The bond between Raine and her father broke. Then her father died. The pain that ripped through her tore off little chunks of her heart—the same as it was doing now.

Don't let them get too close and you won't feel like that again, the voice inside her head mocked. *In and out of your life, that's all. No commitments. Stupid! You broke your own rules.*

Dillon's hand rested lightly on her shoulder. She closed her eyes tight, then reached up and covered his hand with hers.

"You're right. I knew you would leave." She stumbled over her next words. "At first, I didn't care."

"And now you do?"

Things wouldn't change, so why not admit the truth? "You aggravate the hell out of me, but yes, I'm going to miss you." The thought of Dillon leaving left her feeling empty on the inside. She would grit her teeth and get over it, just like she did everything else.

"I haven't left yet," he said.

He pulled her toward him. His arms wrapped around her, pulling her closer. She knew he stirred feelings inside her, and not just because he'd spent the night. It was this. Him holding her in his arms. The warmth of his body against hers. Feeling as though everything would be okay and they would find enough evidence against Ethan. Then she realized what Dillon gave her that she hadn't had in a long time. Security. What would she do when he left?

"Don't think about it too much," he said when the silence lengthened between them.

"I'll survive." She drew in a deep breath. "I always do."

"I don't want you to just survive. I want you to be happy."

"At this moment, I'm happier than I've been in a long time. Why don't we leave it at that?"

He studied her face as if he wanted to say more, but then he nodded.

She moved out of his embrace, knowing that as much as she would like to stay nestled in his arms, her problems weren't going away. When she pushed the cover to the side and rolled away from him, there was a chill in the air. She shivered as she hurried to the dresser. When she didn't hear him getting up, she glanced over her shoulder. He was still in the same spot. Staring with a hungry look. Something stirred inside her.

"Really? After last night?" Her words didn't come out as strong as she would've liked.

He dragged his eyes to her face. "I was okay until you slipped out of bed naked."

Knowing that she turned him on was nice. But she still had a criminal to catch. She opened a drawer and began to get dressed. He still didn't move. "You're supposed to be helping me, remember?" She stepped into a lacy pair of black bikini panties.

"No clothes," he grumbled and sat up in bed. The sheet bunched around him. Now she was staring. How could a man be so beautiful? His shoulders were broad and he had the most delicious muscles. And when he pulled her close it was as though he was giving her a piece of Heaven.

"You're killing me," he groaned.

"What?" She realized he wasn't the only one who was staring.

"I'll be back in a minute." He closed his eyes and disappeared.

Raine grabbed the dresser. He really should warn her before he popped in and out of her life. It was jarring watching him vanish. She started to move away, then opened another drawer and grabbed the first bra she touched. They had a lot of work to do today and she didn't want to tempt him. At least, not before they had some more leads.

She pulled on jeans and a loose shirt, buttoning the front. Maybe Ethan wouldn't slip up, but there had been two men with him. They might not be as good. She grabbed socks and boots and then headed downstairs. Once she had the coffee started, she went to the back porch and sat in one of the rocking chairs, setting her boots and socks on the floor, staring at the land before her. There was something fresh and clean about the country. She didn't want to lose it.

Someone once told her the country was too quiet. They didn't listen. There was nothing quiet about it. Birds were already waking up. They chirped and flew back and forth from tree to tree. They fussed at a squirrel who invaded their territory. The squirrel wiggled his tail at them as if to say he didn't want to climb their silly old tree anyway and scurried back down. A horse whinnied. The cow answered. The chickens were clucking and the rooster crowed.

She drew in a deep breath. Good clean country air. The aroma of fresh brewed coffee. You couldn't beat—

Dillon popped in, blocking her view. She jumped and grabbed her boot, ready to throw it at her intruder. She stopped herself just in time. "What? Is your goal to give me a heart attack?" She frowned at him. "I asked you not to do that."

"You knew I was coming back." His forehead furrowed as though he was genuinely puzzled.

"Okay. Fine," she grumbled as she pulled her socks then boots on. She came to her feet and started past him, but he pulled her into his arms and kissed her. Her body was starting to come alive when he ended the kiss and stepped back.

"Good morning, in case I forgot to tell you."

For a moment she only stared at him, then a frown turned her lips downward. "Has anyone ever told you that you're an ass?"

He grinned. "A few people have."

"They were right. You are." But she wasn't really mad. How could she be angry when he made her feel so alive?

Chapter 23

DILLON WAS GOING TO be the death of her. All that should be going through her mind was collecting enough evidence to prove Ethan robbed the bank, but when he touched her like that, when he pulled her close, when he kissed her, nothing else seemed important.

She pushed out of his arms. "The coffee should be ready."

"I won't let you go to prison," Dillon said.

She turned at the door. "How will you stop them?"

"I'll do whatever it takes."

The determination in his eyes said he would do exactly that, no matter the cost. Maybe she didn't want to know what he would do if it came down to it. There was something in his look that said his decision might be a high price for him to pay.

"It won't come to that," she said with renewed determination. Suddenly, it wasn't her future or Grandpa's or Tilly's at risk. Dillon was also throwing his hat into the ring. It left a sour taste in her mouth. The weight of everything and everyone she cared for rested on her shoulders and the burden was getting heavier by the minute. She wasn't sure she would hold up.

"Trust me on this one," he said.

But she couldn't. It wasn't because he'd mistakenly thought she would be killed the night of the bank robbery and pushed her out of the way. That wasn't his fault. She knew deep down she was afraid to let someone else take charge. She wasn't exactly sure why; she only knew she couldn't, and she didn't want to think too long or hard about her reasoning.

"Coffee," she mumbled, then hurried into the kitchen.

She went straight to the cabinet and opened the door, taking down two cups. She filled one, then the other, marveling that her hands were steady.

The screen door opened and closed. She added sugar and cream to her coffee. "I do what I have to do," she said. She stirred the coffee, watching it change from dark black to a light brown. He picked up his cup. She didn't look at him.

Dillon simply said, "I know."

A moment passed until she gathered her thoughts and spoke again. "I need to find out if this uncle exists."

"Where do you want to start?" he asked.

But Dad, it's too hard.

Raine, you're not paying attention.

I am, but it's like walking through a maze and there's no way out. Every time I think I might have it figured out, the perp throws another hedge in my path and I have to start all over again.

If you want to find where the lie begins, sometimes you have to start at the end.

She blew across the top of her coffee and took a drink. "We'll start at the end." She had a plan and it was a good one. For a while she might have been anxious, but good teaching always won out, and her father was one of the best.

She glanced up and saw that Dillon didn't understand what she was talking about. "Phil Turner owned the car dealership. We'll start with him."

It still took over two hours to track the man down. At least he was still in town. The ink was barely dry on the contract and he was tying up loose ends and not planning to return, or so his cousin told them. The cousin didn't care for his uppity ways and was more than glad to tell them he was at the storage buildings on the North side of town, making arrangements to have the rest of his things shipped to California.

"Mr. Turner, we'd like to speak with you a moment," Raine said with a smile pasted on her face.

He was standing with a man outside the office building. The cousin had described Philip Turner accurately. He was tall and thin and always wore a jacket no matter the temperature. The cousin said he had thin skin and the brutal Texas sun would burn him to a crisp if he wasn't careful. She also said they better hurry because his flight left that afternoon.

"I'm afraid I don't have the time," he answered and took the top copy of the sheet the other man handed him.

"It's been a pleasure, Mr. Turner." The owner of the storage buildings tugged on his cap and hurried back inside. He didn't ask many questions about what went in his storage units and he didn't want to know anything.

"Unless you want to miss your plane, you'll oblige the lady," Dillon said.

Raine glanced his way. Since when did he become a cop?

"By what authority do you have the right to detain me?" he blustered.

"I'm a deputy. That's all the authority I need," she said. Technically, he didn't know she was on a forced leave of absence. She refrained from telling him.

His eyes narrowed as he studied her. "Where's your uniform?"

"We're undercover," Dillon easily answered before she had a chance.

Now they were breaking the law. Legally, she didn't have any authority to question Mr. Turner, but she didn't refute Dillon's words. "Would you like to use my phone to call the office? Sheriff Barnes has to be in court this morning, but he might be back. If not, we can wait here or at the office."

Mr. Turner glanced at his watch and frowned. "No, I'm sure you're who you say you are. What do you need to know?"

"We want to know everything about the deal you made with Ethan Miles."

"He's a cop." He looked back and forth between them.

Raine didn't blink. "He's under investigation."

The man stuck a finger beneath his collar as though he thought it was a noose that was tightening around his neck. "I don't know anything about him except we made a deal and he signed on the dotted line. If he's done anything illegal, I'm not aware of it."

Dillon's smile didn't look at all genuine. "Did we say he did something illegal?" He looked at Raine as though he was puzzled. "All we said was that he was under investigation. Isn't that right?"

What the hell was Dillon doing? Mr. Turner wasn't stupid, and Dillon might be immortal but he couldn't act. She gave him a look that she hoped would tell him to back off and let her handle this. When Mr. Turner looked at her for confirmation, she smiled.

"We're checking out a few of his stories," she explained. "Now, if you don't mind answering a few questions, then you can be on your way."

"How did he pay?" Dillon asked.

"How was he acting?" Raine asked at the same time. Mr. Turner looked between the two of them as though he might turn around at any moment and run all the way to California. She hurriedly jumped in. "One question at a time, Mr. Turner. How did he act?"

A bead of sweat ran down the side of Mr. Turner's face. "As if he was in a hurry," his words tumbled out. "Nervous," he squeaked.

"And how did he pay?"

"A check on a Galveston bank. It's legit. I called to make sure. The money has already been transferred. Over half up front and the same bank is financing the rest."

"Did he say where he got the money?" Not that she expected him to know.

"An uncle died and left it to him. That's all he said. I swear."

By the time they finished with their questions, Mr. Turner was sweating profusely and practically ran to his rented Cadillac. Raine watched him climb inside and drive off in a swirl of dust.

"The sale of the dealership might be perfectly legal, but I'd bet my last dollar he's done shady dealings in the past," Dillon said, voicing her thoughts.

"I agree."

"What are you thinking?" he asked.

"If Ethan paid four hundred thousand for the building, there's a quarter of a million dollars still unaccounted for. Where's that money?"

"Pocket change?"

"Maybe he thought he might need to make a fast getaway and would need to have quick access."

"Sounds plausible."

She socked him on the arm.

"Ow." He rubbed his arm. "Why'd you do that? He answered all our questions."

"That didn't hurt and you know it."

"You frogged me." He shrugged. "It hurt for a second."

"What were you doing? You could've blown everything playing cop. What was with all the dramatics?"

He suddenly grinned. "Acting lessons. I was pretty good, right?"

"Acting lessons? Who from? Laurel and Hardy?"

His eyebrows drew together. "You've heard about them?"

She opened her mouth, then snapped it closed. God, sometimes he made her feel like a fish out of water. "Never mind. I don't want to know. We have enough information to continue the investigation." She glanced down at her notes. "We need to know about this long lost uncle."

But it wasn't going to be as easy as she thought. There were more Miles listed in the Galveston area than she had time to search through. It was time to call in a favor.

"Hello?" Darla said, sounding drowsy.

Raine glanced at her watch. Darla worked last night and she would work tonight. "I'm sorry I woke you, but I need to ask a really big favor."

"Raine?"

"Yes, it's me."

"Whatcha want?" She yawned.

Raine waited, then said, "I need you to leave the back door at the sheriff's office unlocked tonight." She hated asking her, but it was the only way to get to Ethan's personal files so she could find out more about him. It could cost Darla her job.

"What's going on?" Darla asked, more alert than she had been a moment ago.

"The less you know, the better off you'll be. You can't tell anyone about this, and if they question you, say you didn't realize the door was unlocked." She wasn't sure Darla would put her job on the line. Raine was taking a huge risk asking her to do this much. What if Darla left it unlocked, then got scared and told the sheriff what Raine asked her to do? But then, Darla was taking an even bigger risk if she followed through.

"I won't say a word, sweetie. I know you didn't rob that bank, even if you do need the money. If I can help in any other way, let me know."

"I will. Thanks, Darla." She pressed her lips together as an unexpected wave of emotion flowed through her. Oh hell, she didn't want to care about anyone else. What if something happened? How would she protect Darla? She slipped her phone back into her pocket.

"She'll be fine." Dillon put his arm across her shoulder and pulled her against him. "You can't take care of everyone all the time. Friends help friends and that's what Darla is doing."

"But I *don't* take care of everyone. That's the problem."

"It's not your fault your father gave up after your mother left him."

She squeezed her eyes shut. "But I was partly to blame. I let him down. I promised I wouldn't let anyone hurt him again. I didn't follow through. He hurt up until the day he died. Alcohol was the only thing that made his pain go away."

He looked into her eyes. "He made the choice to drink. Not you."

"But—"

"No. It was his choice, not yours. He was the parent. He should have seen to your needs, taken care of you."

"It hurts," she whispered. The pain was raw and it had festered inside her for too many years.

"I know."

"I thought we had something special, but we didn't."

"Sometimes people can't accept the pain of their loss for one reason or another. It consumes them until they start making bad choices. You need to stop blaming yourself and understand he was human and had flaws. Everyone does."

Dillon was right. But accepting it was another matter entirely. It was easy to tell herself that she wasn't to blame for her father's drinking; it was harder to believe it. For the first time in a long time, though, she felt as though the weight on her shoulders was beginning to lighten.

"I want to see Grandpa," she said.

The ground suddenly disappeared beneath her feet. Her stomach rolled as it did every time they transported. She tightened her hold around his waist and closed her eyes tight as the wind rushed past. What if she let go? Would she end up somewhere halfway between wherever they were going, her body splattered all over the place?

Her feet touched on solid surface again and she breathed a thankful sigh of relief. She opened her eyes and saw they were in Tilly's living room. "I meant we should take the car." She stepped out of his arms.

"Oh. You didn't say you wanted to drive."

"I thought it was implied."

"Have I told you how sexy you are when you get ticked off at someone?"

She clamped her lips together. "That's not what we were discussing, so don't change the subject."

"We thought we heard voices," Grandpa said as he and Tilly walked into the room.

"Grandpa!" She rushed to him, throwing her arms around his neck and hugging him tight.

"What's the matter, little girl?" Worry laced his words.

"Nothing. I've missed you."

"This will all be over soon." He patted her on the back. "We've been working on our end to find out more."

"Everyone sit," Tilly said. She beamed when she looked at

Dillon. "I never thought I'd see the day when there was an angel in my home." Her forehead furrowed. "Except maybe when I was dying." She shook her head. "But that's neither here nor there."

When she and Dillon were comfortably seated on an antique red velvet settee, and Tilly and Grandpa in matching high-backed chairs, Grandpa said, "You first."

Raine began with what they'd discovered a little while ago, telling them everything Mr. Turner had told them. "I think Ethan is guilty. Everything points to him."

"But you still don't believe it," Grandpa guessed.

"I'm not sure. I don't agree with the way he does a lot of things, but he's a good cop," she said.

"Or is it out of loyalty?" Grandpa asked. "He's a cop and you were always taught to respect someone with a badge. Good cops can go bad."

"I know," she said. He was right. She didn't want to believe it.

"What have you discovered?" Dillon asked.

As Raine looked at everyone in the room, she knew that whatever happened, she wasn't alone. She wasn't the only one to carry the burden. Except it could all be taken from her at any moment.

"He had to have help," Tilly said. "We put our heads together and it has to be Leo. When we followed him—"

Raine sat forward. "You followed him?"

"We stayed back a ways," Grandpa reassured her.

"No, you're not to follow anyone. This isn't a game. Guilty people get desperate when they're cornered. You could get hurt. Promise me you won't follow anyone else." When Tilly and Grandpa would have protested, Raine crossed her arms in front of her and pursed her lips.

"Okay, no more tailing people," Grandpa grumbled.

Lady came barreling into the room, going straight to Grandpa, but the dog stopped at his knees as if she sensed she couldn't plow into him. He laughed and rubbed her ears.

Raine studied the animal. The dog had fattened up and was no longer limping. Lady looked too much like a purebred to be a stray. She had a funny feeling about all this. "Where, again, did you find the dog?"

Grandpa and Tilly shared a look. Tilly suddenly became preoccupied with her hands. Grandpa cleared his throat. "East of town."

There was definitely more to the story. But before she could question him further, Dillon spoke up.

"Did you find out anything when you trailed Leo?"

Grandpa immediately launched into what they discovered, and Raine forgot about the dog. Where Grandpa got the dog wasn't that important.

"Like I said, we followed Leo. Ethan and Leo met on the sly more times than I can count."

"Five," Tilly supplied.

Grandpa frowned. "I'm telling the story."

"But we want to be accurate," she lightly admonished.

"We saw them meet *five* times." He cast a pointed look in Tilly's direction and she smiled. "They met at the car dealership four times and went out to the wrecking yard once."

Raine looked between them, waiting for more. "That's it?"

"Of course not." Tilly was frowning again when she looked at Grandpa. "You're waiting much too long before delivering the punch. You pause, count two seconds, then tell them the important stuff. That makes your pitch stronger. By the time you get around to saying what needs to be said, you've already lost your audience."

Raine met Dillon's gaze. She silently asked if he knew what they were talking about, but he looked as confused as she felt. She returned her attention to Tilly again. "*Was* there more?"

"I told you they were as lost as Hogan's ghost," she said, reaffirming her point.

"You're right," Grandpa conceded. "There was more. Ethan kept glancing around, all nervous like."

"But he didn't see you?" Dillon asked.

"If he did, then he wouldn't think nothin' about it. We were in disguises."

"Disguises." Raine repeated. She was living in a bad B-rated movie again.

"Yeah, nothing elaborate. We didn't want to stand out. I wore a big wide-brimmed hat low on my forehead and overalls, but that's not all. I kept a pipe in my mouth and leaned heavy-like on a cane." His gaze moved to Tilly. "Tell them what you wore," he urged.

"Oh, it wasn't that fancy." She giggled like a schoolgirl.

What the hell? Didn't they realize this was serious? Apparently not, since they were playing dress up.

"I put on a baggy dress with great big flowers and a wide white belt," she quickly launched into her description anyway. "And a long fake white pearl necklace. I dug out my grandmother's garden bonnet from a trunk upstairs. It's the kind that fits close to your face and ties in a big bow under the chin.

Grandpa slapped his leg and Lady looked up from where she had laid beside him, saw that he was all right, and laid her head back down. "We were a sight. Should've took a picture."

"Tell them the rest," Tilly urged.

"Oh, right." He was thoughtful for a moment, as though he tried to remember what he'd been about to say.

"At the dealership," she nudged.

"Someone else showed up." He lowered his voice dramatically and looked around as though someone might overhear. "A woman."

Tilly clapped her hands. "Much better delivery!"

"Did we miss something?" Dillon finally asked.

Grandpa's face turned a bright red. "We've started going to the nursing home every Tuesday. We tell stories or read from one of the books they've chosen. A lot of them are friends who can't get around like they used to. We try to make them feel as though they're still living, not dying. Sometimes we forget about the ones who can't do for themselves. They're still useful, just in other ways." His gaze dropped.

Raine's heart swelled with pride. "You're right, we do sometimes forget." Grandpa looked up and smiled. How long they took to get their story across stopped mattering.

"Can you tell us what the woman looked like?"

"That's where it gets a little tricky." Tilly's words were hesitant, and for the first time since Dillon and Raine arrived, her forehead creased with worry. "She wore a dark skirt."

"That's how we knew it was a woman," Grandpa added.

"But our eyes aren't as good as they used to be. So we really didn't see her that well," Tilly finished.

Raine leaned back and crossed her legs. "I never thought that it might be two men and a woman who robbed the bank."

"You said their voices were muffled, right?" Dillon asked. "I never heard them speak, so I can't help there."

"They were definitely muffled." She rubbed the place where she'd hit her head when she fell after Dillon shoved her out of the way. "And everything is still a little foggy."

"That's all we have," Grandpa said. "Did we do okay?"

"I couldn't ask for two better detectives," she told them.

"What's next?" Grandpa asked.

"We're breaking into the sheriff's office tonight to steal Ethan's personal file," Dillon said.

Raine wanted to slap her hand over his mouth. Why in the world would he tell them about her plan?

"Can we come?" Tilly and Grandpa asked almost in unison.

"No," she said emphatically, then reiterated, "Promise me you won't come to the sheriff's office tonight."

"Promise," Grandpa grumbled, then added, "Don't put me out to pasture yet."

She went to him, kneeling in front of him. "I would never do that, Grandpa. I just don't want you to get hurt."

His smile was gentle, the kind he used to give her when she did something wrong but he didn't want to scold her. "If you don't get hurt every once in a while, little girl, then you ain't living. You're only pretending."

Was that what she was doing? Pretending?

That night couldn't come soon enough; then it came too fast. Raine knew if she got caught in Sheriff Barnes's office going through his files, he would have no choice except to lock her up. She didn't have a choice either.

Her hand shook when she tested the door. The knob turned. Some of the tension inside her eased. Darla was true to her word. The door was unlocked. She opened it and slipped inside. Bless her heart, Darla had gone one step farther and turned off the bright entry light.

"The coast is clear," Dillon spoke beside her.

She slapped a hand over her mouth to keep from screaming. "You scared the hell out of me!" she whispered. Her pulse raced so fast she was almost afraid she might keel over dead any second.

"I was trying to help."

"I don't need that kind of help." She drew in a steady breath and waited a moment for her heart rate to return to normal. "Thank you anyway."

"You're welcome." His smile was slow and sexy. "You look good dressed all in black."

Her body began to respond, but just as quickly, she tamped down the sexual thoughts that began to run through her head. "Really, Dillon?"

"Just letting you know what I think. Is that a crime?" He leaned against the wall.

"Your thoughts are," she mumbled. "Will you please let me do what I came here to do?"

He swung his arm wide, motioning her to continue on her way. "Darla gave Justin a stack of papers to read. She told him there would be a test when he finished. Ethan is filling in for you tonight since you're on leave. He's patrolling the streets, and Leo's at the truck stop flirting with the new waitress."

"I thought you weren't supposed to help?"

"Up to a point," he said.

"It seems like you make up a lot of the rules as you go along." He was causing her to lose track of why she was there. She frowned at him as she slipped past. He vanished in front of her eyes and she stumbled. She really hated when he did that. It was good to know she wouldn't run into someone when she rounded the corner, though.

She still didn't breathe easier until she was standing outside the sheriff's door. She tested the lock. This one was locked, but Darla wouldn't have the key anyway and Raine hadn't told her where she was going once she was inside. It didn't matter. She could pick a lock in under three minutes. Most of them, at least.

She reached in her back pocket and pulled out a flat bag of tools. She chose the one she would need and set the others on the

floor. It took her under a minute to pick the lock, but then this was
the door she'd always practiced on when her daddy was sheriff.

Once inside, she carefully closed the door behind her, then
used her cell phone light to shine around the room. Dillon was
leaning against the file cabinet. The man was seriously becoming
a thorn in her side. "You couldn't open the door?"

"You didn't ask me to. Besides, it was sexy watching you pick
the lock."

She shook her head and moved to the file cabinet. It was
locked, but she reached behind the cabinet, sliding her hand
down the inside edge, then smiling when she felt the key. Her
father always kept it there too.

She unlocked the cabinet, then grasped the handle, but at the
last second indecision filled her. The idea that Ethan might have
committed the crime, then let her take the fall, didn't sit well with
her. If he was a dirty cop, then she would put him away, but it left
a sour taste in her mouth. She tugged on the drawer, then quickly
located Ethan's file. She brought it out and took it over to the
desk. Her hands shook when she opened his file. She skimmed
through all the unimportant stuff, skidding to a stop when her
eyes landed on one word.

"What did you find?" Dillon asked.

"He couldn't have inherited the money from an uncle,"
she said.

"Why not?"

She raised her eyes to meet his. "He's an orphan. It clearly
states he grew up in an orphanage on this background check. He
was never adopted." Odd that she should have felt elated, but the
only emotion running through her was sadness that Ethan hadn't
known a real family. Her parents might have had problems but
Grandpa had been there to help pick up the pieces.

Maybe that's why Ethan didn't share a lot of his past. It might be why he robbed the bank, too. And as much as she hated the idea that one of their own turned out to be a rotten apple, she was leaning more and more to that conclusion.

The doorknob rattled. She swung around, hitting the button on her phone that would shut off the light. She looked around for a place to hide, but before she could move, the door opened and Darla stuck her head inside.

"Raine, you in here?"

Raine slumped against the desk. They were both going to be the death of her! "Yes, I'm here." Dillon looked at her as if to say she wasn't the only one.

"I was coming down the hall and I thought I heard voices. These halls echo."

"It's a good thing it was you and not someone else," Raine voiced her thoughts.

"Justin is going through a stack of papers two inches thick so he'll be busy for a while. No chance of you getting caught." She held up a radio. "And I have my portable. I told the little twerp if he so much as touched the button on the mike I'd cut off his ears." She chuckled, then quickly sobered. "I wouldn't cut off his ears. He's kind of cute. Kid brother cute," she amended. "Not boyfriend cute."

"I knew what you meant."

"She's funny," Dillon said.

"Be quiet," Raine said.

"I promise no one will hear us talking," Darla said again.

Raine couldn't explain she was talking to Dillon and not her. Darla would think she was shy a few brain cells.

"Did you find what you were looking for?" Darla asked.

"We… I mean, yes, I did."

"You don't look happy."

"I'm relieved," she said, and she was.

Darla's portable crackled.

"*Go to channel two, Darla.*" Ethan's voice was brisk.

Darla frowned. "Something must have happened. Why else would he tell me to go to the scrambled channel?" She turned the dial until a red two lit up. "I'm here. Do you need something?"

"Just checking something out at the salvage yard. I thought I saw a light. I didn't want to broadcast my whereabouts in case it's not a false alarm," Ethan said, sounding a little too casual in Raine's opinion.

Darla keyed the mike. "Should I send backup?"

There was a pause, then her radio crackled again.

"I'm here with him, Darla," Leo said.

Her gut told her there was something going down. Why else would they be together? It was all too suspicious.

"I'd better get back to dispatch," she said, looking at Raine. "Is there anything else you need?"

"No, I'll let myself out."

They hurried down the hall then split at the end. As soon as Raine was out the door, she headed straight for Old Red.

"You thinking what I'm thinking?" Dillon asked.

"That they're making a withdrawal?" she asked as she climbed inside the truck.

"Exactly."

She turned the key. The pickup did its usual ugga-ugga, but this time it didn't start. "Damn!" She slammed her palm against the steering wheel. She tried again but the motor refused to turn over. She jumped out and started toward the office but Dillon grabbed her by the arm and pulled her close. "Dillon, are you nuts? I need to get the keys to a cruiser before Ethan gets away."

"Close your eyes."

She did and immediately felt the ground disappear beneath her feet. "Why didn't you do this before?" she asked as she gripped him a little tighter.

"I'm not supposed to interfere with the investigation."

"Then why are you?"

When her feet were on solid ground again, she moved back and looked up at him. "Will you get into trouble?"

"Probably, but I don't want you to go to prison for a crime you didn't commit, either."

"What will they do?"

"Don't worry about me. I'll be fine. You have some bank robbers to catch."

She nodded and pulled her gun from the holster and looked around. They stood in the middle of the salvage yard. The area was dimly lit, only two lights working. She nervously glanced around. Dwayne used to have a mongrel guarding the place, but that was when they were still in high school. Surely the ugly, mean-assed beast was dead by now or at least too old to attack.

She didn't see the mutt.

There were so many junk cars it would be easy to hide the money here. Ethan had chosen a good spot. She cautiously moved forward. There was a noise to her right. She stopped and listened. She heard it again so she changed direction, moving toward the sound.

"Stay close," she told Dillon, then realized she was talking to an immortal.

He grinned, then suddenly doubled over as if in pain. "Dillon, what's the matter," she frantically whispered.

"Go, get your bank robbers," he gasped.

"Not until I know what's happening."

"I think I'm being called home," he gasped.

Raine saw he was fighting against whatever force was pulling him away. "Tell me what I can do to help." She holstered her gun and grabbed his shoulders.

"I'm sorry."

"Don't be." She shook her head, tears blurring her vision. "I don't want you to leave."

"Don't ever be afraid to lose control."

"I love you," she whispered.

He began to fade. She pressed her lips to his. For a moment, she felt the warmth of his lips, then he was gone. She dropped to her knees. "Why?" she asked, looking up.

But no one answered. They never had before, so she didn't know why she expected an answer now. But the feeling of loss ran a lot deeper this time. When had she fallen in love with her angel?

She heard another noise and came to her feet. "I still have bank robbers to catch," she said, then scrubbed her hands across her damp cheeks. She sniffed, then unholstered her gun. She moved steadily forward. The noise became voices, muffled at first, then more clear.

"Here it is," Leo said, then laughed. "Jackpot!"

She peeked around the side of a rusted Chevy that would never run again. Leo held up a bag. The name of the bank was printed on it in bold black letters. They were guilty. The evidence was right in front of her. She took a deep breath, exhaled, and moved into the open.

"Drop your guns and put up your hands."

Ethan whirled around, surprise on his face. "Raine?"

"Hands in the air," she repeated.

"This isn't what it looks like." Ethan took a step toward her.

"Don't." Her voice cracked. "Don't come any closer."

"Crap, don't shoot us," Leo bellowed.

"Why the hell did you do it?" she asked. "Dammit, I might not have agreed with everything you did, but you were both damn good cops."

"Put your gun away." Ethan spoke slowly but firmly. "We're not the bad guys."

"You are now," she whispered.

Chapter 24

Laughter sounded behind her. Raine froze.

"Now, isn't this nice. The gang is all here."

She recognized Dwayne Freeman's voice and turned. He held a gun. Odd, but she never thought of him as the kind of person to even own one.

"Like he tried to tell you," Dwayne said. "They're not the bad guys."

Shock almost knocked the breath out of her. "You robbed the bank?"

"Don't sound so surprised." His voice was hard and brittle. "Take her gun, Travis."

"You got it, bro." The boy was seventeen. She knew him as a troublemaker, and Dwayne's younger brother.

The other brother stepped into the open. "What do you want me to do, Dwayne?" His voice sounded just like his brother's, but with a little more whine. He was slightly bigger than his older brothers. She knew his name, George, and that he was a little slow.

The night of the robbery she remembered thinking she was hearing double, but thought it had something to do with her injury or the fact their voices were muffled behind the masks. She should've put two and two together and guessed they were brothers.

Travis took her gun. His hand lingered a little too long against hers. She thought it might have been accidental until he grinned and winked at her. Travis was a younger version of Dwayne when he was that age. Cocky little bastard.

She leaned in a little closer to him. "You're going to do really well in prison." She eyed him and clicked her tongue. "Yep, some guy is going to latch onto you real fast, boy."

Anger flared in his eyes.

"Travis, get your ass back over here!" Dwayne ordered.

"Did you hear what she said?" Travis whined.

Okay, now his voice sounded more like George.

"She said some guy would... would..." He glanced over his shoulder.

"Latch onto you," she supplied.

Travis nodded his head. "Yeah, that's what she said!"

"Get your damn redneck ass over here and give me the gun before you blow your fucking foot off!"

Travis handed him the gun, barrel first. Dwayne jumped out of the way. "The other way! How many times do I have to tell you, the butt of the gun first?"

"I forgot."

"I swear Momma dropped you two on your heads after you were born. Dumb sons of bitches."

"You're the one who gambled all the money away," George mumbled.

Dwayne rounded on him. "What did you say?"

George kicked a tire, except the rubber was rotten and his foot went through it and got stuck. Dwayne rubbed his forehead with a pained expression. "See what I have to put up with?" He looked up as if asking for guidance.

Raine scanned the area, but she knew Dillon wasn't there. An ache began to burn deep in her chest. She fought against it and tried to stay focused. She made one hell of a mistake when she thought Ethan and Leo were the bad guys. Now she had to fix her blunder or they would all die.

"Yes, I gambled a little too much, but only because I needed an outlet," Dwayne complained. "No one can blame me for that."

"Except you gambled away your brothers' inheritances as well," Ethan commented.

Travis's expression said he hadn't figured that one out yet. "Did you blow our money, too?"

"Go up to the house and get the shovels."

Cold dread filled her. Dwayne was going to kill them. Dillon once told her their powers could be blocked if they interfered too much. Was that what happened? Maybe she was really supposed to have died that night. She didn't want to die. There was too much living she wanted to do.

"Why do we need shovels?" Travis stared at them. He lost some of his earlier swagger as he figured out what Dwayne was really saying.

"Do as I say."

Travis looked as though he was going to say something else but changed his mind at the last minute and began to jog toward the trail that would lead to their red brick house.

Dwayne's face was mottled with fury when he faced Ethan again. "It's your damn fault. You fucked up everything. I was going to buy that building and fix up some of these old cars. I almost have one running. All we had to do was get enough money together. When I talked to the owner, he said you already bought it. Then I found out that old biddy, Ms. Albright, was hooking you up with her customers up North. You're not even from around here. I was going to make more money than we got from the bank job. You stole my idea!"

"And he arrested us when we robbed the laundromat," George pointed out.

Dwayne turned on him. "Shut up!"

George stumbled back a few steps. "Well, he did."

"Now you're trying to turn my brothers against me," Dwayne accused.

"That wouldn't be too hard once they find out you sold this place and bought a single one-way ticket to the Bahamas. Were you going to leave them behind to fend for themselves? No home, no money?"

"Dwayne?" George's eyes were round with fear. "Was you going to leave us here all alone? Who would've taken care of me and Travis?"

Dwayne muttered something under his breath. "Are you going to believe me or him? I'm your brother. Haven't I taken care of you two since Momma died?"

Raine knew Dwayne lied. Only an idiot would believe him.

"I didn't think you was going to do that," George said.

She rested her case. There was one thing about it that puzzled her. "How did you get Grandpa's handkerchief?"

Dwayne stood a little taller. "The night I got that old clunker you drive to run, you tossed me a rag to wipe my hands. I stuck it in my pocket. When I changed clothes, I saw your grandpa's brand stitched on one corner so I kept it with me. Pretty smart of me to leave it at the scene. You and *Grandpa* took the heat." He laughed.

"And it led us to you," Ethan said.

Dwayne's laughter abruptly stopped. "What do you mean?" he snarled.

"You wiped your greasy hands on the rag."

"So? Lots of people have greasy hands."

"I knew there was only one other person trying to restore classic cars. You. The oil on the handkerchief is blue. I had it tested.

There's a special blend of oil that keeps the pressure from dropping when you run a classic on the highway. You would know that. It just happens to be blue. The test came back positive for that blend."

"You're going to be the first one I shoot." Dwayne's words dripped ice.

"Hey, look who I found." Travis came around the corner holding a shovel like a weapon. Tilly and Grandpa were holding hands walking in front of him.

"I told you to stay out of this," Raine whispered. It felt as though her heart jumped to her throat.

"That's my dog!" Dwayne stomped his foot. "Why is my dog with you?"

"You hurt her. Me and Tilly saved her life," Grandpa said. "She's a good dog."

"She's worthless. She didn't guard a damn thing. She wouldn't attack a freaking bone!" He raised the gun toward Grandpa. "You dog thief!"

"No!" Raine ran toward Dwayne.

Grandpa yelled for her to stay back.

Dwayne didn't know who to shoot first. While he was still undecided, Lady launched herself at him. The dog got to him first, clamping her teeth down on his arm. Pandemonium followed as everyone moved at the same time. Raine knew she had to save her grandfather. Then she heard the gunshot and white fury filled her.

Dwayne screamed as he tried to shake off Lady, but her teeth were firmly latched onto his arm. Travis raised the shovel to hit the dog, but Ethan was already running toward him. Tilly began to scream and flap her arms, drawing Travis's attention. It was enough time for Ethan to tackle him. At the same time Raine came from below, driving her fist in a vicious slam to Dwayne's jaw. A strange flash lit the night. He stopped yelling and slowly crumpled to the ground.

Her fist throbbed, but the satisfaction she got from taking the son of a bitch out made it all worthwhile. As she straightened, she saw Leo, who'd been quiet up until then, slapping a pair of handcuffs on George's wrists. George was crying.

"You okay?" Grandpa asked.

"I'm okay. What about you?" There was no blood and they didn't look as though they were hurt. Ethan was putting handcuffs on Travis, but no blood there. She wondered if the past really did repeat itself and scanned the area, but Dillon wasn't lying on the ground bleeding from a gunshot wound. And who the hell was the young man with the camera who stepped from behind one of the junk cars?

"Who are you?" she asked.

"Reporter."

She looked him over. "I've never seen you."

"I'm new. Straight out of college, and I just got the shot of a lifetime."

"Shot?" Ethan's eyes narrowed on the young man. "Did you fire the gun?"

He shook his head. "Oh, no, sir. That was the man Officer McCandless took out with a single punch. The bullet hit that tree over there." He turned and pointed.

"Why are you here?" Ethan asked.

"Anonymous tip, sir."

"It looks as though you don't need us," Texas Ranger Emily Gearson said as she and Sheriff Barnes arrived.

How many more people are going to show up? Raine wondered.

"Wait, I've seen you before," Tilly said, looking straight at Emily Gearson.

"You know the Texas Ranger?" Raine asked.

"Ranger?" Grandpa asked. "Well, hell, we thought you were in cahoots with Ethan and Leo. We saw you that day at the dealership."

"In cahoots with them?" Emily looked around at them as if someone could explain a little more.

"We thought you, Ethan, and Leo robbed the bank," Tilly said, then smiled. "I suppose we got that one wrong. But wasn't this exciting?" She was practically jumping up and down.

"Dwayne planned to shoot us," Raine said. "What's so exciting about that?"

"We're not dead, are we?" Grandpa asked.

"No, but we could've all been murdered." He didn't understand the magnitude of the situation.

"When you get our age," Tilly explained, "you'll take excitement any way you can get it."

"A hell of a lot better than ending up in a hospital bed hooked up to all kinds of tubes and machines and choking on your own spit."

"Grandpa, that's gross."

"But it's the truth."

"Get them to the station and book them," Sheriff Barnes said. "I want a confession."

"Got it," the reporter said. When everyone turned to look at him, he blushed, then held up his cell phone. "I recorded everything, too."

"Kid, you might have a hell of a career in front of you," Sheriff Barnes said and took his phone.

"Thanks. Can I have my phone back?"

"As soon as we get a copy."

Raine rode to the sheriff's office in one of the patrol cars.

She kept looking around but she didn't see Dillon anywhere. Was he okay?

When they were at the sheriff's office, she answered questions and wrote down her statement to be added to all the others. Sheriff Barnes let her borrow one of the older patrol cars until she could get her pickup fixed.

"Grandpa, you coming home tonight?" she asked when he joined her in the lobby.

"I was thinking Tilly might need me. She's still pinging off the walls and I don't want her to have a spell of some kind."

"You sweet on her?" Raine was surprised to see him shuffle his feet like a teenager discovering love for the first time.

He met her eyes. His were old and tired but they shined with a light she hadn't seen in a long time. "Would you be mad if I was?"

She slowly shook her head, smiling. "You know I like Tilly. I'm happy for the both of you."

He reached out and patted her hand. "Good. I best be getting back to her. She worries about me if I'm away from her too long." He winked. "I'm a catch, what can I say. It's the McCandless charm."

"I love you, Grandpa."

"I love you too." He wasn't quite as stooped when he walked toward Tilly. Tilly smiled and took his hand when he moved next to her.

"Did you really think I robbed the bank?" Ethan asked as he came up behind her.

She knew she would have to face him sooner or later. "Not at first, but the evidence against you kept mounting." She studied him. He still looked the same as he had the other day, but there was something different, too. "You don't have an uncle," she blurted.

His eyes widened. "What?"

"I sort of read your file," she admitted. "All in the name of justice. You were raised in an orphanage. How could you inherit enough money from a mysterious uncle if you have no relatives? Did you find some?"

"I don't have any relatives."

Was he guilty of another crime? No, she didn't think so. "Forget I said anything. I don't believe you stole anything from anyone."

"Ever hear of Arthur Winspur?" he asked.

"I heard something on the news." She couldn't remember exactly what was said about the man.

"He donated huge sums of money to the homeless, the needy, orphanages…"

"Okay, now I remember." Understanding dawned. "He's the uncle?"

"We called him Uncle Arthur. He thought it was important for us kids to have family. He donated a lot of money to the orphanage where I grew up. He did more than that, though. He gave of himself. He was an orphan, too. I hadn't heard from him in a long time, but I guess he kept up with his kids. When he died, he left me money. Enough to pay a good down payment on the dealership building so I can work on my vehicles and…" He stopped talking and cleared his throat.

"Your artwork," she finished.

"Yeah." His face turned red.

"I think that's great."

"I hope other people do too."

Sheriff Barnes came up to them, patting her on the back and shaking Ethan's hand. "Good job catching the bank robbers." Ethan excused himself and joined the others. "Your father would be proud."

"You think so?"

"Know so. I am, too."

She looked around the room. "The Ranger?" She wanted to thank her for believing in her.

"Already gone. As soon as their job is done, they leave. Never did see one who hung around in one place very long."

"I'm kind of tired myself," she said.

"Go home and get some rest. I know this has been a difficult time, but it's over now."

As she started up the patrol car and drove away, she thought about Sheriff Barnes's words. He'd said it was over. That was exactly what she was afraid of.

Chapter 25

A WEEK PASSED, THEN another. Grandpa and Tilly bought an RV and left with Lady on a mini vacation. Raine pretended to be happy so they wouldn't worry, but she was dying on the inside a little each day. There was still no sign of Dillon. Would she ever see him again? She milked the cow and fed the livestock, trying not to think about the future or that she might never see him again. She carried the milk inside the house. After straining it, she put it in the refrigerator. All routine. She didn't have to think, only move through the motions of living.

As she walked past the dining room table she glanced at the paper. She'd tossed it there the morning after Dwayne tried to kill most of the sheriff's department. She needed the reminder that it was all over. She had her job back and she wasn't going to prison. The front page had a picture of her knocking Dwayne out cold and the headline read: OFFICER RAINE MCCANDLESS PACKS A PUNCH! The article said she was a true heroine. She and Grandpa received medals from the mayor and there was a big ceremony. She didn't feel any different, except for not worrying about prison. Now she worried about Dillon.

"Chance!" she yelled, hoping at least his friend might hear.

She turned and ran into a hard chest. Relief sprang inside her, but it wasn't Dillon's hands that grabbed hold of her so she could regain her balance.

"Hi again." Chance grinned.

It was okay, she told herself. He was her connection to Dillon. "You came," she breathed.

"Dillon would have my hide if I didn't," he said.

"He's okay?"

"Fine." He frowned. "Sort of."

Dillon had warned her he might get in trouble. *Please let him be okay.* "What happened? Why hasn't he returned?"

"He can't." Chance glanced at the newspaper, then picked it up, letting out a soft whistle. "Hell of a punch." He looked at her with a little more respect shining in his eyes.

She needed him to stay focused! "Why can't he return?"

"Tobiah won't allow it." He tossed the paper on the table. "Dillon has tried, but nothing works. Even my powers are blocked when it comes to helping him."

"But I love him."

"I'm sorry." Sadness was etched on his face. "There's nothing I can do to help him return to you."

She hung her head as the enormity of his words hit her. She'd finally found love, only to lose it. "We never got to say good-bye."

How could Tobiah be so cruel as to keep them from seeing each other one last time? Was that so much to ask for? Was that...

She stilled, then met Chance's eyes.

"What are you thinking?" he cautiously asked.

"Take me to his father. Take me to Tobiah." She trembled. If he would block his son from returning, what would he do when she met him face to face? She was nothing. A soon-to-be nuisance.

Chance shook his head. "Nope. That would be suicide."

"I'm dying without him."

"No way will you talk me into taking you to Tobiah."

"Please."

"You don't know what you're asking."

"Yes, I do."

"I'm sorry. I can't," Chance insisted.

No, this couldn't be the end. She wouldn't let it be the end! "Haven't you ever loved someone so much that a piece of you died every minute you were apart?"

Chance's expression softened for a moment. She pressed forward with her argument. "Now what if you could never see them again? Not even to say good-bye?" She held her breath.

He studied her for a moment, then expelled an aggravated breath. "If Tobiah doesn't have my head on a platter, then Dillon will. Why do I let women talk me into doing crazy shit?"

She drew in a deep breath as excitement swept over her. "I think I know why Dillon likes you so much."

"Don't talk." He grimaced. "I might change my mind." He opened his arms.

She knew the drill and hurried to him, wrapping her arms around his waist and holding on. His arms tightened around her. Air whooshed past. She closed her eyes tight and wondered if she was doing the right thing. Some people said she was fearless, but she wasn't. She was scared, but never seeing Dillon again scared her even more.

As soon as her feet were on solid ground, she opened her eyes. They stood in a clearing in the woods. Was this Heaven? "Where are we?"

"I can't take you up there. They'd fry us both. I figured this was more neutral." He glanced around. "The nephilim created this place a long time ago, before we bought the ranch. I'm not going to promise anything, but I'll see if Tobiah will meet with you."

She nodded and he disappeared. Time passed slowly. A day, then two. Food appeared from nowhere. Once, she thought she saw someone, but wasn't sure. She might have been hallucinating because she thought she saw a lion, too. Ridiculous, of course.

There was a waterfall nearby. She bathed, then dressed.

Then she got pissed. "Are you afraid of me?" she taunted. "Why won't you at least talk to me?"

She didn't notice the bright light forming at first. She thought the sun was rising. The sun had never been that bright. She raised an arm to shield her eyes. The light drew to the center, then became a man. Except Raine was pretty sure it was an angel.

"Tobiah," she breathed.

"No, I'm not afraid of you. Are you afraid of me?" he asked.

"Scared shitless," she said before she thought.

He laughed. She didn't relax.

"I love him," she blurted.

"He's an immortal."

"I don't care."

"You can never be together. It's not possible."

She raised her chin. "I love him," she said again. She saw something in his eyes and walked nearer. One step, two. "I love him." She kept walking toward him, not stopping until she stood in front of him. "I love him as deeply as you loved his mother."

"I couldn't be with her, either," he said softly.

She bowed her head. "Then take me now. I don't want to live without Dillon." She closed her eyes. A moment later she felt a rush of air and wondered if this was it. She should've left a note for Grandpa. He'd be sad, but he had Tilly and she would help him.

Her feet settled on solid ground. She opened her eyes and looked around. She was back in the dining room at the ranch. "No!" She dropped to the floor as pain ripped through her.

Hours later, she came to her feet. She fed the stock, she milked the cow, but poured it down the sink. She sat in the rocker on the back porch. She couldn't eat. She might have dozed. She didn't know. She didn't care.

Someone shook her shoulder. "Raine, wake up."

She dragged her eyes open. "Dillon?" *Oh God, is it really him?*

"You look terrible. When was the last time you ate?"

"I don't remember. You're really here?"

He grabbed her close. "I'm here."

"I'm not dreaming again, am I?" She pushed out of his arms, searching his face. "How?"

"You. It was all you. Tobiah thought you would snap out of it and get on with your life, but you didn't. He remembered what it was like to be without my mother and felt your pain. He intervened."

"I don't understand." Could this really be happening? Happiness swelled inside her until she realized it couldn't be this easy. "I thought you couldn't be around mortals very long."

"I can't."

"But now you can?"

He hesitated. "I'm no longer immortal."

"How could you give up who you are?"

"It was the only way we could be together."

She shook her head. "I never wanted you to die for me. Why would you give up who you are?"

"I want to be with you until we both take our last breaths. I love you." He caressed the side of her face as though he couldn't stand not touching her.

"I love you, too."

"I'm still nephilim. That will never change. Immortality kept me from being a part of your world. Tobiah convinced his superiors that I could do more good for mankind if I lived among them. You could say they're testing the waters with me."

"You gave up a lot to be with me." She looked around. "A rundown ranch might not be as grand as what you're used to."

He frowned. "Actually, I've accumulated a little money. We shouldn't be hurting."

She leaned back and looked at him. "Exactly how much do you have?"

"A few billion."

She choked. "Billion?"

"We should be able to fix up the ranch before Sock returns." He paused. "Raine, are you okay?"

"Maybe." She had a feeling life with Dillon was going to take a little getting used to.

"Try not to overthink it," he said. "Damn, I missed you."

She'd just won the lottery, in more ways than one, and he said don't overthink it. Yeah, like that was going to happen. But when he pulled her into his arms and began to kiss her, Raine decided she would have time to think about it later. Right now, she just wanted to think about the man holding her close.

About the Author

Karen Kelley is the award-winning, national bestselling author of twenty books and contributed to the *USA Today* bestseller *I'm Your Santa*. Her *Close Encounters of the Sexy Kind* was nominated for an *RT Book Reviews* Reviewers Choice Award and her books have placed first in numerous contests. She currently resides in Texas.